Elizabeth Beacon has a passion for history and storytelling and, with the English West Country on her doorstep, never lacks a glorious setting for her books. Elizabeth tried horticulture, higher education as a mature student, briefly taught English and worked in an office before finally turning her daydreams about dashing piratical heroes and their stubborn and independent heroines into her dream job: writing Regency romances for Mills & Boon.

Also by Elizabeth Beacon

The Scarred Earl
The Black Sheep's Return
A Wedding for the Scandalous Heiress

A Year of Scandal miniseries

The Viscount's Frozen Heart
The Marquis's Awakening
Lord Laughraine's Summer Promise
Redemption of the Rake
The Winterley Scandal
The Governess Heiress

Discover more at millsandboon.co.uk.

A RAKE TO THE RESCUE

Elizabeth Beacon

MILLS & BOON

First published in Great Britain 2018
by Mills & Boon, an imprint of HarperCollins*Publishers*
1 London Bridge Street, London, SE1 9GF

Large Print edition 2019

© 2018 Elizabeth Beacon

ISBN: 978-0-263-08156-5

MIX
Paper from
responsible sources
FSC **FSC™ C007454**
www.fsc.org

This book is produced from independently certified FSC™ paper to ensure responsible forest management. For more information visit www.harpercollins.co.uk/green.

Printed and bound in Great Britain
by CPI Group (UK) Ltd, Croydon, CR0 4YY

3476547 C

Chapter One

'Oh, I am sorry…please excuse me,' the stranger murmured.

How could Hetta have left her toes where a society beauty might tread?

'It was nothing,' Hetta lied politely.

'All this bustle is distracting and I hate the sea,' the lady explained as if she was grateful to have another woman to talk to, even a travel-worn and weary one dressed in a shabby cloak and old gown.

'I'm none too fond of it myself,' Hetta admitted ruefully.

The lady grimaced at the mud-grey water. It was calm at the moment, so she would have a far better crossing than Hetta had endured coming the other way, but it was still the sea and she obviously did not want to be on it.

'I wish I could stay,' the lady said wistfully,

glancing back at the town as if she was having second thoughts about leaving it.

'Then why go if you don't want to?'

'Because I must,' the lady said, then seemed to recall Hetta was a stranger and stepped out of her path, looking regal and chilly again.

'The swell has almost calmed now, so you should have an easy journey,' Hetta said and turned to go.

'Thank you,' the lady said absently, her attention now fixed on a woman walking towards them with a grizzling baby of about eight or nine months in her arms.

'She needs you, Lady Drace,' the nurse said.

'I know,' Lady Drace replied, with a tender smile for her little girl. Love for the pretty, dark-haired and dark-eyed baby lit her face to a beauty far more compelling than the icy mask she seemed to use to keep the adult world at bay.

'No, my lady, she *needs* you,' the woman insisted.

Hetta saw the lady blush as the meaning behind those careful words sank in—Lady Drace must be suckling her child herself. Hetta had been happy to dislike her as a privileged being who stood on other people's toes and then frowned as if it was their fault. Now she sympathised with a dilemma she knew all too well and warmed to a fellow mother.

'There is nowhere private enough to feed you, my angel, but I expect you'll work yourself into a tantrum and refuse to be comforted if I don't, and the sea is quite enough to contend with without you adding to it, my pet,' Lady Drace told her fretful infant with a besotted smile and shot a panicked look round the bustling harbour. Her pale blue eyes looked tearful, as if this was the last straw for her. Hetta could not make herself pretend it was none of her business and simply walk away.

'Over there,' she said, pointing at a pile of baggage waiting to be claimed and unwilling to admit it belonged to her family since it was much used and had their names on and she had learned to be wary on her travels. 'That looks a quieter place than most and out of the way of all the hustle and bustle. If you hold your cloak around your mistress on one side, I can do the same with mine on the other, and Lady Drace will be hidden from view. Between us we can make a tent and glare at anyone rude enough to try to overlook us,' she told the maid. Having to feed Toby in all sorts of odd places when she had been tracking her father across Europe after her husband died, Hetta knew how rude and crude some could be to a lady suckling her baby. 'You will be nigh as private as at home in your own bedchamber, your ladyship.'

'Ah, home,' the lady said wistfully, eyeing her hungry and fretful baby as if torn between love for her child and her dignity. She must have made up her mind the little girl was more important since she sighed and shrugged. 'Thank you,' she said. 'You are very kind.'

'High time I found Toby,' Hetta's father muttered and left the ladies to it.

"Coward," his daughter whispered at his retreating back, but since she was worried where her boy had got to, she hoped her father really did mean to look for Toby. It felt wrong to dismiss this stranger's dilemma and find Toby herself now she had made her impulsive offer. So once Hetta and the maid formed their circle, Lady Drace sat down to nurse her child while all three of them thought their thoughts and the baby fed. Hetta wished this trip to her homeland was over and she could go back to the warmth of a real summer somewhere more interesting. Now the greyish-brown waters of the Channel seemed to mock her with gentle ripples after the bitter squall on the way over here and she was quite surprised she was still alive. She stared towards Dover as tame little waves lapped at the quayside gently enough to soothe a fretful babe to sleep.

'And they call this summer?' she muttered as soft drizzle began to crown her miserable homecoming. She had barely been back in England half an hour and she was wet and chilled and her head ached. She felt dull and weary and almost wished she could go with this almost haughty lady and her child to Paris and beyond, although it would mean crossing the Channel again while her stomach was still heaving from the journey over, and even if she could find her son in time, that felt like a bad idea.

'I believe you are finished, my little minx. She might even sleep now,' Lady Drace announced hopefully at last. Hetta heard rustling as the lady got herself back in perfect order then settled her little girl in the crook of her arm and shook her head at the maid as if she didn't intend letting her child go. 'You can let the world back in,' she said resolutely.

'I wish you well on your travels,' Hetta said gently, wondering where this blonde, blue-eyed lady was going with the dark-haired, brown-eyed baby now looking about her with wide-eyed wonder and not in the least bit weary.

'Thank you. It was kind of you to help a stranger,' the lady said as if she was surprised anyone would put themselves out for her.

The lady's life must have been a hard one to make her put on so much elegant armour to keep it at bay. Hetta was glad the woman felt she could love her child wholeheartedly and she was pleased she'd stopped to help a lone mother. Now a nagging anxiety for her own child was urging her to leave the lady to get on with her journey. Her father had already said Toby should be allowed to run off his high spirits so he would be more bearable on the journey to London, so he would not make much effort to track him down, and Hetta knew her son too well to trust him very far with all this bustle and excitement to intrigue him.

'And they do say you should be careful what

you wish for, don't they?' the lady added with a rueful smile.

'But learning when to ignore the naysayers is half the fun,' Hetta said as she peered around the dock and saw no sign of her son or father and felt more like an anxious sheepdog than an English lady of gentle birth and unusual education.

'Do you really think so?'

'Travelling is a lot easier if you can see the lighter side of the obstacles in your way,' Hetta said encouragingly, even if she did think there was little to be cheerful about in the sea crossing her new friend was about to undertake. 'Paris is on the other side of the Channel, don't forget, and if you can't have an adventure there I despair of you,' she added and found out the lady had a surprisingly earthy laugh.

'Thank you. I will do my best,' Lady Drace said, bade Hetta farewell with her baby cuddled close and turned resolutely towards the sea.

Hetta turned to go as well, but the noise and bustle of the busy dock faded away to nothing as a furious-looking and ridiculously handsome man strode into view so fast he was nearly running. The sight of Toby wriggling like an eel under one of the stranger's muscular arms made her gasp in panic and her heart race with anxiety. Protective fury masked fear as she watched her son bundled along so fast he didn't even have breath left to cry out. Toby was pummelling the man with his fists and kicking out, so at least he was not cowed by such rough treatment. Her heart thundered as she watched furious energy power every line of the man's body, but there was always a chance Toby was in the right for once—a slim one from the temper in the stormy gentleman's dark eyes. He *was* devilishly handsome, though, wasn't he? She told her inner idiot not to be stupid and glared at the stern force of nature loping towards them like an angry tiger.

Her stomach had not got over that appalling sea crossing yet, so the stir of something hot and sharp deep in her belly was caused by it being emptied so often as the ship rode the waves of a vicious summer storm like a cork at the mercy of furious Mother Nature. This tall and formidable man could not stir her sensual instincts back to life without even a smile or an interested look, so there was no other explanation for it. And he had Toby firmly under his arm as if her boy was a mere bundle of faggots, so those instincts would be wrong anyway.

'Is this yours?' he barked at her as soon as he was within earshot.

As Hetta was the only woman gaping at him with her mouth open, it must be easy enough to pick her out as Toby's mother. She was vaguely conscious Lady Drace had jumped as if she had been shot at the sound of his deep voice, then turned to stare at him with horror in her light blue eyes. So that made two women scared by the great clumsy oaf roaring and raging as if he had every right to make rude comments about anyone he wanted to, and she wondered why the rest of the world had not stopped to watch him open-mouthed as well.

'What have you done, Toby?' Hetta didn't quite answer the man's rude question and told herself she was too worried about her son to care about gruff strangers or her new friend's reaction to them.

The Honourable Magnus Haile frowned at the strange woman staring back at him like a simpleton. Given the gasp of relief the boy had given on first sight of her, she was his mother, and what a neglectful shabby-genteel idiot to leave her offspring running loose without a keeper. He didn't have any time to spare, so why was it his job to chastise a brat who threw himself under his weary horse and nearly killed them both? Luckily his younger brother's man, Jem Caudle, told Magnus he would stable the exhausted and unnerved beast for him, then reminded him the packet would sail if he didn't hurry. Jem even told Magnus to leave the lad to him and get to the vessel faster, but Magnus was too shocked and angry to leave the boy to Jem's mercy. So, he'd grabbed the brat in order to berate the boy's parents before he thought of some way to stop Delphi and his little girl leaving England without him, even if he had to throw himself aboard the boat and leave his homeland with no more than the shirt on his back.

He was a father now, whatever Delphi had to say about it. His frown went fierce again as he grappled with that fact and his helplessness to do anything about it when Delphi refused to marry him. He longed to be able to keep his daughter out of wild scrapes like this when she was big enough to be naughty. Not that his little Angela could ever be as wayward as this brat, but the boy's parents obviously didn't know how lucky they were to have the right to protect him from harm. Yet they let him run around like a street urchin! Now the boy was scratching and trying to bite, as if Magnus was the villain, and he was tempted to drop him on the cobbles and walk away. 'Try that trick again and I'll dust your backside for you, whether your mama is looking or not,' he threatened dourly.

'No, you won't. She won't let you,' the lad shouted, lower lip wobbling and his dirty face scrunched up with the effort of producing a tear.

'Once she knows what you did she will thank me for saving her the effort of doing it herself.'

'No, she won't. She will skin you alive, then boil you in oil if you even *try* to smack me.'

'Then I won't need to worry about anything, will I? Least of all a wicked little liar like you,' Magnus said grimly.

'Put my son down this minute,' the sunburnt woman in dull clothes, a drooping bonnet and the most ridiculous pair of eyeglasses he had ever seen demanded furiously as she finally snapped out of her trance.

Magnus could now see where the boy got his temper, if not his wild blond curls, wide blue eyes and the daredevil spirit that made him look like a fallen cherub. Perhaps his father was absent for a good reason, but Magnus's inner sneer felt cheap when he eyed the termagant in petticoats and wished for a brief, mad moment he'd fallen in love with such a tigress in spectacles, instead of the woman hiding behind her, trying to pretend she had never seen him before in her life, even with his baby in her arms chortling at her father with *Haile* written all over her darling little face like a banner.

'Gladly, if you promise to keep him under better control in future,' he told the woman grimly and tried to ignore the pain in his heart when his Angela reached out her arms to him and Delphi snatched her away as if she hated him. 'A collar and lead should serve. He nearly killed himself running under my horse just now. Luckily for all of us the poor beast was too weary to throw me when I curbed him, or you would have a lot more to worry about than a filthy little thug in a foul temper. A blow from the nag's iron-shod hooves would have killed him outright.'

The woman went even paler under her unladylike sunburn and Magnus regretted his harshness for a moment. But, no, she needed a shock like this to force her to keep a better eye on the boy in future. He had to harden his heart again when she pushed her spectacles up her nose with a shaking hand and he counted himself lucky she wasn't having an attack of the vapours. She braced her shoulders instead and he had better things to do than admire her resolution and the fine figure he should not even notice when he had ridden all the way here at breakneck speed to plead with Delphi not to take his child so far away he might never see her again.

'Stop that ridiculous wriggling and pretend-crying, Toby Champion,' the boy's mother snapped at her flailing offspring.

Magnus felt the boy still as if she had waved a magic wand. Deciding the brat was not likely to get away with his sins after all, Magnus swung him down. 'Buy him a chain if you can't keep him under better control in future, madam,' he barked.

'How can you be so harsh, Magnus?' Delphi broke in as the lad threw himself at his mother so enthusiastically she lurched and nearly fell over.

Magnus had been so intent on the boy's mother he hadn't noted how Delphi's wide and horrified eyes were fixed on him as if she expected him to lash out as the late, unlamented Sir Edgar Drace was prone to when something about his young wife did not suit him. It said much for his baby's sunny nature that she was gurgling and wriggling in her mother's arms as if this was a fine show, instead of cowering and grizzling as she caught the megrims from her mother.

'If someone doesn't check the boy, he will kill himself,' he explained with an impatient glance behind him to convince Delphi he wasn't in the least like the straw man she had married for some reason he had never managed to fathom.

'Only your horror at the idea of doing so could excuse such a wicked display of temper,' Delphi said, reproaching him with the stiffness in her voice.

'I could hardly pat him on the head and bid him be more careful next time.'

'No, he could not,' the boy's mother admitted with a sigh, as if it cost a lot to stand up for such a grim stranger. She turned to Delphi with a resigned shrug and said, 'He's right. My son *is* far too adventurous for his own good. And I want you to see your eighth birthday, despite all your best efforts not to, my lad, so you can take the wounded expression off your face and listen to your elders and betters for once,' she added as her boy let go of her narrow waist to stare up at her with the wide eyes of a wronged cherub.

Magnus revised her age down a decade and decided, if she still had a husband, the neglectful idiot should be here, trying to back up her efforts to keep their child alive so she wouldn't look elsewhere for comfort for herself and a little help with the lad. A ridiculous, totally unacceptable part of him wanted to be the source of both for her for a moment and hadn't he already had a harsh enough lesson about throwing himself at complicated and unfathomable women? And what did he know about how to bring up well-balanced and happy children after the childhood he and his younger siblings had endured at their father's hands anyway?

'I see,' Delphi said almost as if she did.

Hope leapt in Magnus's heart for a heady moment as his daughter blew kisses at him as if she would always be on his side. 'Please, Delphi, let me come with you?' he begged the child's mother as softly as he could with all these wild emotions roiling around inside him right now. He would plead in front of the devil himself if it got him a place in his child's life.

'I told you before, Magnus. No. Have the manners to listen to me and stay away from us in future, before you do even more damage than you already have.'

'Should I send for the Harbour Master?' the strange woman said as if ready to leap into battle on Delphi's behalf. Why must she be such an interfering, reckless female? He almost had to admire her for it. All his attention should be focused on Delphi and trying to persuade her to let him have any sort of role in his daughter's life, but parts of it kept straying to this vital and puzzling stranger who was threatening to get in the way at the worst possible moment.

'No, although I really do thank you for the offer,' Delphi said with such horror in her expression a disinterested bystander might laugh at the show they were putting on. 'He won't hurt us,' she explained.

Magnus was glad she gave him that much credit and supposed he ought to be grateful for small mercies. 'I won't,' he added shortly.

'Well then, perhaps you could work harder at seeming a little less threatening in future, Lord Drace,' the woman said and made it all worse somehow.

'He's not my husband,' Lady Delphine Drace said with such an appalled expression Magnus almost gave up and went home.

'Oh,' the stranger said, looking from one to the other and then at the baby in Delphi's arms as if she had put two and two together and got four. She blushed and looked as if she wished herself a few hundred miles away as well right now, but she still met his eyes with defiance blazing from behind those disfiguring spectacles of hers and his reluctant admiration for her courage fretted like an itch under his skin. 'It seems to me you have even more reason to leave her ladyship in peace, then, sir,' she said severely.

'None of your business, madam,' he snapped because her words stung all the more sharply for being right.

Chapter Two

'Stop embarrassing me, Magnus, and go away. I have made it clear to you time and time again I will not marry you. Do me the courtesy of listening for once and leave us be.' Delphi sounded so weary Magnus's heart thudded with dread, then slowed to a horrified acceptance that she really meant it this time. Now he would have to watch them both sail away and the thought of it nearly took him off at the knees.

'What about Angela?' he said bleakly as he stared at his baby with what felt embarrassingly like tears in his eyes. The baby laughed back at him and gigged up and down in her mother's arms as if she liked him, even if Delphi didn't any more. She was so like him his paternity should have been obvious to the whole world at birth and he longed to proclaim it to the rooftops and be her father for life.

'She will be safe, loved and with her mother. That's all you need know,' Delphi said implacably, and defeat had never tasted so bitter for Magnus.

'Unlike her father,' he said flatly as his life stretched away from him in a long, slow road he almost wished was over and done with.

'I am sorry, Magnus. It was never you, you see?' Delphi said, as if his pain at the idea of never seeing his child again was so plain to see even she could no longer ignore it. 'You were never the man I really wanted when I had to wed Drace, nor afterwards when he died and I was rich as well as free and *he* still didn't come to comfort me for all those wasted years I had to endure without him.' She spoke as if that grief was the one she might never get over. 'You look so like him at the age when he loved me back, you see. I admit I could not help myself taking what I could get from one of you Hailes when you arrived, so eager to comfort me after Drace died, and he still stayed away, as if he didn't care a snap of his fingers about me and how I still longed for all I could not have because he turned his back on me. He said he had to do his duty and never mind where his heart led him, but if I was in his heart he managed to ignore me when it all ended and I still had nothing—not even a child to make the emptiness less cruel.'

'So you used me to make one and never mind if I was the wrong man to make it with? I was only ever a poor substitute for another man as far as you were concerned, wasn't I?' Magnus said bitterly, a terrible suspicion dragging him back to the shore like a heavy anchor chained to his waist as she turned to walk aboard the ship so she could get on with forgetting he even existed on the other side of the Channel. 'For my damned brother, I suppose, since you always hated the old man nigh as much as I did,' he gritted out at her stiff-backed figure and felt as if this last, bitter truth might poison him.

'You Hailes look so alike, you see?' she turned back to tell him earnestly, as if he might nod and agree, as if he had been a fool to ever think himself aught but a stand-in for the man she really loved and wanted all along when she'd taken him as her lover for six glorious weeks after her husband died.

'All except Wulf,' he said numbly, relieved his favourite brother was both too young and too like their mother to be the man Magnus had been a substitute for when he had helped Delphi make a Haile baby to love so soon after her husband's death—even the rightful Drace heir had not argued Angela was Sir Edgar Drace's get. Maybe the man had been so relieved Delphi had birthed a girl he'd made no effort to see the babe in full daylight and Delphi *had* kept her child very close. She'd had Angela baptised soon after birth on the excuse she might not survive. That lie had sent him galloping all the way to Drace Dower House to discover his child thriving and he'd fallen instantly in love with her as only a father could. Nobody would believe Delphi's lie about her baby girl's health if they could see her in her mother's arms now, laughing at the strange sayings and doings of her elders and so full of life.

Magnus numbly marvelled that Delphi's relief at leaving her native land and him behind seemed to have lulled her into trusting a stranger not to noise her affairs abroad, when she usually kept her feelings so firmly in check. He only wished he shared her confidence in the woman hesitating nearby as if she knew she should leave them to have this very private discussion in as much peace as could be got in such a place, but felt she could not walk away lest he became violent. Couldn't she tell he would never hurt a hair on either of these two females' heads if his life depended on it? Luckily her boy had already got bored with such adult puzzles and had gone to create more mischief behind his mother's back.

'Marry me anyway?' Magnus pleaded and to hell with his pride and their audience.

Even if Delphi didn't love him—and he was rapidly going off the idea of loving her back if his elder brother Gresley was truly the love of her life—he was the father of the little darling watching him as if she knew he mattered. Why wasn't her mother agreeing with her? Delphi must have deliberately lured him into her bed to fantasise he was his elder brother when Gresley stayed sternly away and left her to find comfort in another man's arms. It was never him she'd wanted and that felt bitter as gall as he nearly choked on the taste of it after all these years of being half in love with a woman he could not have. Delphi had loved and been loved by Gresley for a time before the dutiful heir married money to save the Carrowe estates from bankruptcy instead of lovely, not very wealthy Lady Delphine Bowers. So, she in turn had made a marriage of no affection to keep her true love alive in her heart while she flaunted Drace's almost legendary wealth in her lover's face and effortlessly outshone his new Countess at every turn. It seemed a poor reason for marriage, but what room had Magnus to criticise when he'd nearly married a friend for the sake of her fortune only a few months ago?

'Wed me for her sake?' Magnus begged huskily even so and leaned forward to kiss his baby daughter before she was snatched away for what could be for ever. The little minx gurgled at him and his heart lurched with love and his need to protect her against every harsh wind that might blow on her for the rest of her life. She was still his child, whether her mother liked it or not.

'No, I won't have her watch us tied together only by duty and not love. I lived in a hollow marriage for a decade after I could not marry the love of my life and I swore never to do it again the day Drace died. Angela is mine and her own, but she is not yours, Magnus.'

'Explain that to anyone who ever lays eyes on her and has seen one of us Hailes first, then. You can call her by another man's name as much as you like, but you can't pretend Drace had any hand in her with those features and dark brown eyes and all that jet-black hair to give you the lie.'

'I won't have to if you stay away from us. If you truly love her, you will go away and leave us to live a good enough life in another country without you. I can afford to give her the best of everything and make sure she has a good education and all the things you can never afford, circumstanced as you are. You have nothing to offer her and I can give her everything. Now my maid is getting frantic and signalling we must get aboard, before she and my worldly goods are forced to cross the Channel without us, so get out of the way, Magnus, and leave us be.'

'And that is all you have to say to me?'

'Yes. You must live a good life and forget all about us.'

'How can I?'

'Take lessons from the man who knows how it's done,' she said with a thin, bitter little smile and waved a dismissive hand in his direction before she turned away with his child to be scurried up the companionway by the impatient Captain of the packet boat. Then she took herself to the other side to look towards Calais and away from him. At last the boat embarked with Magnus gazing after it like a fool, watching every step and sail they took away from him as if he had a wicked spell laid on him and there was nothing he could do to tell the world his heart had been ripped out.

'Guv,' a skinny young man said to the brooding figure Hetta was suddenly so reluctant to disturb. Magnus Haile stood stock-still now and looked as if everything he ever cared about had left him for ever and his life was meaningless and empty without them. She must have caught at his name, like carelessly thrown jewels, when Lady Drace dropped it into her bitter farewell. This man Lady Drace had refused so coldly looked as if he'd been broken by his lover's final rebuff. Hetta almost cried for him and she was no watering pot and was nearly sure she didn't like him. 'We need to get home, Mr Magnus,' the youth urged, clearly uneasy in the face of such raw emotion which seemed to come off his master in waves as he stood there trying so hard to be impassive and rocklike and failing at it rather badly. At a distance he might look so, but this close to he was clearly spent. He ignored his unlikely-looking rescuer as if his ears had shut down after Lady Drace's last bitter words stung him to the heart.

'Mr Haile, your man is trying to get your attention.' Hetta spoke up at last, and thank goodness *she* was too much of a stranger to need to search for words of comfort when the man looked back at her as if he knew there was none to be had.

'Eh?' he managed to say, as if reluctantly realising he had a new world to live in now the two people he most wanted in it had left him. 'Oh, yes. There you are, Jem. Horses calmed and dealt with, are they?'

'Aye, stabled and fed and asleep already when I left—which you looks as if you ought to be as well, if you don't mind me saying so, Mr Magnus.'

'Wouldn't that be a handy trick?' Mr Haile

said softly, as if he hadn't slept properly for longer than he cared to remember.

'Whatever it is, you needs to come away now. Mr Wulf will skin me alive if I get you home in an even worse state than you was in last Easter when—'

The young man stopped himself and eyed Hetta as if he had suddenly realised she was a total stranger and couldn't be trusted to keep a still tongue in her head about his master's family and their obviously very tangled affairs.

'I am no gossip,' she reassured him earnestly and turned to meet Mr Haile's dark eyes. Shock and a terrible weariness looked back at her. There was a faint glimmer of the man he ought to be looking at her with a tepid sort of interest, as if she was a being who knew far too much about him and he ought to care, but could not quite make the effort to do so. He seemed to have shut down all the power and vitality that made him so memorable at first sight, even if her motherly instincts had been on the alert for her son's welfare at his furious hands at the time. This man now looked as if he was too tired and battle-weary to care what anyone did to him. Toby could dance on the topsail of the next ship to come in and drop on his head to break his fall and he would shake him off after a few stunned moments and go on with hardly even a blink to admit he had a headache.

'I think you had best find this gentleman a good meal and a clean bed for the night, young man,' she advised his unlikely companion gently, as if she knew he was being left to deal with a casualty and might need a little advice from a woman who was all too used to wrenching comfort out of spartan lodgings and a sometimes less than perfect life of her own.

'You're in the right of it there, missus. Rode here as if the devil was on his tail, he did. Ought to know better, but I can take care of him now,' the youth said as if he was decades older than the man Lady Drace had just whistled down the wind as if lovers like him were ten a penny. Magnus Haile seemed almost broken and the last thing in the world to make him feel any better would be the pity of a strange woman. A part of her that should be ashamed of itself mourned for him as *her* fantasy lover. She could only imagine having a man like him in her own bed in her wildest dreams. Lady Drace was obviously made of finer stuff, though, and, since he was used to a lover of such graceful beauty and elegance, he would have no eye for a plain Mrs Champion even if he wanted another lover to comfort him, sensible Hetta argued. Being second-best would feel more hellish than being alone with all these feminine longings and frustration when she sought her lonely bed tonight. No, it was time she got back to real life and forgot Magnus Haile and her odd welcome to a country that had never felt like home to her.

'Reassure your master, once he is refreshed and well enough to listen properly, that I never gossip,' she said with a nod to say *You can trust me.* The lad returned with a wary *Maybe I can* nod back.

'Heaven send I never see you or your brat again to test you on that assertion, ma'am,' Magnus Haile said as if her words had woken him from a stupor. He looked so revolted by the idea that she felt stung, but before she could summon up a sharp answer he marched off as if it was her fault he had suffered such a felling blow at his ex-lover's hands today.

'The feeling is entirely mutual,' she muttered into the damp and empty air even as she gazed at his fast-retreating back and noted his loping stride had already taken him well out of hearing distance, proving he had more energy than she'd thought. 'Of all the rude, abrupt, bad-tempered m-m-monsters...'

No, that won't do. Hetta stopped herself in mid-stammer as words failed her. She refused to let him take words away from her, even if he wasn't here to sneer at her. An ill-mannered, bad-tempered, unshaven and arrogant apology for a gentleman would *not* turn her back into the silenced little mouse she'd nearly become under her grandmother's roof when Papa had sent her back to England after her mother had died and he didn't seem to know what else to do with his only child.

Back then the Dowager Lady Porter was determined to turn her skinny, suntanned and rebellious grandchild into a meek and mild young lady who did as she was told without questioning why. Why on earth Hetta's father thought a stay under his mother's roof for Hetta and his grandson would work this time, she had no idea. It was a disaster last time and, after enduring two years of being forever in the wrong, Hetta had been desperate enough to elope with the first man who had asked her to in order to avoid spending one more day under her rigid and forever disapproving grandparent's roof. This time she had a bright and rather rebellious seven-year-old son with her as well and felt no more inclination for polite society than she had last time she had to live with the Dowager Lady Porter. Sir Hadrian Porter had made the arrangement behind Hetta's back, though, leaving her no chance to refuse and stay on the other side of the Channel while he was in England.

He didn't even tell her about his plans to keep her out of the way this time until France was fading from view and it was too late for her to refuse to cooperate with them. If only he hadn't been so devious about it, she and Toby could have found refuge from the relentless heat of midsummer on the Normandy coast and let the polite world pass them by, again. But her father had other ideas and Hetta was very suspicious about them now she was actually in England and the pall of drizzle, stilted manners and her dread of being forced into an empty society marriage was on her once more.

How she cursed the promise her father had

wrung out of her that she would agree to be sent somewhere safe with her son whenever Sir Hadrian thought they could be in danger from one of the secret villains he pursued for his country. This time he had invoked the promise to get her to agree to go somewhere she did not want to be even more than usual. She ground her teeth at the memory of making such a blasted promise when she had finally managed to track her father down after her husband, Brandon Champion, had died and her son was a mere babe in arms. With all the failed romance and blighted hope behind her, Hetta was desperate for the old life she'd lived with her wandering parents until her mother died and had been so desperate to escape England she'd rashly made the promise Papa demanded of her as a condition of her staying with him at all. He had held her to it ever since.

Of course, Toby was a wondrous gift from those wretched years and he made every minute of it seem worthwhile. But even though Hetta felt horror at the very idea of being sent back to England, her father knew she would never break her promise to him. Her word was her bond as surely as any gentleman's and she knew Papa's trade was a dangerous one, but she was growing very weary of being bent to his will when he chose. It was time to settle into a life of her own making somewhere, she decided, and with a sidelong look at Toby she knew it must still revolve around his needs. He was old enough for school now and she would have to settle for this dull and rainy land at least in term time. He would probably be his grandfather's heir one day, if Sir Hadrian didn't make an April and December marriage and beget a direct heir, so Toby would have to learn to be an English gentleman whether either of them liked it or not. To do that he had to go to school here and she would have to live here as well, at least for most of the year. The prospect didn't please her, but neither did the idea of leaving her son at school and travelling the world without him. Somehow or another this trip to England had to be the start of a new life for both of them.

Anyway, never mind all that now. Brought back to the present moment, Hetta refused to let Magnus Haile's hurtful words make her lose control of her words for the first time since Toby was born. If that was the sort of gentlemen she was likely to meet here she wished herself in France more than ever. Never mind the sea. She would brave it again right now to avoid ever having to meet him again. Probably.

'Mama, he said he'd smack me himself if he ever heard of me pulling another stunt like that,' Toby told her as he ran towards her as if sensing her fury with the stranger might outdo her anger with him if he worked at it hard enough.

'Good. If you truly ran under a horse's hooves as he said you did then you should be beaten to make sure you never do it again,' she said briskly and gave him a hard stare to say *And stop right there if you're thinking of denying it.*

She knew her son far too well not to know when he was lying. However furious Magnus Haile made her with his last contemptuous look, she was still not going to fall for any of her son's clever tricks.

'I saw a puppy,' Toby said sulkily, as if of course that explained why he'd darted across a road just as a high-nosed aristocrat was cantering down it.

'Well, it won't be the last one you see in England, so you had best get used to the sight if you want me to think you deserve a dog of your own one day.'

'I want one now,' Toby insisted.

'I wanted an angel boy for a son and a house in France where we could stay all summer without a care in the world, but instead I got you and the next place we need to be on your grandpapa's list. Life is hard, my son.'

'Why can't we have a dog?'

'Because a dog needs a home and we move around so much the poor beast would never know if it was coming or going.'

'Then we should stop moving around and *make* a home for it.'

'You would be bored within a week, Toby, and I would end up looking after the animal. Now that's enough of the whole subject, unless you would like me to spank you instead?'

'No,' Toby said, eyeing her warily.

'Then accept the fact your hen-witted conduct makes it less likely I will agree to what you want instead of the other way about and stop trying to look like a waif. I am a wonderfully kind and patient mother and, luckily for you, there is far too much for me to do right now to see that you get your just deserts. We must find our carriage and get to London so Grandpapa can start work. I doubt even you will be bored for long in such a great bustling place as London, although I would quite like you to be right now, so you should spare me a few moments to repent your stupidity in diving under a moving horse when you are nearly eight years of age and quite old enough to know better. You *are* supposed to be bright, are you not?'

'What good is one of Grandpapa's mysteries without a dog to help us track down the criminal?' her son muttered disgustedly and carefully ignored her question, as if intelligence had nothing to do with his longing for a pet.

Hetta silently gave him full marks for determination, although her headache wished he would accept defeat and be a good, quiet boy for once. Other women did seem blessed with adoring little angels for offspring, though, and sometimes they made her son seem a little devil in comparison.

And how boring such perfectly behaved little cherubs must be to live with, her inner rebel whispered.

She wished it would be quiet and go away

while she got on with her headache and a nice cup of tea in a peaceful and preferably darkened room, but that was never going to happen, was it? No, now she must find Papa and get him and her son to London, then hope for a rest when they got there.

'Where has your grandpapa got off to now?' she asked, smoothing Toby's wildly curling mop like the doting mother he certainly didn't want her to be. She chuckled when he shrugged her off and made a wry face. 'Find him for me and I might try to forget you put ten years on my life with your latest duel with death, my son, but first promise me never to do anything so stupid again.'

'I promise,' he muttered with a fine show of reluctance, so she wouldn't think it was too easy. 'The man scared me when he shouted, but I suppose he was right,' he admitted at last.

Progress indeed, Hetta decided as Toby scampered off to do as he was bid for once and she organised the transfer of their luggage to the inn where a fast carriage would be waiting to whisk them up to London. At last Sir Hadrian emerged from a ship's chandler's shop with a neatly wrapped package in his hands and Toby at his heels like a well-trained sheepdog. Sir Hadrian Porter looked vaguely about him as if he might have forgotten something, but he wasn't quite sure what it was. His smile when he saw his daughter was genuine, but Hetta did wonder for a moment if he was even capable of the sort of love she had longed for so badly when her mama died and he sent her back to his own mother like an unwanted parcel. Perhaps it was time she made an independent life for herself and Toby? But even though she had loved so many of the places they'd visited over the last seven years, none of them felt quite like home. She sighed at the drizzle now soaking determinedly through her cloak and put it aside as a problem for another day—this one had quite enough trouble in it to be going on with.

Chapter Three

If there *was* a lovely cool room with fresh sheets and a kindly breeze fluttering through it to be had in London, Hetta certainly hadn't found it, she decided wearily, as the shabby old carriage rumbled along for a few steps, then ground to a halt again. She was being pushed from pillar to post in this confounded country yet again and the headache she'd come ashore with in Dover was still plaguing her three days on. Two days ago, her grandmother had declared she could not and *would* not endure her great-grandson's presence in her usually quiet and stately home in Grosvenor Square a moment longer. Henrietta must send the ungovernable brat to school straight away, even if most of them were closed for the summer, or take him away. So Hetta had gone to crumbling old Carrowe House to ask her father for advice on finding suitable lodgings, and the new Earl of Carrowe's sister, Lady Aline Haile, insisted they stay there while she found somewhere.

Then Toby managed to find a way up on to the roofs of the decayed old mansion and Lord Carrowe had been so furious with him they'd had to leave that house as well, so here they were, back on the road again. The traffic was stubbornly blocked on the way to their next temporary lodging for the night. Most businessmen still in London now summer had finally arrived seemed to be fleeing the city for the villages around it to spend time with their family. She promised herself she would find somewhere cool and clean and suitable for a longer stay as soon as she had her breath back and got a decent night's sleep. She could use the few days Lord Carrowe had offered them at his mother's nearly restored house to regroup and decide what to do next.

'I'm glad we had to leave Carrowe House, Mama. It was boring there when Lady Aline left for Worthing. It would be so much better if she stayed with us.'

'Not for her,' Hetta said as she wiped beads of perspiration from her forehead and wished she was enjoying a summer by the seaside as well as her new friend—at least there was one Haile she would like to meet again. 'Lady Aline's mama and twin sisters are in Worthing for the summer and who would *not* prefer to be by the sea on a day like this?' she said with a gesture at the shouting, overheated drivers and unnerved horses outside the small windows of the ramshackle hackney.

'Lord Carrowe is very stuffy. I don't see how I could have harmed his roof when it was already full of holes.'

'You could have gone through one of them or fallen off altogether, or been snatched up by one of your grandfather's foes while you wandered around such a half-empty and insecure place heedless of any danger. I try not to be forever scolding and picking at you, but really, Toby—must you do everything you should not simply because someone forbade it?'

Toby eyed his mama and seemed to consider the question seriously. 'Probably,' he admitted at last. 'How else can I find out why I'm not supposed to do it?'

'Ask. Get a rational explanation and listen for once, because right now I have trouble believing you have any brains and never mind being clever.'

'Lord Carrowe didn't give me any reasons at all, let alone a rational one,' Toby pointed out with his usual ruthless logic and carefully ignored her slight.

He was right. The gentleman had lost his impressive Haile temper and ordered them to his mother's house in Hampstead for the night so he could wash his hands of them with a clear conscience. There was something to be said for being the daughter of Sir Hadrian Porter, the King's discreet and coolly efficient roving agent, when even an earl didn't dare risk his wrath and put his daughter and grandson out on the street. It was her father's job to keep his country's diplomats and spies safe when the usual threats and dangers they faced became too acute to ignore. Lord Carrowe didn't know the full extent of her father's powers, but he knew enough to be careful, Hetta recalled with a frown. She shivered as she remembered the wary and brooding feel of poor, half-ruinous old Carrowe House during the day and the creaks and moans of the crumbling old mansion during the night, not much chance of her sleeping for long amid all the Gothic brooding and unease of an old house where murder stole in and out without anybody knowing how.

'Hmm, perhaps you're right,' she admitted, 'but now I have the impossible task of finding somewhere for us to stay where you won't cause chaos before we hardly have our feet over the threshold, my son. You are seven and three-quarters, Toby, but at this rate you won't live to see eight and I am tired of all these accidents you keep falling into.'

'The rat wasn't an accident,' Toby muttered mutinously.

'I know,' she said dourly.

'And you didn't want to stay at the Dowager Lady Porter's London residence either, Mama,' he pointed out slyly, imitating her grandmother's stiff and disapproving butler's hushed reverence for the place.

'No, but I would rather we had somewhere to go to next before it became impossible to stay another moment, and I would prefer it if my grandmother was still speaking to me as well.'

'Why? You didn't like her either and we would never have met Lady Aline if we stayed at stuffy Porter House with Great-Grandmama frowning at us all the time and looking down her nose at you. I'm glad I found the poor rat in a trap and let it go in her horrid drawing room when she had her horrible friends to tea. She did nothing but blame you for everything from the moment we got inside her stuffy old house and I never want to see her again. You can't live there when I go to school, Mama. You would hate it and so would I.'

Hetta met her son's bright blue eyes and managed a wobbly smile to reassure him she didn't hold that particular piece of mischief against him and a sceptical lift of her brows to let him know she could fight her own battles, thank you. Toby was offering her something nobody had since her own mother died: unconditional love and real concern for her feelings. 'Her visitors will spread the story of your misdeeds and I don't want the world to think you a monster, love, even if you are one.'

Toby seemed immensely cheered by the notion and Hetta didn't have the heart to berate him for his sins again. She blinked hard at the unfamiliarity of being protected by her own son. Nobody had truly worried about how she felt about the world since her mother died. Her father made sure she was physically safe, then went on with his own life. And her late husband had been a prime example of April when he'd wooed her, December when they'd wed. She winced at the memory of Bran shouting in his cups that she'd ruined his life. At least she'd still had enough spirit left to argue he'd reneged on every promise he made to love and cherish her for life if she would elope with him. Even now she flinched at how desolate she'd felt when he staggered to his feet and glared down at her, challenging her with his superior height and strength to blame him for using his looks and charm to bend a lonely schoolroom miss to his will, even if he had done exactly that. He didn't meet her eyes and carry on with the lie, but belched and slammed out of the house with a lewd comment about finding a woman with some go in her instead of a useless little milksop who still cried for her mother. At least she had faced him down. It hurt to know he'd wed her because he thought her father and grandmother would relent and advance his career once their marriage was a fait accompli. She was seventeen to his two and twenty when they'd wed over the anvil.

Her father had never laid a hand on her in anger, but he seemed to think she was too grown up to need him to tell her he loved her, even when he sent her back to England after his wife died. Hetta was sure he had loved her mother in a vague *this woman fills the gap in my life so comfortably I must love her* sort of fashion, and he probably loved his daughter as well, but he had no idea of how to comfort a grieving child when he was feeling bereft himself. He was so relieved to leave her with his mother and bury himself in work again that he'd ignored all her letters pleading to be allowed to join him on his travels and escape the constant criticism and disapproval of her grandmother and the stiff-necked governess hired especially to teach her to be the perfect English gentlewoman so she could attract a stern English gentleman one day. No wonder she had spent most of her time at Porter House fantasising about being adored by a dashing hero out of a Gothic romance. Lieutenant Champion had looked like the answer to a maiden's prayer, but appearances were deceptive.

She had been even more lonely in the neat little cottage in Lyme Regis Brandon had bought to store his wife in. Once he realised none of his plans would bear fruit he tried to live almost as freely as if he'd never met and married her. Bran would come home, slake the lust of however many weeks he had spent at sea without a woman on her, then walk away whistling to find the knowing and flirtatious sort of women he preferred to his wife. Never again, she swore to herself as she shook off those uncomfortable memories. Never again would a man woo her, then walk away as if she was nothing. If not for his Admiralty masters' raised eyebrows Bran would have left her in Lyme that day and never gone back and she would not have Toby. She would not undo a day of her failed romance if it meant losing her son, so she had best forget the past and live for now. The fleeting picture of a man as mighty and passionate as Magnus Haile desperate to share life with her was folly and she consigned that to outer darkness as well.

Now the next tangle of wagons and porters and furious drivers snarled the traffic to a halt again and it seemed even more stifling inside the tired old hackney than ever. At least Toby was chastened enough by his latest misadventure to only fidget and sigh and peer out of the small window to listen to colourful arguments being traded all around them. Hetta dreaded to think what gems were taking root in his busy head, but she would have to trust him to save the worst for his peers at the school she must find him before summer's end. He knew enough insults in several languages to keep a pack of scrubby boys happy, but at least their wandering life had given him a wider view than he would have got in Lyme or at Porter House with her rigidly formidable grandmother. Her son had a robust sense of his own worth. Now she owed him stability, she decided as she eyed the sweaty chaos outside the window and sighed. She would have to endure this benighted country while her son grew up and there was no point having the blue-devils about it.

Since before he was even born Toby had been her counterweight against the failings and sadness of the past, and hope for the future, but she had to be careful not to smother him. The fact that most schools were closed for the summer let her put the idea of him going to one at least as a weekly boarder to one side, so she could at least get her breath back and give herself more time to look around for a place that wouldn't stifle his character and try to turn him into the crushed pattern card of a gentleman. Not that it seemed likely, but the attempt to force him into such a mould would end in disaster for him and his mother, so she would need to be very careful about this school and the place she would eventually settle—nearby, but not too near.

The new Earl of Carrowe's odd behaviour seemed a good way to distract herself from thoughts of her imminent parting from her son, so she let him steal her anxiety about the future, as the ancient vehicle finally trundled on. Shouting at Toby to come down off his less than noble roof had almost shocked her son into the tumble Lord Carrowe had claimed he was trying to prevent. The panic in the dark eyes the Earl shared and yet didn't quite share with his younger brother Magnus had looked odd as well. Understandable for her to feel her life was hanging in the balance while Toby teetered between safety and a crashing fall, but why had his lordship been so concerned about a boy he didn't even like? He'd continued to stare at the chimney Toby was clinging to even after he had let go and taken the lesser risk of a jump into the ancient attic below rather than a fall to unkempt grounds far too many feet below. At the time she had been so concerned for her son that his lordship's odd behaviour had seemed irrelevant, but now she thought about it the more the man had seemed almost as hard-pressed to keep his feelings in check as his younger brother had under very different circumstances at Dover.

Hetta sighed and concluded she was making mountains out of molehills. Toby had been exploring where he wasn't supposed to, so the Earl could hardly pat him on the head and claim it didn't matter. Her fault for weakening and agreeing to stay there instead of facing a tramp around London looking for suitable accommodation. She should have recalled Haile was the Earl of Carrowe's family name and steered clear of the rest of them the moment she heard Magnus's name at Dover. Still, she recalled all the heart and intelligence under the misery in Magnus Haile's dark brown eyes as he'd watched his little girl sail away and decided he had hopes, dreams and a passionate nature his elder brother must have sidestepped at birth. She marvelled Lady Drace was so obsessed with the current Earl of Carrowe that she refused to see how much less of a man he was than his younger brother. Perhaps ten years ago the eldest Haile brother had been as dashing and deliciously dangerous as the Honourable Magnus was now, but Hetta couldn't imagine it. There was coldness in the Earl's gaze his brother would never share, and if she was lucky enough to have a lover as potent and passionate as Magnus Haile, she hoped she wouldn't be as big a fool as Lady Drace was by whistling him down the wind.

No, close off that notion right now, Hetta Champion. One failed love affair in a lifetime is enough.

She refused to be second-best ever again and Magnus Haile wouldn't even notice if she fell at his feet and begged him to take her instead of his precious Lady Drace.

A week after he had to watch Delphi and his daughter sail away Magnus was halfway down a second bottle of cognac and still the memory refused to fade. He'd felt so hollowed out and despairing that day he had been trying to fill the void ever since.

'Oh, no, what the devil are you doing here?' he asked when he heard rapid footsteps outside, then looked up and only just managed to silence a groan of protest. Maybe he was asleep and dreaming. He blinked and the apparition still didn't go away. The boy glared back as though Magnus was somehow at fault. Well, he *was* drunk and noxious in his mother's newly decorated dining parlour. He needed a hot bath and someone to shave him, then push him into clean clothes, since he was too cast-away to do it himself. He didn't think he deserved a hallucination as ill timed as this one, though.

'Mama! Mama! It's the man from Dover and he's got horns,' the boy's treble voice yelled and managed to make Magnus jump as if he'd been struck by lightning.

He put up a shaky hand to feel his hair standing up in two peaks where he'd run his fingers through it and smoothed them down as best he could. He still didn't see why the boy had to trumpet his sorry state to his mother when she was standing right behind him and could see for herself. 'Oh, the deuce, please get him out of here,' Magnus begged, putting his hand over his eyes and hoping the boy would disappear if he pretended not to be here hard enough. He thought he'd done quite well not cursing his imagination for dreaming the boy up, but next time he looked the brat from Dover was glaring at him as if he was the interloper here. Even thinking about the day they'd met made Magnus's stomach give a heavy roll of nausea in protest. He only just managed to force it back and go on glaring at them owlishly.

The sight of him glowering must have made the bespectacled lady hesitate in the doorway, far more daunted by the rough welcome than her appalling offspring. For a moment Magnus felt guilty about making it so plain he didn't want them here, but she shouldn't march into strange houses if she wasn't prepared for a rebuff. Before he could repent his harshness and recall his manners, she raised her chin, braced her shoulders and sailed further into the room as if she had every right to be here as well. He was almost ashamed of himself and could see the effort it cost her to brazen this out, but he *was* three-parts drunk and looking forward to adding the last quarter as soon as she and her son left, preferably as fast as their feet would carry them.

She was eyeing the chaos Magnus had wrought during his day of drunken misery instead of obliging him, though. A tidal wave of sickness ground again in Magnus's belly as dread of Delphi and his little girl being unmasked by this woman who knew too much joined all that brandy and very little food, if any, he recalled hazily. This woman knew things he didn't want anyone knowing and here she was expecting… Exactly what *was* she expecting of him?

'We did knock, but nobody came to see who was at the door, so I dare say they thought it was you being loud and ridiculous,' she explained frostily. She looked tired and pale even to Magnus's jaundiced gaze and shame got a little stronger under the dread she might have tracked him down somehow and come to extort a price for her promised silence.

'And why the deuce were you knocking on my mother's door?' he barked harshly.

'Lord Carrowe told us to stay here until I find more suitable lodgings.'

Magnus felt more at sea than ever as he wondered why Gresley had sent this woman, of all the women he could find and send to the Dowager Countess of Carrowe's Hampstead home, in their mother's absence. She didn't *look* like a member of the muslin company and the boy couldn't have an ounce of Haile blood in him if she turned out to be another of Gres's guilty secrets he was shuffling about the country now she was on these shores, in the hope his wife never found out about her.

'Who the devil are you, then?'

'Mrs Champion.'

'And who the deuce is she?' he said, still uneasy with the notion Gres could have had anything to do with her or her son.

'Sir Hadrian Porter's daughter,' she said flatly, as if that was all he needed to know about her. The name sounded vaguely familiar, but he couldn't dredge the man out of his memory to go with it. So, who was Sir Hadrian Porter and where was he while his daughter was running wild about the countryside with her brat knocking on doors where she wasn't wanted?

'So now I know?'

'My father was called back to England to

track down your father's murderer,' she told him wearily, as if she was quite accustomed to being unwelcome among Sir Hadrian's victims, or should that be his clients? 'Lord Carrowe sent me here when he decided Carrowe House was unsafe for adventurous boys. We had nowhere else to stay at the drop of a hat,' she explained reluctantly, and even in this state he thought she was probably skimming over a chapter of disasters.

Another wave of guilt washed over Magnus as he looked round his mother's dining parlour and wondered if it looked any better than Gresley's ancestral wreck in town at the moment, thanks to him. Not much of a welcome to be had here nor any comfort. Wouldn't his mother be ashamed if she could see him? He heard himself groan as if he'd been kicked by his uneasy conscience, then glowered at them for hearing it and seeing him like this. Though, if they thought him objectionable enough they might go away and leave him to find oblivion in a bottle at last. He eyed them with disfavour and wondered if he ought to go on with his potations to underline how little he wanted them here.

'I beg your pardon for interrupting, Mr Haile,' Mrs Champion said. 'But the front door is open and this one was ajar.' She carried on as if that was a good enough excuse for rushing in here even when his glare argued it wasn't.

'Your son would march into hell to argue with the devil uninvited, if you ask me,' he said harshly. Unfair, but he might as well try to get drunk in a busy London street and he didn't feel like being fair.

'You *are* the devil,' the boy argued, chin out and a fine glare of his own.

For a moment Magnus almost smiled and might have managed to laugh at himself if those words hadn't hit home so hard. It *was* devilish of him to speak to a child like this. He had sworn never to be like his father at a very early age, but he caught the glower and meanness of the man in his own frown and gruff unfairness now and felt his sins grind in his gut all over again. A cold sweat broke out on his forehead and he hated the man he'd become with a bitter passion close to despair. He heard an unearthly noise, more like an animal in pain than a human being, and realised he had made it as the awful fear he was about to disgrace himself washed over him like icy water. Desperate to prevent the final disgrace of having them see him spew, he lurched to his feet and shot past them at a speed he didn't know he had in him. A brief image of the woman and her boy staring as he fumbled blindly past them haunted him as he ran for the back of the house, blessing the fact the door was open as he dashed past the kitchen. Lingering cooking smells didn't help, but he was vaguely aware of Cook and Peg, the middle-aged maid who stayed with his family through thick and thin, staring after him open-mouthed, but they at least must have been expecting it after the amount of time he'd spent in the darkened dining room trying to drown his sorrows. At last he was outside and in the kitchen garden, gulping in clean air, and dared to hope he had managed to overcome his ills.

Wrong, an evil little voice in the back of his mind chortled triumphantly. Heat and icy chills washed over him in waves and he managed to stumble as far as the stable midden before casting up his accounts as the smell hastened wave after wave of wretched sickness, so he doubled over in self-inflicted misery and gave in. No effort of will could halt the cramping nausea now and he hardly had time to moan his woes into thin air between bouts as brandy scorched out of him a lot faster than he had put it in.

Magnus had no idea how much time passed before he finally dared hope he was done. A wonder if there was anything left in his belly to retch on now and he dearly wanted to believe it was empty. The cold of his own sweat on his skin belied the glorious summer day all around him and he had a horrible suspicion he might be about to faint. The threat beat in his ears as the world seemed to come and go with an angry buzz every time he moved his head, so it would be foolish to straighten up just yet.

Not that, he silently pleaded with the gloating voice of his conscience. *Don't let me be found lying on a muck heap by a nosy boy.*

Determined to save a small scrap of dignity from the wreck of fashionable and almost Honourable Magnus Haile, he straightened up slowly and carefully and waited for the world to stop spinning.

'Come on, Mr Magnus. Let's get you under the pump.' He heard Jem's resigned voice behind him and he realised Peg or Cook must have run to fetch the lad so he could deal with Magnus while they welcomed their unexpected visitors.

'I am a damned fool, Jem,' he managed to mutter as he lurched towards the pump in the far corner of the yard and felt better as the smell of manure faded a little.

'There's a lot of it about,' Jem said wisely, and Magnus felt like a child with a patient and resigned adult telling him boys will be boys.

Then even thinking was impossible as ice-cold water rushed over his still-reeling head and shoulders and soaked him to the skin. Feeling as miserable as sin, he made himself stay under the relentless flow while Jem pumped and he shivered. At last he called a halt and shook like a great, misguided and miserable dog. Standing still for a long moment, he signalled Jem to pump again and made himself gulp icy handfuls of water to test his still-complaining belly. Shaking water from his sodden hair, he dared stand back and strip off his soaking shirt.

'Finished?' Jem asked.

'Aye.'

'Best have this, then,' Jem said and first presented him with a towel, then exchanged it for a pristine shirt Magnus pulled over his head, at the same time wishing he'd never even heard of brandy as the thunder of it rang in his temples. Why had he thought getting drunk would solve anything?

'Cook said you was to drink this,' Jem said glumly and passed over a concoction that smelt of peppermint and something a lot less tempting, so Magnus gulped it down as fast as he could and grimaced as the taste clashed with everything else he'd put into his belly lately.

'I will do now, go and help Peg,' Magnus managed to say gruffly, and Jem took one last look at him, then nodded as if he agreed the worst was over, before leaving him.

Magnus felt his stomach give one of those ominous rolls as it objected to whatever the drink was before it settled and felt surprisingly better. At least he had the taste of peppermint in his mouth now instead of the sour aftermath of his sins. He stood still for long moments like a chastened dog bathed after a really good roll in something awful. After a while he dared hope he might be himself again in a week or two and the sturdy wall at the end of the kitchen garden looked just the right height to support a failed gentleman in a fragile state of health. Somehow, he made his way there without toppling over, but he could not face going back inside to apologise to the woman from Dover and her unruly boy quite yet.

It would make sense to build this wall higher and block out the wind, he reasoned to distract himself from the thunder of his own pulse in his ears at the thought of her and all he had to be sorry about this time. Peaches and grapes and apricots could shelter under its sunny warmth and fruit almost as happily as they would in their Mediterranean home, but why would anyone wall out such a view even for those natural riches? And where *did* grapes and apricots and peaches come from originally if not those warm and sunny lands?

Magnus leaned on solid stones under a benign July sun and gazed across wide acres of blessed space as the Heath spread out before him. Out there was real life—the glory of nature he ought to have clung to as his world fell apart, instead of trying to lose himself in a brandy bottle. He listened to the quiet buzz of bees happily occupied among the bean flowers and mused on the origin of garden plants in an attempt to forget his troubles. His shirt was still clinging to him like a lover and his head was thumping as if Thor's hammer was busy inside it, but the world was wondrous again and he needed to remember how small a part of it he was.

Soft footsteps sounded from behind him and he heard the rustle of feminine skirts. His brief moment of peace was over. 'Can't I be spared even one indignity?' he pleaded with nobody in particular under his breath. He knew she heard when she met his aching eyes with a hint of hurt behind the eyeglasses he suddenly suspected were there to keep him and the rest of the world at a distance. Regret nagged at him as he caught sight of her flinching and a feral nag of attraction to this sharp, yet somehow vulnerable, female dug into his conscience like a hot whip. He groaned in audible protest that she took the wrong way from the look of that poker back and her best antidote's glare. She should know what a contradiction all the pretend hardness was against the soft fullness of her mouth and a figure not even the most determined attack of dowdiness he had ever come across could quite disguise. A true rake would be so intrigued by the contrast between the faulty disguise and a warm, desirable woman underneath it and try all the tricks in his armoury to seduce her. Luckily he was an uneasy seducer and in no state to undo any sane female with his mythical charms right now.

Chapter Four

'I am sorry to disturb you, Mr Haile, but your manservant said you were feeling a little better and I wanted to talk to you before we go,' Hetta said with more sympathy than he deserved after calling Toby a little devil and greeting her with such revulsion she almost turned tail and ran, until weariness and common sense took over and reminded her what a challenge it would be to find somewhere else to go this late in the day.

But then he'd stared at Toby with what looked suspiciously like a sheen of tears in his bloodshot dark eyes before dashing outside to be disgracefully ill, as if her son was a painful reminder his own child was gone. Her heart went out to him even as she fought an impulse to run after the hired carriage she could hear trundling down the drive and forget she had set eyes on him again. She noted the sunlight played on his wild, wet black curls as they dried in complete disarray, but highlighted his starkly handsome features more acutely than ever as he squinted against the light with a flinch that gave his headache away. Even after seeing how drunk he was when she got here she still had to fight a ridiculous flutter of enthusiasm for the dratted man. He could have walked straight out of one of Lord Byron's epics and he wasn't to know she had peeped through the window on the half-landing and glimpsed him bare-chested and rather magnificent as he reeled back from his dousing under the pump. Bran had been five years older than her, but he'd lacked the sleekly muscled power of this mature man even when he died. And Magnus Haile managed to look deliciously masculine even when shivering like a drowned rat in the July sun. With sunlight merciless on his ashen face now and those darkly shadowed eyes showing how little he had slept since she saw him at Dover, a dangerous sort of pity softened her heart. Despite his dissolute ways and low opinion of her and Toby, he was clearly a deeply lonely and bereft man and at least he *had* a heart to be broken by a lover's desertion. Her late husband would have shrugged and found the next willing female if she had left him. Heart or no, Magnus Haile had no feelings for her, though, so she ordered herself not to be more of a fool than she could help and waited for him to argue.

'Why?' he obliged, producing one of his best frowns especially for her.

'My son and I need a safe place to lay our heads for the night. The jarvey has demanded his fee and driven back to town. I could not persuade him to take us to the nearest respectable inn. He said his horse wanted its stable and he did as well, so I need your advice on where I can find a respectable and clean place to stay for the night. Oh, and I also wanted to remind you I *never* gossip.'

'Everyone gossips in the right circumstances, Mrs Campion.'

'Champion,' she told him impatiently. Getting her surname wrong wasn't an insult even if it felt like one. 'And I don't.'

'What did you say you are doing here, Mrs *Champion*?' he demanded sharply as a man could when he was suffering so many self-inflicted ailments.

She should wait until he was completely sober, but she really must find lodgings for the night and, once she had, they need not meet again. Even now she would leave him to his misery and his favourite glower, but he was ghost pale under the tan even she knew a dandy would condemn as bucolic. Maybe the rumours she claimed not to listen to were right about the Honourable Magnus Haile after all, then. Perhaps he had been trying to turn over a new leaf since his father was murdered and wanted to live a more useful life. She reviewed Mr Haile's solitary drinking spree and decided, no, he was quite happy with the old one.

'My father came to England to find your father's murderer,' she told him.

'You said that before as well,' he said impatiently.

'Drunken gentlemen rarely recall what was said five minutes ago,' she said and cursed her own stupidity for trying to reason with him. 'I suppose you are so used to being one you have developed an obliging memory.'

'If you say so, but if your father is Fat George's Bloodhound *he* will need an exceptionally hard head to keep up with his master,' he said with the suggestion of a sneer in his voice. She could imagine him backing it up with a quizzing glass in his heyday as a dandy. 'Like his royal patron Sir Hadrian Porter doesn't seem to take much interest in his immediate family, does he? Even I know he doesn't spend more time in his home country than he can help, yet he is supposed to catch the killer who has confounded our efforts and half of Bow Street as well? Forgive me if I doubt it, ma'am.'

'Papa has solved all the mysteries His Majesty's Government set him so far, I will have you know. He does important work, so why should he worry about things I am capable of sorting out myself? We go on very well together, Mr Haile, and, if I were you, I would be glad he is here to unmask your father's murderer and he always refuses to listen to rumours. Because of my father your family has a chance of finding true justice instead of some cobbled-together tale made up to satisfy his masters.'

'I hated my father, so no wonder the gossips whisper I must have killed him, despite my valet's evidence I was even more drunk that night than I managed to be today.'

'Your mother and sisters have my sympathy, then. Two drunks in the family must have been almost too much to endure,' Hetta said bluntly, but he had insulted her and her family first, so why not?

'I am not a habitual drunkard and I would never hurt them if I was,' he protested, and deep down she felt guilty for implying it.

She knew he would never use his strength to coerce or dominate a woman. If ever a man was tempted to do so he must have been when Lady Drace walked away with his child. Now, instead of one of Lord Byron's devil heroes, he looked like a weary knight who had defended too many lost causes for the good of his soul. Fanciful nonsense, she told herself, and it came of being in the wrong place at the wrong time to witness his darkest moments, but what on earth was she going to do with herself and Toby now? The idea of trying to find a hired coach to heaven knew where at short notice nearly overwhelmed even her sturdy determination never to allow a man to order her life again.

'Why are you here instead of in Worthing?' she asked impulsively, because it was easier to think about him than worry about where to spend the night.

'Guess,' he said wearily. 'This summer by the sea is supposed to be a much-needed tonic for them and it won't be if they spend it worrying about me.'

'Honestly, men,' she said disgustedly. 'Do you really believe your mother and sisters won't worry if they can't actually see you drunk and miserable? If you truly believe we women live on fluffy clouds of ignorance about what men get up to behind our backs, I am sorry for you. I took you for less of a fool than most of your sex, Mr Haile, but apparently I was wrong.'

'Obviously, and why would you give me so much credit when my idiocy was writ large the day we met, Mrs Champion?' he barked as if he meant to drive her away and never mind if she had to sleep under a hedge tonight.

'Your sister Lady Aline has such a high opinion of you I must have fallen into the error of thinking she knew you better, despite all evidence to the contrary. She seems such a rational being and really should know better.'

'No doubt she will see through me in time, but what *I* can't understand is why my elder brother sent you here and your father let him. Your husband must be deranged to let you and his son visit England in his father-in-law's so-called care.'

'My husband is dead,' she said, indignant he thought she ought to have one to take charge of her when Bran was as irresponsible as a cuckoo whenever he was far away from his command and the sea.

'I am sorry for your loss,' he said so soberly she almost believed him.

'As I am for yours,' she replied, and if he chose to think she meant the death of his father he was welcome.

'I don't deserve pity,' he said harshly.

'Yet your dilemma was made by two people,' she said with a brutal frankness she refused to regret even when he glared at her, then shook his head as if silently admitting she might be right.

'Most of them are,' he said with a half-weary, half-wolfish smile that made her heart skitter, then race on in panic. No, she refused to be a fool for a handsome face ever again. She had been one for Bran for a heady, brief time, and now this man was baiting her she almost wanted to flirt back. Luckily, he waved a hand as if he was being more unworthy than usual in using such tactics to deflect her. 'I cannot deem my child a mistake, then shrug and carry on with life untroubled, Mrs Champion, even if her mother wants me to,' he added bleakly.

Her heartbeat sped up again as she put herself in Lady Drace's elegant shoes for a moment and decided she would say yes to almost anything if he asked her to in the right way. 'Why would you?' she managed to argue even so.

'You heard Lady Drace, Mrs Champion. I have been dismissed from their lives and I hope you and Champion did a better job of being parents, for all your sakes.'

'He died before Toby was born,' she said, frowning at the prickly memory of how little Bran wanted the baby in her belly during his last shore leave.

'That explains a lot,' Magnus Haile said as if it might well.

'And do you always use rudeness to deflect personal questions, Mr Haile?'

'Only when frigid politeness fails me, Mrs Champion. None of which explains why my elder brother sent you here when our mother is from home and the place half-finished,' he persisted.

He waved an impatient hand at the lovely little Queen Anne manor house behind them. It was obviously still undergoing improvement from piles of sand and gravel and a dusting of sawdust, and Hetta wondered if he had sent the builders and carpenters away for the day, so he could get drunk in peace. The strength and elegance of his long-fingered hand caught her feral imagination and painted her a picture of him sensually rendering parts of her helpless with longing and melted to the core. She was so shocked she glared at him to make up for the shameful image and thought she saw a reluctant echo of her own fascination in his dark brown eyes for a moment before they were sternly guarded again.

This will not do, barked her inner puritan, so she grasped at the reason she was here to divert them both.

'Lord Carrowe caught Toby climbing the roof at Carrowe House, despite all the nailed-up doors and windows and his dire warnings not to go anywhere near the worst parts of the poor old place. His lordship suggested I get

Toby out of London before he killed himself in such a deathtrap and it was kind of him to suggest we came here for a few days, given Toby's mischief. I would have had to stop him bothering the builders here, I suppose, but we cannot stay now, so at least that's one less thing to worry about—and that reminds me. I must find somewhere to stay tonight before the inns are full, so I shall bid you good day, Mr Haile.'

'Wait, there's no need to quit the place. I am in the way of the builders and upholsterers anyway and of my mother's cook and house-keeper, who insisted on staying to be sure the builders do not make a mess. My mother hired servants for the summer season because she wanted those two to enjoy an easy summer after years of devoted and often unpaid work, so looking after me is hardly a rest.'

'They don't seem unduly worried, rather the opposite, in fact.'

'Peg was our nursemaid and playmate when I was young and we still had a few servants will-ing to stay in such a decaying old wreck as long as my mother managed to scrape together their wages. By the time my youngest sisters came along, Peg and Cook and a very ancient butler were the only staff left. Peg is more a member of the family than a housekeeper and Cook is too happy with her new kitchen to complain about anything much.' He smiled and looked as if his memory had taken him back to more innocent days, before he recalled Hetta was a stranger in his home and snapped back to the present. 'This business with the old Earl must have made my elder brother think harder about his responsibilities if he got you out of the old dust heap before your son did himself permanent damage,' he said as if it almost explained her presence. 'And I ought to leave this place, not you. There are plenty of low dives where I can stay and you cannot.'

'No, finding a new place to stay is hardly a great hardship and we will soon be back on the Continent and back to a proper summer, so it hardly matters where we stay for now.'

'Is this an improper one, then?' he asked with a ghost of rakish innuendo in his naturally husky, fascinatingly deep voice.

The sound of him reciting a laundry list would make goosebumps rise on her oversensitised skin, so his almost-suggestion they misbehave together made her shiver with something very far from cold. 'No, just a British one,' she said flatly.

'Aye, the rain must have found all the holes in the roof and made Carrowe House even more uncomfortable than usual,' he said as if he had already repented his lighter mood.

It was wrong of her to wish he hadn't changed his mind and his mood, she reminded herself, as she tucked away a fantasy of being locked in his arms until they both forgot the season and everything else on a lazy afternoon in the middle of the sun-sleepy Heath. Magnus had been brought up at Carrowe House with a bullying father and a mother wilfully mired in scandal by her own husband, so it was silly of Hetta to feel sorry she had never had a real home to go to. Her father's country house had been let out ever since he inherited it in order to cover the costs of his mother's grand London home. And Magnus Haile's own home was so tumbledown and faded she wouldn't wish it on her worst enemy. She kept her suspicion that someone was slipping in and out of Carrowe House to herself. It *was* only a prickly feeling of being watched from shadowy corners and once fancying she heard a soft footstep where feet should not be able to go. She had no proof and if she mentioned it the impulsive idiot could gallop off there to lie in wait for a murderer. Hetta shivered and was more glad than ever to be out of the poor old house, despite Magnus Haile's drunken revulsion at the sight of her.

'Yes, I suppose it did feel damp and a little depressing in the rain yesterday, but I doubt you need a stranger to confirm its shortcomings,' she said almost politely.

'Gresley says most of it was habitable when he was a boy, but nobody should have to endure the place now if they don't really need to.'

'Although you wish he had sent us somewhere else?' she asked, and as he said nothing she knew she was right. 'I suppose you will be glad when Carrowe House is torn down,' she said to fill an uncomfortable silence.

'Aye, and Gres will have to pay someone to do it and that will delay matters. There isn't a shred of gold leaf worth more than a farthing to salvage after my father stripped it bare to fund his excesses, so at least my brother and your father should be safe from thieves there since there's precious little left to plunder.'

'Couldn't your brother stop your father doing so? He was the heir.'

'You never met our father,' he said with a gesture of that fine-boned hand to distract her again. 'Although Gres was wild in his youth and closer to our father than the rest of us back then. Shortly before he married he seemed to wake up to the folly of it all, though...' He paused and they avoided one another's eyes as Lady Drace's bitter parting words reminded them of a possible reason why. 'As the heir he was the only one who *could* rescue the rest of the family fortunes from the same ruin. Our father would have picked everything clean and mortgaged the land as well and I have to admire Gres for stopping him, but I'm not so sure about the way he did it now.'

Hetta could hardly agree out loud, but she managed to school her features to her best imitation of a marble statue in spectacles. She would never have agreed to stay under the new Lord Carrowe's roof if Lady Aline Haile had not made it virtually impossible to refuse until something more suitable came along. The Earl's sister was back for a fleeting visit when Hetta had called to ask her father's advice on suitable lodgings when the affair of the rat made her and Toby homeless at short notice. She had been away from England so much of her life she had no idea which areas were respectable and which only looked so by daylight. At the time it seemed sensible to seek his help, even if her father would rather not be distracted when he was hunting a murderer of aristocrats because the King thought the idea might be catching and he must be next on any revolutionary's list.

Sir Hadrian and the Earl of Carrowe had been out when Lady Aline insisted Hetta and Toby stay at Carrowe House rather than take the first place on offer. Lord Carrowe had tried to pretend they were welcome when he returned, but Hetta never quite managed to believe him. This morning Lady Aline left for Worthing and Toby grew bored in the small range of rooms the family had kept watertight and nailed up against the ruin everywhere else. Of course, she should never have fallen asleep in an almost comfortable chair after a disturbed night, but it could have been worse. The dream she had been having about sneering ghosts and stalking murderers could have come true. Instead she

woke up to hear Lord Carrowe shouting and
ran out of the room just in time to watch her
son take that fall into the attics as their reluctant host stood looking horrified and stared up
at the chimney where Toby had been clinging.
To give him his due, his lordship soon awoke
from his horrified stupor and ran upstairs while
she was still trying to make her legs stop wobbling long enough to follow. Before she could
stop shaking like a leaf Lord Carrowe had
come downstairs as fast as he could go whilst
towing her son behind him with every last iota
of the fine Haile temper he must share with his
brother flashing from his dark eyes and a scowl
even Magnus Haile could not outdo. What a relief to find the worst damage her son had suffered was to his pride—oh, and a few scratches
and bruises he richly deserved and yet another
set of his clothes waiting to be patched and
mended when she had time. Lord Carrowe let
her know he had only kept his hands off her
boy because Toby fell through his lordship's
rotten roof on to his lordly rotten floor and
landed on his merely genteel backside. Even in
a fine Haile temper Lord Carrowe could hardly
give the boy a beating for going where he was

expressly told not to go when he was already bruised and a little bit chastened.

Once she had got over her reluctant host's impressive show of temper and made sure her son wasn't really harmed, Hetta had been secretly delighted to leave Carrowe House. If not for her father's vague order to go where she was bid and keep the boy out of trouble, she would have resumed her hunt for another lodging straight away. That wretched promise again. Why the deuce had Papa invoked it simply to get them out of his way as fast as possible? She frowned at the thought there was something real and a little bit anxious behind her father's irritation today. She was almost glad Magnus was staring at the wall as if he wished he was alone, so he couldn't read her thoughts. However hard she tried to tell herself he and his family mysteries were nothing to do with her, she felt involved. Somehow, she couldn't simply put the Haile family to the back of her mind and carry on with her life as if she had never met any of them.

And poor old Carrowe House had felt so oppressive and strange she could easily believe a man was murdered there. It felt as if the tremors of such a violent crime lingered there like the aftershocks of a great earthquake. Fanciful to even think such a thing and she blamed her fascination with Gothic romances she picked up during long, lonely nights sitting up with Toby as a baby as he grew teeth or was fretful or simply his usual ravenous self. A series of shocking events happening at a distance to timid, yet recklessly curious, heroines seemed an ideal diversion when the rest of the world was fast asleep and hired lodgings could feel soulless by candlelight. Except last night, as she lay listening for the next creak or moan the old house made as if it tried to settle on its ancient foundations and couldn't get comfortable, her secret vice had not seemed such a good idea. Even the latest chilling tale she had picked up could not divert her from the fancy she was living inside one and could be silently, watchfully observed from places that looked perfectly innocent in daylight.

And she knew far too much about its new owner to be at all comfortable under his roof at Carrowe House now, even if she hadn't let her imagination run away with her. Lord Carrowe had ruined the lovely young girl who became

Lady Drace, then wed an heiress rich enough to buy him control of the main Haile estates from his father. Despite her trick of presenting a stiff facade to the world, Hetta knew she wasn't much of an actress. Sooner or later the Earl might have realised she knew more about him than he wanted anyone to know. So why had she agreed to come here when it was best to be done with the Hailes and all their houses? Panic, she supposed and called herself a craven. Anyway, Lord Carrowe didn't own this house and he seemed fixed in London, despite the heat. It had seemed a safe enough compromise to come here while she got her breath back. But now it felt even more impossible to like the new Earl when his betrayal had skewed Lady Drace's choices. Those choices, in turn, had made Magnus Haile into a cynic who refused to look at Hetta while they discussed trivial things and now tension sang between them like overstretched wire.

'I suppose your father kept control of your London home because town life suited him better.' She finally broke the silence almost tactfully.

Her mouth might say careful things, but her

mind and too much of her imagination was still busy with the man in front of her. Even ten years ago, when he might have been a callow youth and she was busy being blinded by Bran's golden good looks, ready smiles and flattery, she would have leapt at the chance of loving Magnus Haile instead. She silently cursed him for not being there, so she could have picked him and not Brandon Champion. Shocked by her own thoughts, she ordered herself to look hard into the next mirror she passed so she could see for herself why meeting him then would only have meant more heartache for her instead of less. Next to Lady Drace's cool and perfect looks, Hetta Porter would have been nigh invisible.

But Lady Drace isn't here now, is she? bad Hetta argued.

An urgent need for something deep and intimate with this gruff and unshaven idiot tugged at Hetta, and the *I wonder...* whisper that had shocked her so deeply at the first sight of him was plaguing her with unsuitable fantasies yet again.

Don't, she told it sternly, looking for some way to resist his rough appeal. Despite all the reasons she should go, she didn't want to leave him staring into the middle distance as if his sins were writ large on it for the whole world to see.

'Your sisters' old rooms at Carrowe House are comfortable and one of the kitchens is usable,' she said as if his brother's house fascinated her.

'Their old bedchambers are as secure as Wulf and I could make them, but not comfortable,' he argued as if he was amazed a lady voluntarily spent half an hour there, never mind a whole night.

'I had to make all sorts of unlikely places home on our travels,' she explained, glad they were safely off perilous ground. 'As the alternative was coming back to England with my tail between my legs, I learned to adapt. Can you imagine how bored Toby would be in a neat little house away from any action?'

'Not without a shudder,' he said, and it was unfair of him to have a sense of humour under all that gloom and rough-edged glamour.

'Neither can I, and as I travelled with my mother and father as a girl, it seemed natural to join my father when my husband died, so I set out as soon as Toby and I could travel once he was born.'

'Intrepid of you to make such a journey with a babe in arms, Mrs Champion,' he said as if he didn't quite approve of intrepid females.

'I did my best,' she said ironically, and if he turned out to be a washout as a wild seducer it was all to the good, since she didn't want to be seduced. She tried to recall why she *was* out here wasting her breath—ah, yes, reassuring him his secrets were safe with her and trying to find out if there was a nice clean inn on the doorstep. Time to get on with that, then, and never mind the rest.

Chapter Five

'And now I have to find somewhere to stay,' Hetta said as briskly as she could with that ridiculous notion of him staring at her with all his sensual attention on her instead of Lady Drace haunting her.

She wished she couldn't see past his whiskers and dour frown to the good man underneath. She smiled wistfully and he looked puzzled, then turned back to stare at the wide landscape on the other side of the wall as if he didn't want to know why. Her husband would have agreed and she grimaced at this man's back. Once she was *enceinte* Bran was revolted by her changing body. If she'd ever hoped a child would bring them closer, she didn't enjoy the fantasy for long. She recalled Bran taunting her that his slender filly had become a fat mare and his contempt had picked at her fragile self-confidence ever since. She could be a lioness on her son's behalf and refused to be overlooked or under-valued because she was female, yet as a sensual and sensitive woman she felt more like a wary tabby cat who had avoided mankind since Bran showed her his true colours.

She glared at Magnus Haile's strong back as he peered at the Heath as if he wanted to forget her as well. Drat the man for destroying the notion she was safe from his kind. Jealousy of Lady Drace still gnawed at her, despite his dismissal of her own limited charms. She really must stop gazing at the play of his powerful muscles outlined by a damp shirt when he shifted as if he felt her gaze. He was a drunken rake and that ought to put her off his lethal mixture of power and vulnerability.

'A child should never suffer for its parents' mistakes,' she told him earnestly.

'Yet so many do,' he replied. 'I am glad my elder brother had the sense to send you away from Carrowe House, Mrs Champion, and amazed you stayed as long as you did. Most ladies wouldn't step over the threshold of such a wreck even if it wasn't the scene of bloody murder.'

As his brisk change of subject was for the best, she allowed herself a shrug of resigned acceptance since he didn't have eyes in the back of his head. 'It doesn't pay to ask too many questions about past events in grand old houses, does it?' she said. 'And that one's shortcomings are less of a problem now than they must be in winter when I imagine the whole place is cold as charity.'

'Colder if anything, but not a suitable place for a lady in any weather, especially not one who lacks the chaperone you seem to have forgotten to employ when your last one left,' he said with a severe look over his shoulder and a careful shake of his head as if he was the most respectable man on earth.

'My father has an aversion to the breed since the last two he insisted on hiring tried to marry him. Now he is quite happy for me to do without one and I am a plain widow with a son who makes devastatingly honest comments about any man who tries to take advantage of me, so all three of us are happy.'

'Your son is hardly the sort of sop to the proprieties the high sticklers insist on,' he turned around properly to tell her with a coolly assessing look she wished he had kept on the landscape. Now the Honourable Magnus Haile was back, she sighed for the unshaven pirate who made her shiver with something it was best not to name. At least that version of him had feelings to drown in brandy. This one had his emotions walled up behind so much chilly indifference she almost gave up and walked away. 'And your father is not exactly attentive to his daughter or grandson's comfort, is he?' he added disapprovingly.

Papa was very busy about Haile business and might save this one's neck from the hangman, so she couldn't see why Magnus Haile was so intent on his shortcomings as a father. 'Papa has never made me feel a burden and he loves us deep down,' she defended Sir Hadrian loyally.

'At least we have hating to be a weight on our loved ones' shoulders in common, then, Mrs Champion,' he murmured. 'Champion?' he added as if her married name had finally caught his attention. 'My friend, Sir Marcus Champion, had a brother.' He was silent for a moment and Hetta wished they had stayed on the subject of Magnus Haile's loves and losses instead of hers. 'Brandon, yes, that's it. I remember now there was some tale about him eloping with a schoolgirl. He was Captain Champion last time I met him in London waiting for some appointment at the Admiralty.'

'Yes, he left me in Lyme. He thought I should not travel so far in my condition,' she lied, avoiding his eyes as she told the comfortable version of Bran's absence she'd tried to fool her neighbours with at the time.

'I dare say he was right,' he said almost gently, as if he didn't blame her for papering over the cracks in her marriage to a man he looked as if he hadn't liked very much, however much he enjoyed the company of Bran's elder brother.

'Maybe he was,' she said as airily as she could.

She shifted under Mr Magnus Haile's sceptical gaze. It had not taken her long to realise Bran had wed her for her father's fortune and the Dowager Lady Porter's influence. He must have thought her the perfect wife for a naval officer determined to outrank his elder brother and be a Lord of the Admiralty as soon as his relatives by marriage could push his name forward. But then her grandmother had washed

her hands of Hetta and Papa had written that
he would not save his son-in-law from being
eaten by lions, so what madness had possessed
Hetta to run off with such an ambitious fool?
She had naively believed Bran's lies about loving her and never mind who her father was, but
madness? No, misery at losing her mother, then
being sent away by her father, had made her
vulnerable to Bran's flattery and her youthful
longing to be loved had done the rest. She had
been so lonely under her grandmother's roof
she'd agreed to elope with him because she was
so afraid of being left alone with her grandmother until she was so cowed she agreed to
be married off to some middle-aged protégé
of Lady Porter's simply to get away. She had
been a fool to be so wilfully taken in, but having Toby meant she could never truly regret
marrying his father.

She still shuddered at the memory of Bran
cursing her as his clog and telling her he had
put himself out to wed a plain nonentity for
no return at all. He managed to blame her for
their elopement as if he had never made all
those false promises and pretended devotion.
His passion for her was heady while it lasted,

she reminded herself. Being wanted so urgently by a handsome lover had filled a lot of gaps in her life until her grandmother's rebuff and Papa's horrified denial made him show his true colours and made the gaps yawn wider than ever. The last time she ever saw him her husband was striding away from her after a mere day at home, leaving her feeling fat, miserable and humiliated by his open revulsion at her visibly pregnant body, so she had hurled insults after him like a fishwife. She doubted her neighbours believed her fairy story about Bran leaving her behind because she was in no state to travel either after hearing her impressive collection of insults in a variety of outlandish languages. Then she had to live with herself when she found out her husband wasn't coming back. The guilt at realising a terrible tension had unwound inside her the day she knew Bran would never be able to teach their baby to despise its mother still haunted her even now.

'Anyway, I'm sure you know my husband died and was buried at sea since you are so well acquainted with his elder brother,' she said stiffly.

'My condolences,' he said with the contained

look she already knew was a smokescreen to hide his true feelings. 'It must be hard to be left with a child to raise alone,' he added with real sympathy in his deep voice this time.

'Toby wasn't born until three months after his father's death,' she said, and her secret euphoria that her son had come into the world fatherless felt wrong even now. She'd never wished Bran dead, just a few hundred miles away and not married to her, but at least he had died young and vigorous and full of promise instead of a disappointed man. Something told her he wouldn't have got to the places he'd planned to even if her family had been more inclined to help him, but now he was a force that had burnt out too young and no one would ever know what he might have achieved.

'From Mark's tales of him, your husband was nigh fearless as a boy and must have been a fine naval officer. Sir Marcus would welcome you both at Wellaby Hall if you are in need of a refuge while your father is busy. Mark enjoys having a pack of brats running wild about the place. *Come one, come all* should be the motto carved over his door since he and his lady retired to the country to raise their children in the fresh air.'

'I have no wish to be a duty guest,' she said stubbornly. Being one didn't work out with her grandmother or Lord Carrowe, so she was very reluctant to wear out another welcome and maybe too proud as well. 'I told you how I dislike being a burden, and since Papa forgets to eat for days when he's on the scent of a felon or a solution to a knotty problem, at least he needs us.' Hetta recalled whose mysteries Sir Hadrian was trying to solve this time and blushed. The bloody and violent end of an aristocrat in his own home seemed so unlikely in this peaceful place. With the sun gentle on her back and the warmth of an unusually benign English summer's day all around her, the loss of it felt a terrible crime for any man to quit this world before his time.

'The Champions would never think of you and your son as a duty,' Magnus Haile said gently, as if he recognised her pride and almost applauded it.

'You must know them well to say so, but I would still feel like one,' she said briskly. 'I did not follow you out here to seek sympathy, Mr

Haile, only to ask for your help and to repeat your secrets are safe with me. I would never play with the life of a child even if I was spiteful enough to gossip about her parents, which I am not.'

The spark of curiosity in his rather fascinating dark brown eyes died. He was once more the arrogant aristocrat she first saw on the quay at Dover, and only a brief shiver, as if he had been reminded his life was now barren, gave him away as human at all. He stared at his precious view again as if she was an unwanted guest who refused to leave and she was, she supposed, so she ought to get on and go.

'That would be reassuring, if I had any idea what you mean,' he said coldly.

'Given my father's occupation, I learned to be wary even as a child, Mr Haile. Once Toby could walk and talk there was even more reason to be discreet, so you can stop pretending with me.'

'As your son is stalking us like prey right now, I see why you would need to be very careful about what you say.'

'The little devil; I told him to stay with your housekeeper and cook,' she said and spun round to glare at her son. He was too far away to overhear them, and she really ought to find a tutor to keep him busy until it was time for school. He needed to be kept fully occupied before he got into more trouble. 'Come out from behind that currant bush, Toby Champion, or no puddings for you for the rest of the week.'

'He looks perfectly all right to me,' Toby said accusingly as he did as he was told and seemed disappointed Magnus Haile wasn't as sick as a dog.

Her son had mastered the art of deflection far too early, Hetta decided, and wondered if girls were easier to deal with than boys. Since she'd inherited her mother's fortune at the age of five and twenty and Bran's prize money was held in trust for his son, there was no need for her to go out as a governess or, heaven forbid, find another husband to support her, so she would never find out. Now her son was old enough for preparatory school she could be an independent woman. She tried not to think about the empty sound of it, and forming a picture in her head of a dark-haired tot of her own with velvet brown eyes and her father's stormy temper was simply no help at all. She was done with men and marriage, and the man her inner idiot seemed determined to yearn for was about as likely to ask her to change her mind as he was to sprout wings and fly after his former lover instead.

Chapter Six

'I would have thought you had seen enough people being miserably ill on our way across the Channel last week,' Hetta told her son with a straight look to say, *Stop right there, before you say something even more insulting.*

'You were so sick I thought you would turn inside out, Mama,' Toby announced cheerfully instead.

'And I will never have a single weakness to keep secret with you about to trumpet them to the world, my son.'

'It's not a weakness—it's a constitutional anomaly. Grandpapa said so.'

'And thank you, Grandpapa,' she said under her breath. Less scientific observation and more practical help would have done wonders at the time, but she chose this life, so she could hardly blame her father for being who he was.

'Then you have seen enough to study something else for a change. Since Lady Carrowe's cook has been kind enough to feed you and her housekeeper agreed to put up with you while I talked to Mr Haile, I hope you remembered to say thank you.'

Toby mumbled something defensive and shrugged.

'Then go back and do so this minute, young man. You won't be welcome in any kitchen if you do not say thank you for food and friendship. A boy who eats as you do should never risk a frosty welcome in one of those, should he?'

'No, but Grandpapa is always forgetting his food, so I can always eat his,' Toby said sulkily, as if he thought something important might happen if he ran back inside and did as he was bid.

'You should encourage him to eat instead of stealing from his plate when he's lost in thought. Rumours will get about there's a ravenous and thankless young wolf visiting Lady Carrowe's house it's best not to let in if you are not careful.'

'I need to eat as much as I can because you

want me to go to school soon and they say boys don't get fed properly there, but I think I would like to be part of a wolf pack,' Toby said, suddenly wistful about the friends he had never made as they had never stayed in one place long enough for him to make them.

'I'm not sure the pack would own up to you,' Hetta teased her son with a rueful smile and tried not to feel guilty he was fated to be a lone one. She must learn to be stricter with him in future, though, since he was grinning at her as if he had won their latest skirmish and he was probably right.

'Stay around here long enough and you'll be rolled on, sat on and joined in with by my sister-in-law's vast tribe of nieces and nephews and many other relatives, Master Champion,' Magnus told Toby as if he had forgiven him for being unruly and nigh ungovernable both here and in Dover.

Hetta sometimes felt as if she spent half her life trying to excuse or explain her son's restless ways to wary adults, but Toby was a lot more vulnerable than he liked to appear, and his bright blue eyes became eager at the thought of lots of children to play with. It was time to settle in this damp and unpredictable country and make him a real home. 'Don't let your hopes of mayhem and mischief rise too high, my son. We need to find lodgings and be gone before Mrs Wulfric Haile's relatives join her,' she warned.

'What lodgings would those be, Mrs Champion, in Hampstead, in July?' Magnus Haile raised his eyebrows to say what a fool she was to expect such wonders to drop into her lap. This leafy place must be the perfect escape for families to stay in reach of any almost-gentlemen who worked for their bread while their wives and children came out of London to avoid the heat and stench of high summer.

'We must go further from town, then,' she said, wondering why she had sold the house Brandon had bought when they'd married so hastily. She was sure to like Lyme with its fine views and beautiful situation when she wasn't being left there by a husband who wanted her as far away from his real life as possible without causing a scandal.

'When you dragged me round that fusty museum to look at broken bits of old statues the other day you promised I could see the beasts in the Tower Menagerie and the waxworks and the tunnel under the Thames and…'

'No, I said we would go and see them if we could, Toby, not that we would trail round your long list of macabre and apparently fascinating places day after day in the heat and dust and smell of the city.'

'I never wanted to come to this horrible country. It's cold and wet and boring and I wish you'd left me in—'

'And that's enough curmudgeonly nonsense from you, my son.' Hetta interrupted his catalogue of woes. 'I wish I had left you in a nice strict seminary for unruly boys, to be called for when you had learned better manners in a decade or so. If wishes were horses, beggars would ride, though, so we must both make the best of things as they are and not repine.'

'And it's not actually cold, wet or boring today,' Magnus pointed out and gestured at the wide vista beyond the garden wall.

He was taking a little too much interest in what was happening now he had some colour in his cheeks and a spark of interest in his fascinating dark brown eyes. To distract herself from this urge to stare into them and find out the details of their velvety depths, she wondered if his ribs and stomach ached as much as hers had after the awful sea crossing she still recalled with a shudder. Despite the wild disarray of his ebony-dark hair and an unshaven chin, the man was handsome as ten devils when he smiled. Luckily, she had too much to do to be a *femme fatale* and cast silken lures in his direction, even if she had a talent for seduction, to make it a temptingly bad idea. He wasn't dangerous at all, simply a minor character in her father's latest drama, and they need never see each other again after today.

'Don't encourage him,' she muttered to Magnus Haile as soon as Toby was busy standing on tiptoe to take in the wide and tempting landscape on the other side, picking out the details of a world that had no idea a boy with mischief never far from his mind was watching it with so much interest.

The man grinned and ignored her, helping Toby stand on the broad capping stones and take in his surroundings from even further up. 'Maybe the view will help you realise how small we all are next to wild nature, Master Champion,' he said.

'It looks like pure temptation to me,' Hetta muttered glumly.

'Don't you trust him?' he murmured as Toby stared fascinated at the wide green of his homeland after the more sun-scorched landscapes he was used to.

'No, and nor should you. You know what sort of risks he's capable of running,' she reminded him.

A frown knitted Magnus Haile's dark brows again and misery took the spark of humour from his eyes at her clumsy reminder of the day he had lost contact with his own child. 'Aye,' he said with a brief, bitter glance at her before he turned to look back at the mellow and elegant manor house where his mother must have grown up. 'If you don't mind your son running about with a lad who knows more about real life than he ever will, my brother's man, Jem Caudle, might take him out on to the Heath if I ask him nicely, and you can trust Jem to keep him safe. Having run the streets as a boy himself he knows all the dangers as well as most of the tricks grubby urchins play on their elders, so he won't stand any nonsense from your son.'

'Maybe later, if Master Caudle has time and

patience enough left after dealing with you, sir. Your brother's manservant was busy helping boil water for your bath and is waiting for you to go inside and be turned into a gentleman. Toby will have to wait until that brave young man finishes civilising you as best he can.'

'And I should not inflict my company on a lady until he does so,' he replied, suddenly guarded and every inch the haughty son of an earl.

Maybe she had imagined an easier and more intriguing gentleman lay underneath all that arrogance and pride. 'Best go in to be shaved and groomed anyway, then. You are shivering and it isn't even cold, for once. We can entertain each other and I still have time to take Toby for a short walk before I must be busy finding a respectable inn for us to stay in for the night,' she said to make it clear she didn't intend to be a burden on his family.

'No, you must remain here. I dare say it's too late to find a good enough place where this brat won't be up to his neck in trouble every time you take your eyes off him by now,' he argued with an almost affectionate smile for Toby to take the sting out of his words. 'My younger brother and his wife live not half a mile away as the crow flies and I can stay at their house. They are having dinner with Lord Carnwood as he is in town on business, so they will stay the night at Carnwood House. I cannot stay here since you neglected to bring a maid or chaperone, but nobody can gossip if we are not even in the same house, so we can both be comfortable and take stock of your situation come morning. For now, if you take yonder path out on to the Heath and don't venture too far from the main track, you will be safe enough even with Master Champion here as your sole companion,' he said with a rueful smile for Toby that made Hetta feel cut off and excluded, which was a ridiculous idea. 'When I am fit to be seen I will come and find you and it will be almost time for you to eat again,' he said as he gave Toby a hand down.

'It's always time for food, as far as Toby is concerned,' Hetta said, rather grumpily because Magnus seemed determined not to give her a chance to say thank you for saving her the task of tracking down somewhere respectable to stay tonight.

'I still want a puppy,' Toby said, and she grimaced at that oft-repeated demand.

'And what have I told you about making impossible demands?'

'We move around too much to have a dog. I am about to go off to school, so what would be the point? He would not like to be always travelling with you and Grandpapa and never having anywhere to settle for long. Innkeepers and ship's captains don't look kindly on dogs as guests or passengers,' he parroted wearily.

'All very sensible,' Magnus Haile broke in. 'You must meet my brother's mixed collection of hounds, and I dare say, if you are very good for the rest of the day, he will introduce you when he gets home tomorrow. They will be in need of a good run after being kept at a farm nearby while he is busy elsewhere.'

'Really, sir? Oh, can I, then, please, Mama?'

Toby sounded so eager she would be the worst of mothers to deny him, but she wondered if it might make him more desperate for a dog than ever and the idea of that rather lonely home in the country with only Toby's dog for company in term time loomed large again. 'Very well,' she said, and he danced on the spot with joyous impatience. 'But only if you are good for the rest of the day,' she cautioned since she knew where high excitement could lead.

'I will be, I promise.'

'They will be overjoyed someone is so eager to meet them, but my brother will expect a promise not to get them into trouble, since they are nearly as restless and inclined to find it as you are,' Magnus Haile said almost as if he liked Toby now the shock of meeting him again had worn off, and Hetta felt cross-grained and a little put out he didn't seem to have warmed to her in the same fashion.

'I promise. What sort are they?' her son said as he practically danced with excitement. 'How old are they? Where are they now? Why can't they come today?'

'They are no sort in particular, about six months old, and staying with a friend of my brother until *he* fetches them.'

'And if you take them on an adventure and it ends up the usual way, I shall make very sure you are never trusted with them or any other dog again, oh, white-headed son of mine,' Hetta put in before Toby could even suggest one Mr Haile was very much like another and this one could release those poor lonely animals right now if he chose to.

'It's not white—it's yellow,' Toby protested, 'and I can be good when I try.'

'Can you, my love? When is that going to start, then?'

'Right now.'

'Oh, good. Begin by walking with me like a good boy who loves his mother too much to run off and worry her with his antics and Mr Haile might convince his brother you are worthy of such a treat in the morning.'

'I'm sure your son knows it is a gentleman's duty to put a lady's safety before his own need for adventure,' Magnus Haile said solemnly.

'Mama keeps *me* safe,' Toby objected confidently after a quick think.

Maybe it was time she stopped fighting his battles for him and let him feel the consequences of his actions, then. He was her boy and infinitely precious to her, but he had been at the centre of her world ever since he was born. She didn't want him to grow up selfish and careless of others as she admitted his father could be. Bran had been so self-absorbed their ill-starred marriage was doomed from the moment they made it.

'You must be more of a baby than I thought,' Mr Haile said, managing not to laugh at Toby's shocked expression somehow.

Hetta had to disguise her chuckle as a cough because even a smile would undo the good work Magnus Haile was putting in on her son. Why couldn't Lady Drace see what a wonderful father he would be if only she would let him? Yet the thought of them being happily reconciled in some sunny land made her feel at odds with herself again and that really wouldn't do.

'Did you have to look after your mama, then?' Toby asked.

'Someone certainly needed to,' Mr Magnus Haile said. Apparently, the last Earl of Carrowe had declared his youngest son a bastard and his Countess an adulteress when Mr Wulfric Haile had been born, only admitting they were a maligned wife and his legitimate son in an announcement sent to the newspapers after his death. 'Right now, I must civilise myself, and your legs obviously need stretching if any of us are to have a moment's peace for the rest of the day,' he said lightly enough and walked off with the hint of a swagger in his long stride.

Hetta frowned at his broad back with a concern he would find embarrassing if he knew about it. One reason she had agreed to stay here tonight was the hope of stopping him falling back into a brandy bottle as soon as they were gone. A better man than he thought was lurking under the frown and gruff manner he used to fend off the world, but maybe it would be as well for her if he hid him a little longer. A shabby widow had even less in common with polished and aristocratic Mr Haile than she had with his unkempt alter ego, so any distance between them was bound to be a very good thing, wasn't it?

Chapter Seven

It had taken him over an hour to become even halfway civilised, Magnus realised when he glanced at the clock in the hallway. He had been bathed, shaved and dressed like an unruly child. Jem even tied his neckcloth for him before he let Magnus out of his sight. The old, dandified Magnus Haile would shudder at its lack of pristine perfection, but this one was glad to be clean and decent again and never mind elegance. Getting drunk because Delphi had taken his daughter away wasn't the behaviour of a sensible man and he must become one of those if he was going to put some sort of life together without them.

'Ah, there you are. That's more like it, Mr Magnus,' Peg told him as he strolled into the kitchen. 'You look much better now.'

'I'm right as rain,' he said and absently

sipped at the cup of strong coffee she pushed towards him.

'Are you, now? Well, I suppose you believe it and you always were stubborn as a pack of donkeys. I knew you'd turn up with an empty belly as soon as you was feeling a bit more dandy,' the elderly maid said after casting an anxious look over him to make sure he was at least looking close to his old self.

'I had to be gentle with it as it emptied in such a hurry.'

'Aye, well, least said about that the soonest mended,' she said, with a *boys will be boys* shrug that made him feel about Toby's age. 'Your ma will eat these even when she turns up her nose at everything else,' she told him, putting some delicately made lemon biscuits in front of him. She turned back to her gossip with Cook as if she didn't care if he ate them or not, and Magnus looked down some time later to find out he had demolished the lot.

'Better?'

'Aye, thank you.'

'You're a good man, Mr Magnus, despite your wild ways.'

'I doubt it, but I promise to take my megrims

somewhere else next time and not mess up your smart new house again,' he said lightly enough.

'It's bad for a body to brood alone, so you come here and never mind a bit of extra dusting.'

'More than that and I can't keep drowning my sorrows like a green boy.'

'Maybe not but it's your home, so where else would you take them, lad?'

'No, it's my mother and little sisters' home. High time they had the peace and quiet to enjoy one without me making the place untidy.'

'If you think that's what they want, you don't know them as well as you think. They love you, my lad.'

'Then they shouldn't. I'm not worth it.'

'Listen to him, Cook—still thinks he should set the world to rights for the rest of us and at his age as well.'

'Aye, can't be done,' Cook mumbled past whatever plans she was turning over in her head for dinner.

'You always were one to think you ought to make other folks' hurts better if you could,' Peg said and shook her head as if it was a habit he ought to have grown out of by now.

Delphi *had* been hurt by her marriage and by Gresley before that, but what possessed her to pick the very rich but rather stupid Sir Edgar Drace to wed in the first place? Who knew what went on in her lovely head and at least Drace wasn't the one who'd broken her heart and Magnus knew why he couldn't find a way to mend it now. 'Then I promise to stop doing it,' he told Peg half-seriously.

'Get on with the life you've got and don't make promises, Master Gus,' she said as if she knew something serious had happened to him and of course she did. Peg couldn't stop him drowning in brandy, but she hadn't sent for his mother or Aline to talk sense into him, so she knew this went deeper than a fit of the blue-devils.

'Thank you. You are a darling,' he said because she was and had always been there for him and his family.

Peg blushed and shook her head at him. 'Now you stop your nonsense and eat what Cook puts in front of you before you fades away again, Master Gus.'

'I'll be fat as a farmyard goose before you two are done,' he complained half-heartedly.

He was sipping a cup of his mother's favourite China tea when hasty footsteps told them their young guest had found his way back to the kitchen like iron to a magnet.

'I'm hungry,' Toby Champion announced as if that was the most important fact in the world right now and, for him, it probably was.

'Are you, my lamb?' Cook said indulgently. Magnus wondered how the lad had got into her good books so quickly. 'I'll have to see if there's something in the larder as won't spoil your dinner, then.'

'Have you eaten it all?' the boy accused Magnus as if they were more or less the same age and he had stolen a march on him.

Magnus managed a manly shrug. 'I ate the lemon biscuits, but Cook's larder is never empty, even though my little sisters and our mother eat more like wrens than hungry human beings.'

'Wrens have to eat their own weight in food every day to stay alive,' Toby announced as he ate a griddle scone so fast they must have imagined it.

'Really? And to think we understood you through all those crumbs,' Magnus said, and the lad screwed up his face as if thinking about glowering at him, but he must have decided there were better things to do with his mouth than pout.

'Mama will be cross if she catches me eating before dinner again, although I can't see why because I will still be hungry,' he explained past the next one.

'So, you eat as much as you can before she stops you?' Magnus replied, and the lad nodded as he wasted no time getting on with yet another scone.

'Toby Champion, I despair of you,' the boy's mother announced breathlessly from the doorway Cook had left open to let the heat out and fresh air in.

'I was starving, so I ran instead of walking like you told me to, but I didn't go anywhere I wasn't supposed to,' the boy explained earnestly. He had refused a plate in the boyish belief his mother wouldn't realise he had been eating if he didn't have one. Magnus could remember having that delusion at a similar age and his mother hadn't believed him either.

'I doubt leaving your mother in the middle of nowhere could be considered looking after her under any code of gentlemanly conduct I ever came across,' Magnus reproved mildly and wondered why he had almost hated the boy at first sight. Toby Champion was a more intense version of the horrid brat most boys were at the same age, but there was nothing sly or calculating about him and he didn't bear a grudge. He must have got his character from the maternal side and only his restlessness and golden looks from his father. Magnus had never liked Brandon Champion, even before he ran off with a schoolgirl, but he had no reason to dislike his son other than the desolation he'd felt the day they first met, when Mrs Champion demonstrably had a very lively child in her life and he did not.

'Does that mean I can't play with the puppies tomorrow?' Toby said with what looked like genuine tears in his wide blue eyes.

'Don't fall for his tricks,' Mrs Champion warned all the same. 'Stop pretending you're an abused waif this minute, Toby, or I really will pack you off to your great-grandmother to be taught not to cozen your elders and mind your manners.'

'No, I really and truly hate *her*,' the boy said

with a mulish look of appeal in Magnus's direction and he tried not to feel flattered. 'She's an old witch.'

'Tobias Champion! How dare you speak so rudely of a lady who put up with you for a whole day before she decided you are impossible? Heaven knows she must like you to endure your bad manners and wicked tricks as long as she did.'

'She didn't try to kiss or hug me after I let the rat out of the trap in her drawing room, though, did she?'

'Considering you somehow managed to carry it all the way from the larder to the drawing room without being caught, I can't say I blame her and I would not have let you kiss me either. And she did invite her friends especially to meet you, you horrid brat. Now they think me a terrible mother as well as a failure as Lady Porter's only grandchild,' Mrs Champion said with a sigh.

Magnus almost felt sorry for her until he saw humour in her fine grey eyes behind that glassy disguise. She didn't blame her son for creating chaos, nor seem to mind what her starchy grandparent thought of them now they were safely out of her way. Evidently Mrs Champion was as glad to leave such a grimly correct and old-fashioned household behind as her son had been. Why on earth hadn't he realised what an unusual female she was at first glance? he wondered. He felt as if a veil between him and the rest of the world had been ripped away when he finally accepted Delphi didn't love him and never had. It was almost exhilarating to put a full stop and carry on with his life, or it would be if not for the ache of having his little daughter ripped away from him as well.

'I am sorry, Mama,' Toby Champion said and even managed to sound it.

Magnus fought to control a chuckle at a mental image of a room full of elderly ladies screeching like starlings, then having strong hysterics all at the same time. Mrs Champion eyed her son sternly, then sighed and shook her head.

'Why do you never think about the consequences before you do things, Toby?' she asked. 'I despair of you ever being a proper gentleman if you can't at least pretend to respect your elders.'

'I respect you and Grandpapa, and I *am* only

seven and three-quarters, Mama,' he said with a roguish smile, and somehow Magnus knew she was trying not to laugh as well. 'Great-Grandmama says it must be your fault I am growing up a monster and since she is so old she must be right.'

'Checkmate,' Magnus muttered facetiously.

'Stay out of our game unless you know how to lose,' Mrs Champion ordered softly and Magnus badly wanted to know her first name. It felt ridiculous to keep calling her Mrs Champion in his head, especially when it was so full of outrageous thoughts that needed to know what to call her in the throes of passion. 'And not necessarily,' she warned as if the game wasn't up yet. He was glad he had a table between his sex and the rest of the world as all the games he would really like to play with her lined up to make him a lusty fool who ought to know better. 'You were born a little monster, young man, so Lady Porter is wrong for once,' she went on blithely, apparently without a clue Magnus was having very mature thoughts about her while she dealt with her son.

'It must be my father's fault, then.'

'How can it be? He didn't live long enough to meet you.'

'I've got bad blood, she said so. Don't you remember? She said you should have listened instead of running off with Papa as soon as her back was turned. And after she had ordered you never to see him again as well, Mama? Well, really.'

Mrs Champion flushed like a peony and Magnus relished the image of a much younger, more romantic and easily swayed version of her as a girl he wished he had known before Champion got to her. Under all that grey stuff she had a fine figure and without the glasses she would be quietly lovely and compelling, even before he added in a sense of humour nobody had ever accused Delphi of possessing. No, he was being condescending and ridiculous towards both of them now. For the benefit of his own sanity he should avoid the company of all ladies under the age of sixty he wasn't related to from now on. This one could be another Helen of Troy under all that poplin and depressed hair, but he told himself he could still slide past her with only a sideways look and a gruff good day if they met again. He shot her a furtive glance to check she wasn't a beauty, despite her efforts not to be. No, she was still a lady of character rather than spectacular good looks. That was what the kinder chaperones called their more workaday charges, wasn't it? Yet character was not proving anywhere near as dampening to his baser male instincts as he wanted it to be.

'There was nothing wrong with your father's blood, love,' she told her son as if she had no idea Magnus was far too wrapped up in the feel of her arm brushing against his as she sat in the only other chair at the table not in the direct line of Cook's well-floured rolling pin. 'And if I always did what your great-grandmama says you would not exist, my son. You should thank your lucky stars your mama turned a deaf ear to her fell warnings about your papa and you still owe me a good reason why you ran off after promising not to in front of Mr Haile. I have a witness this time, so you can't pretend you never did.'

'I was hungry,' the boy explained as if that was a special circumstance she should under-stand. Magnus nodded solemnly to confirm growing boys needed feeding at regular intervals throughout the day before he stopped to think he might be undermining her authority. 'See, even he agrees,' the lad said.

Magnus didn't want to argue with a lady of so much character while he was still fragile round the edges. Maybe they could have a stimulating argument over the fish course at dinner tonight when he was feeling more the thing. Or a debate on the rights and wrongs of playing verbal chess with her offspring he couldn't imagine his child ever playing with Delphi. Now he was finding his former lover dull next to this woman again, in thought if not looks, and that would never do. And the hank of richly chestnut hair escaping her repressive widow's cap looked a lot warmer to the touch than Delphi's immaculate blonde locks ever had.

'I know how it feels to be as hungry as a hunter,' he argued as he held on to the conversation with the half of his attention he had to spare from imagining all that heavily soft and silky hair loose about her shoulders, 'or I did before Peg found enough food to last me until dinnertime. Those good manners we talked about should have trumped the most urgent of bodily needs, though, my lad, so please don't try to drag me into any more arguments with your long-suffering mama.'

'That's what Lady Aline said Mama was, long-suffering. I like her,' the boy said and managed to sound wistful and deprived all at the same time, saw it wasn't working and gave a triumphant grin when he beat Magnus to the last of the griddle cakes before his mother could forbid it.

'So do I. She is a sister in a million. I am very fortunate in my relatives,' Magnus lied because his elder brother didn't look like much of a gift now and nor had his late father. He wondered what on earth Aline was doing at Carrowe House to meet Mrs Champion and her son in the first place, especially when she had disliked Gresley for a lot longer than him. She was supposed to be fixed in Worthing for the summer, so she and their mother and younger sisters could breathe sea air and have a well-deserved rest away from the dust and noise while alterations to Develin House were finished. So why was Aline staying in a ruinous house she couldn't wait to get away from in the company of a brother she had never even pretended to like?

'I don't suppose *you* have a great-grandmother, then, do you, sir?' the boy said as if
he thought them a very dubious item.

Magnus only just managed to turn a bark of
laughter into a cough under Mrs Champion's
sternly reproachful gaze this time. 'No, even
my grandparents had the tact to depart this
vale of sorrows before I was old enough to be
an embarrassment to them,' he admitted and
contrasted his own family with Mrs Champion's lack of one and realised how blessed he
was after all. His father had been a devil and
he wasn't too sure about his elder brother now
Delphi had cut him out of her life like a canker
because of Gres, but he had close family who
loved him, despite his sins, and a new sister by
marriage he would always be proud to own up
to. All Mrs Champion and Toby had was her
absent-minded father and a grandmother well
worth avoiding. Fleeing to a far-off country
with a babe in arms must have been her way
of avoiding Lady Porter taking over her life
and her baby son's and he couldn't blame her
for not wanting to bring him up in such a stifling household. They would both have been

bent out of shape if she had and he liked them the way they were.

'You can have mine if you like,' Toby Champion said generously. 'I don't want her and she was horrid to Mama. I'm glad she had the vapours when I let the poor rat out of the trap. I do like Grandpapa, though. He's funny and he knows lots of interesting things and he doesn't shout at me, or squeal like a screech owl, or make Mama cry.'

Toby obviously noticed more than he pretended to about the adults around him and must have hated knowing his mother was near to tears. Magnus was sure she would do her best to hide them from her son as well, so the Gorgon must have made her very miserable indeed for even a hint of them to sneak through her guard.

'All good things in a parent,' Mrs Champion agreed airily, but Magnus could see she was embarrassed about him knowing the old besom had brought her close to tears. How could such a young mother *not* cry from sheer weariness from time to time and he had added to her miseries that day at Dover, had he not? Feeling guilty as hell now, Magnus stared into his empty coffee can and wondered why the fool now standing in the Honourable Magnus's once fashionable shoes seemed so intent on making ladies cry.

'My father liked nothing better than making us cry, but I doubt yours would have done, Master Toby. From the little I remember of him as a boy he was more likely to be in trouble as well,' Magnus said to distract them all from what sounded a disastrous visit to a bad-tempered and tyrannical old woman.

'You *knew* my papa, sir?' the boy said with awe.

'A little, although I know your uncle Marcus far better.'

'Do you think *he* might like me?' the boy said wistfully.

His mother looked as if the lack of a genial uncle and pack of lively cousins in his life was a gap it had never occurred to her to worry about until now and Magnus almost wished he hadn't changed the subject. 'I can't see why not,' he said. 'You are quite likeable in a grubby sort of way when you're not causing mayhem and you don't actually smell. Sir Marcus Champion would probably think you an acceptable sort of nephew, since he's not very fussy, and your cousins might even like you.'

'You didn't,' the boy pointed out as if their first meeting with each other still rankled.

Chapter Eight

Magnus wondered how to explain even to an advanced seven-year-old that he hadn't been in the right frame of mind to like anyone the day they met. The boy's emotions and perception hadn't had time to catch up with his enquiring mind yet and Magnus could hardly tell him what he felt that day even if they had. 'You scared me half to death by diving under my horse's belly as if he was a staid donkey who wouldn't hurt a fly. I was furious with you for taking such a terrible risk for no good reason.'

'There *was* a puppy,' Toby Champion muttered as if he already knew it was a poor excuse for being so heedless, so at least his mother had drummed that much sense into his dog-obsessed head since Dover.

'There will always be puppies, lad,' he said in the hope of reinforcing her efforts. 'Next time you could throw yourself in the way of a fresher horse that won't do as he's bid quite as readily. Lucky that mine came down only inches away from your head instead of smack on it and you should remember horses are living creatures and it isn't in their nature to kill. A gentleman should consider their well-being as well as his own before he launches into such reckless action. It will be devilish hard to get about when you're older if you're not a competent rider and treating a horse well is the start of being one. Your uncle Marcus is a very fine horseman indeed and he might be persuaded to teach you some of his skills if you seem a sensible sort of lad who wouldn't dream of dashing under a horse's belly when it was in full motion.'

'You won't tell him I did that, will you, sir?'

'Not if you promise never to do it again.'

'I won't,' Toby said and looked so serious Magnus almost believed he would think before he acted next time. He hoped he wasn't there to be terrified if he didn't.

'Then I won't tell him.'

'*You* could teach me to ride properly, Mr Haile. Although you shouted and cursed me, you still got your horse to miss me by no more than an inch, so I didn't get hurt,' Toby said as if he might hero-worship Magnus if he wasn't careful.

Magnus didn't feel like anyone's hero. The very idea of being on a pedestal made him squirm when he thought of the failures in his life so far. Sir Marcus Champion was a far better man for his nephew to look up to.

'You didn't tell me the horse came so close to landing on you, Toby,' his mother said, looking very pale and shaken as her son admitted the unvarnished truth about his misdeeds for the first time.

'I apologise,' Magnus said shortly.

'What for, not killing my son?'

'No, for cursing him at the time and frightening you now. I admit I was furious with him and strongly tempted to dust his backside until I came upon you and it was easier to leave him to his mother.'

'I'm quite tempted to do it myself right now,' she admitted with a shaky smile that said, *Thank you again for not killing him* and a stern look at her son that said, *Why didn't* you *say how reckless you had been instead of trying to shift the blame?*

Magnus felt a dangerous sort of liking for her threaten. She was brave and even a little bit reckless herself, but her responsibility for such a curious and over-confident son must fall heavily on her shoulders. He wondered again why she hadn't called on Mark Champion to help her get her son to adulthood without killing himself in the pursuit of scientific discovery or a puppy. Pride, he suspected, mentally reviewing his own past encounters with Lady Porter and concluding the woman had a lot to answer for. She must have made her granddaughter feel unloved and unwanted when she was sent home by her father. Little wonder Mrs Champion decided not to ask for her help when her son was born, given Lady Porter's false pride and coldness sent her into Brandon Champion's arms in the first place. Out of the frying pan into the fire, he concluded and wondered why her father had never put *his* child before his so-called duty. The man was a hereditary baronet; he must have a grand enough estate somewhere to keep his mother in ridiculous style. Sir Hadrian should evict the old besom from that chilly house in Grosvenor Square and spend the money on his daughter and grandson instead. But Magnus's admiration for Mrs Champion raising her son alone could undermine his feelings for a very different woman even more if he wasn't careful. He didn't want to go on loving Delphi now she had kicked him aside with such cold revulsion and admitted Gresley was her first and apparently last love, but he refused to replace her with another woman who didn't want him either.

'Fortunately for you, my son, I am far too relieved you survived to give you the beating you deserve for putting your life at risk to stroke a dog who probably would have bitten you if you'd rushed up and frightened it,' she said wearily.

True, but Magnus couldn't help liking the lad, despite his strong physical resemblance to his dead father, and Brandon Champion had kept his young wife close, hadn't he? Magnus imagined her wary gaze wide with innocence and that slender body of hers rather angular and more gently curved than it was now and knew why the man kept her shut away from the wolves of the *ton* while he was busy at sea.

And Sir Hadrian Porter would have looked like the perfect father-in-law to Brandon Champion, wouldn't he? The man had connections to some of the most powerful men in the land and a title and, to crown it all, one day his estate would pass to his only child if he didn't remarry and beget a male heir. Yet Sir Hadrian had refused to advance his new son-in-law's career. Magnus's fist tightened in his lap at the thought of Champion taking his disappointment out on his wife. No wonder she was so wary and skittish now. For some wayward reason he wished he could be the man to teach the guarded and intriguing Mrs Champion not all his sex were selfish and unfaithful. He wanted to be the man who unwrapped the woman she could be, if loved and appreciated as she deserved, except he'd sworn off love and fidelity only days ago. It was too soon to go back on a promise never to hurt as Delphi hurt him again and for Hailes love and hurt nearly always walked hand in hand.

'I thought the man might sell it to us,' Toby muttered as if he knew he had been in the wrong that day, but wasn't ready to admit it.

'First, I would have to want to buy it, for

whatever inflated figure his master would demand after seeing your enthusiasm for the deal. You know we have no room in our lives for a dog if we are to carry on travelling with your grandfather, Toby. I would miss him if we let him go without us, even if you think it a fair trade for me to be stuck in the country so you can have a pet to come home to.'

'Nasty smelly creatures, messing up my kitchen with fur and dribble,' Cook put in stalwartly.

Magnus hid a smile while Cook did her best to divert attention from the boy's misdeeds. 'Wulf and Isabella's dogs wouldn't dribble if you didn't feed them titbits,' he pointed out and all three women glared as if he was being no help at all.

'Lady Porter said Grandpapa should settle down, Mama. If he did, we could live in a house like this one and the dogs could run about on the Heath. We wouldn't trouble anyone until we were hungry and ready for bed.'

'Now that really is a fairy story, my son. Your grandfather has had itchy feet all my life. Even when I was little he hated to stay in one place too long and *my* mama used to say he must have been stolen from the gypsies as a baby, since he clearly had travelling blood in his veins. She loved new places and people almost as much as he does and you would soon be bored with the ideal life you paint such a nice picture of.'

'I wish I could have met her *and* my papa,' Toby said with a sigh.

'So do I, my son, so do I,' his mother said with an ever deeper one.

'If you have taken in enough food to last until your next meal, young man, perhaps you would consider taking *me* for a walk to work up an appetite,' Magnus said to give her a few moments' rest and ignored a sharp jag of jealousy in his gut if she missed Champion as a lover more than Magnus wanted her to. 'Cook will never forgive me if I am not hungry tonight, and if you don't take me outside and walk me about a bit, I shall fail her.'

'Can we go down to the mill? I want to see how the gears work and if the wheel is under-shot or overshot and what they have been mill-ing today.'

'If you promise not to put your hand in the works or dash off to pet dogs at peril of your life,' Magnus agreed warily, realising he had to cover all risks he could think of with this boy before he took responsibility for him.

'I promise.'

'But what are you promising, young man? I am wise to you.'

'I promise to be sensible and not give in to impulse,' the boy said parrot-like, so nobody could accuse his mother of not trying. Magnus doubted anyone could tame the boy's thirst for knowledge, so he would have to hope that promise would hold him for now.

'Mr Magnus will keep the lad safe, ma'am. You sit a while and have another cup of tea while the boys play without you,' Peg urged as if Magnus was much the same age as his new friend. He muttered something dark and grumpy under his breath to make it clear she was wrong and followed Toby before he could scamper off alone.

'Aye, and he's a handful as well,' Cook said when their steps echoed back to them on the stone yard, then went out of earshot.

Hetta wasn't sure if she meant Toby or Mr Magnus Haile. 'Indeed,' she said since they both were in very different ways.

'Cook's right, ma'am, and we always has tea now, so you're not in the way. You looks as if you could do with some quiet, if you don't mind me saying so?'

Deciding it was an offer too tempting to refuse, Hetta sat back down again. 'No, of course not, and you are right—I could,' she replied. The kitchen table was scrubbed spotlessly clean and there were enough doors and windows open to catch a breeze and be almost cool before Cook stoked the range for serious cooking. 'Ah, that's lovely,' Hetta said after sipping her tea and relaxing to the sound of birdsong and the distant countryside instead of the restless roar of a vast city. She shivered at the thought of how close she had come to losing Toby that day at Dover and thanked God and Magnus Haile's quick thinking and magnificent horsemanship for saving her boy to be a nuisance again as they set out to explore the Heath together.

'Should I shut the door, ma'am?' Cook asked.

'What for? Oh, the shiver. No, then, it was a goose walking over my grave. It's bliss to sit quiet after the dust and traffic and arguing on the way here.'

'I dare say that boy of yours was as fidgety as a flea.'

'Yes, he was,' Hetta agreed. How could she argue Toby never caused her a moment of anxiety when it was obviously untrue?

'Mr Magnus and Mr Wulf were the same as boys,' Peg said, 'or they was whenever his lordship wasn't about. Master Gresley, or Lord Meon I suppose I should say since the new Earl was called so back then, used to look down his nose at their mischief, then go and tell his pa, but full of life and fun they were. Not a wicked bone in their bodies, not even after beatings and his lordship shouting at them fit to bust. They're good, sweet-tempered boys for all those bad-lad looks.'

No doubt about the looks, but neither gentleman was exactly a boy, so Hetta said nothing and hoped her new friend would tell her more about Magnus Haile before life, and Lady Drace, made him the gruff and grumpy man she had seen at Dover. She would be a fool to fall for his dark and *to hell with you* looks now, but she was human enough to want to know more about him. It couldn't do any harm to listen to a woman who doted on him for a bit longer.

'Master Gresley was jealous of his younger brothers and her ladyship never quite took to her eldest boy like she did to the rest somehow.'

'Now then, Peg, that's none of our business.'

'Not that his father didn't favour Master Gresley, so that made up for some of it, I suppose,' Peg went on as if her friend hadn't spoken. 'Cook will say I shouldn't speak ill of the dead, but there wasn't much good to say about the old master. A good thing Master Gresley wed and moved to Haile Carr, if you ask me. Better off out of his father's pocket.'

'The present Lord Carrowe seems pleasant enough, from what little I saw of him,' Hetta lied. The Haile family intrigued her and it stopped her worrying what Toby was up to with the most intriguing one of all.

'Aye, he works hard and they do say Master Gresley don't even like cards. The old Earl gambled on things you wouldn't believe a body could worry himself over. Raindrops on a window or which old lady would cross the street first, or how many spots on a ladybird and such childish nonsense you wouldn't think a grown man would bother with if you didn't know how simple even the best of them are at times. Bet on anything that moved, the old lord did—aye, and lost nine times out of ten.'

'Mrs Champion don't want to know, Peg,' Cook said, and Hetta had to pretend she didn't by getting up and losing an argument about who would wash her teacup.

She decided to go for a stroll around the pleasure gardens as she knew more about the kitchen garden than she wanted to. The Dowager Lady Carrowe must have begun reordering them before she left for the seaside from the look of raw earth and stacked branches here and there among lushly flowering plants now thriving in the light. Intrigued by the notion of who planted it all and maybe even designing one of her own, with a lot of help from someone who knew what they were talking about, kept her busy for all of five minutes. Her parents had never settled long enough for her to learn much about plants as a child and she was horrified to realise that the fellow owner of her fantasy pleasure garden looked darkly familiar. That proved she was far too interested in Mr Magnus Haile. She scolded herself for being a deluded idiot and tried to think of something else.

And even if he was remotely interested in a quiz with an active and impulsive boy in tow to make her impossible, Magnus Haile was far too busy yearning for the love of his life to pursue her. It wasn't as if he'd given her any encouragement to yearn for him that day at Dover. On the contrary, he'd stared rudely at her as if he couldn't imagine what they were doing on the same planet, let alone the dock he was striding down as if he owned it. His dark brown eyes had been hard with temper and stony dislike, and she flinched at the memory of staring at him like a codfish while he put Toby down like a piece of luggage and set his mind to more important things.

Somehow no garden could divert her from him being far too close by for comfort, so she went back into his mother's house to find something else to do. After being shooed out of the kitchen again, she was soon nodding over the pile of mending her father and son always created as the muted noises from the kitchen through so many open windows soothed her like a lullaby. Tiredness washed over her in waves now she had finally relaxed her guard a little and her busy fingers stilled. Days of anxiety and too many sleepless nights took their toll before she could shake herself awake one more time and she slept.

Chapter Nine

'Oh, it's you, Mr Haile. You should have woken me,' Hetta said drowsily.

Wondering why his intent gaze hadn't roused her and how long he had been standing watching her as if he was trying to work out what made her who she was, she hoped her mouth hadn't been open or, worse still, she wasn't snoring when he came to find out why she hadn't reclaimed her son. He was probably wondering what a gentleman was to do when he found a lady nodding over her sewing basket in his mother's private sitting room as if she had a right to be there. A guilty flush heated her cheeks and she wished he hadn't caught her dozing. Toby needed her awake and fully aware, so she could get him fed and into bed without too much of a song and dance. Instead she was sitting here sleepily ravenous not for food but for Magnus Haile, who went on staring back at her as if he was hungry, too.

'Don't worry, your son is quite safe. Jem has him helping to hammer in fence posts down in the paddock,' he said rather huskily.

Hetta smiled rather too openly and a hot and very intriguing light glinted back at her from his darkly fascinating eyes. She stretched lazily before her sensible self woke up and told her not to draw his attention to her body with such a masculine man watching her as if he was already fascinated by it. 'His poor thumbs,' she said ruefully, as if they were having a normal conversation while their eyes met and they both knew she was lying.

'We had best hurry, then, had we not?' he whispered as he bent so close she had to look up at him with a question she didn't really want answered in her eyes.

Too late to ask it when he lifted her out of her seat in one smooth move, so the mending dropped on the floor and she was breathing in heat and summer and warm man even as she raised her lips for his kiss. Until now Bran was the only man who had ever kissed her full on the lips like this. She had made sure nobody else had a chance to after Bran's kisses grew rough and careless and all his hopes for their marriage fell into dust. Bran was left with a naive and squeamish bedmate and no advantage he couldn't have got elsewhere with a lot less trouble, according to his theory. Wrong, she exulted as Magnus Haile's mouth taught her to want, and want, then want some more. He showed her how to be ravenous and meet every challenge he set her with one of her own. The lover she always wanted to be was off and running, and she threw herself into discovering her own secrets in the arms of a master. Bran had been a selfish lover and now he seemed so small from where she was standing that she forgot him.

'More,' she muttered greedily against this man's mouth and opened hers to let him find her inner woman.

His tongue quested gently, as if he was asking for all she had instead of demanding. He would linger over every inch of his lover's pleasure, stoke her to burning curiosity, slake the relentless need tempting her to scissor her legs together to stop her moaning for it out loud. *Windows are open*, her inner wanton reminded her, so she kept it to a frustrated squirm against his mighty, unmistakably roused body to let him know she felt like that, too. His hands on her back shaped her even closer; his kiss whispered down the tender cord of her extended neck and settled on the pulse at the base of it to nestle and lick and relish the fast beat of her racing heart. The strong, long-fingered hands she had fantasised over earlier moved to cup one of her breasts with reverent sensuality. Oh, how right she had been to secretly picture bliss flowering wherever he touched her. No, it was better than that. Fire and an aching need made her fit her mouth back on his to mute the demand she felt rising in her like hot lava about to blow out of her in a mighty roar if he didn't cover it up for her, keep them close. He soothed, seemed ready to slick butterfly kisses across her swollen lips, to gentle the passions she had been damming up ever since she dreamed of a lover like this at seventeen and got Bran instead.

Distant noises as Cook clattered pans and Peg bustled about the newly polished dining room warned her she had stirred up far too much to class this as an easily stolen kiss and an unwary moment. One last stretch of her aching nipples against his muscular torso to feel the fierce joy of wanting and being wanted fully for the first time in her life and she would let go. Except it was his turn to bury a moan of need against her. She felt it against the tumble of her half-unwound curls on her neck and who would have thought hair could feel so sensuous between her and a lover like this? He whispered something husky and unsteady and she opened her eyes to stare up at his with too many questions in her eyes as they finally took in where they were and what they had done.

'Now I can see why you wear those ridiculous spectacles,' he told her as he tried to soothe down the chaos he had created and she could hardly lie and say she needed them now, could she?

'To keep my inner wanton hidden?'

'No, to protect your secret self,' he argued with a frown as if she was demeaning what they had just done together.

'I never needed them more than I do right now, then,' she whispered and meant it.

'Don't,' he protested even as he held her a little way away and tried to steady the shake in his own hands as well as the trembling of her body as all that wasn't going to happen now made her feel forsaken and vulnerable.

'Why not? You don't even like me,' she said in a hard little voice she wished would be quiet and let them fall into that heady delusion again.

'Oh, I don't know,' he argued with a stray-cat smile that turned tender when she felt tears sheen in her eyes and determinedly blinked them back. 'I think I do. I think we could be important,' he told her very soberly indeed and as if he really meant it.

'I have a son,' she said dully.

'I have a daughter. It doesn't stop me wanting you,' he told her as if he had more faith in this bone-deep attraction to each other than she could allow herself.

'Maybe not, but it probably stops you getting what you want,' she said sadly and met his eyes full on for the first time. 'I can never up and leave my life behind like Lady Drace has done for the sake of her child. There is no way out for me because of Toby. I would never leave him or take what I want from you, so it might be best if you went to your brother's house as soon as dinner is over, Mr Haile. I am none too sure I can resist temptation now I know what it is, but I must learn to somehow.'

'There's no need to say no to me twice, madam.'

'Ah, now I have offended you. Well, I am very sorry for that. Thank you for showing me what I have been missing all these years, Mr Haile, but I would like you to leave me alone to compose myself again now,' she told him rather bitterly, the thought of all the years of self-denial and frustrated need ahead of her making her sound harder than she intended.

Dinner was a strange meal after those kisses in the long midsummer twilight. Hetta felt as if everything had changed, but Magnus Haile was probably the same as always. And what was he? A gentleman, she decided because she needed to be fair. She had longed to be kissed every bit as much as he had wanted to kiss her, maybe even more. So, she could not accuse him of doing things she didn't want so she could let herself off any responsibility for what had happened between them.

'It was kind of you to carry Toby upstairs. He ends up too weary to get to bed on his own after throwing himself into his adventures all day and he's getting heavy.'

'Peg says you need a proper rest before you have to cope with his starts on your own again.'

It sounded so lonely, being alone with the care of her lively son, but hadn't she been on her own long before Toby was born? 'I shall do very well after a good night's sleep, Mr Haile. It was too hot and noisy in London to rest before it was time to get up again.'

'I dare say, and Carrowe House creaks and moans so loudly it can startle me awake even though I am used to it, so for a stranger to try to sleep there must be nigh impossible.'

'At least with this sort of peace and quiet Toby might not wake with the dawn as he has every day since we landed in England,' she admitted wearily.

And now their mouths were saying a lot of polite nothings while a deep sort of sadness settled into her thoughts. Magnus Haile had shown her such sensual promise, so many heady possibilities. It felt so lonely to sit and talk about nothing much while Jem drifted in and out with this and that and Peg appeared now and again to shake her head at plates only half-empty and an odd sort of tension in the room to go with the lingering heat of the day.

Before Magnus could argue himself out of the door and over the Heath to his brother's house for the night, a piercing shriek cut through the soft evening air and Hetta froze with panic. It was Toby and he sounded furious or frightened and maybe both. Magnus Haile's long and unimpeded legs got him upstairs before she hardly had the time to pick up her skirts and hurry after him. Breathless and stumbling on the unfamiliar landing, she had to remind herself where Toby's room was and calm down to deal with whatever lay ahead. She snatched in a deep breath and ran towards her son's furious voice. At least he was yelling defiance, so there couldn't be too much wrong with him.

'No, let me go! He'll get away,' Toby was arguing as he struggled in Magnus's arms. Hetta was terrified her headstrong son would wriggle away and throw himself into the dark to pursue whatever had frightened him, never mind still being three-parts asleep. 'Get off me. He's getting away,' her son roared at Magnus, who still managed to hold his writhing body without hurting him somehow.

'Stop that nonsensical row this minute, Toby Champion,' she ordered sharply. Toby's struggles stilled and he slewed in Magnus's arms.

'There was a masked man, Mama, there really was, and he will get away if you don't tell *him* to let go.'

'No, he won't,' Magnus said grimly and went to the top of the stairs to bellow at Wulfric Haile's unconventional manservant to search the grounds.

'Toby has vivid dreams,' Hetta told Magnus as he strode back into the room to help hold Toby until he was awake enough to know he could not fly.

'Not this time,' Magnus muttered in her ear, then told Toby to stop making a fool of himself. 'Your mother says you are bright for your age, but I haven't seen much sign of it so far,' he said critically.

Hetta almost laughed when she felt her son stiffen as if mortally insulted.

'Grandpapa says I have a fine questing mind,' he protested.

'Well, he should know, but you seem like a stubborn, run-of-the-mill sort of brat to me and very much like my nephews who are a set of slow-tops, although *their* mothers swear they are exceptional.'

Hetta felt her son tremble with fury at the very idea of being thought ordinary. Then he must have decided it sounded acceptable after all, since he grinned as if it was a huge compliment. Magnus met her eyes over Toby's head and nodded faintly at a shred of fine white cloth caught in the window latch and the faint imprint of a foot on the coverlet. Hetta saw proof someone really had been here and only just stopped a horrified shudder Toby was sure to feel. They hadn't had time to make enemies yet and Hetta doubted even her grandmother would kidnap Toby and have him sent to a strict school to make a cowed young gentleman out of her bright boy. It made a horrid sort of sense someone was desperate enough to kidnap him to stop her father getting too near the truth of the last Earl of Carrowe's murder, though. Sir Hadrian Porter would drop the case like a chestnut plucked straight from the fire and the promise she had made her father not to get close to his cases suddenly made sense, except it hadn't stopped someone coming after them anyway.

'You had best come downstairs, young man. You can doze on the sofa in the parlour while I have tea and Mr Haile drinks his port, but do spare us any more of your nightmares,' she declared as if she really thought it was one.

'I am *very* hungry,' Toby muttered, so things were back to normal. Luckily his talent for sleeping as if his life depended on it meant he was halfway there already. He didn't argue when Magnus picked him up and Hetta was too glad he was here to argue she could manage. Toby tucked his head against Magnus's neck as if he trusted him to sort things out and drifted back to dreamland.

'A man needs to keep body and soul together,' Magnus said as he waited for Hetta to go down ahead of them.

Even though the open window was now closed and shuttered behind them, it felt like an outrage someone took advantage of the night to break in. She was tempted to find every open window in the house and have it shuttered and barred. Closing the stable door after the horse had bolted. She would not let a rogue run their lives, but what a relief Magnus Haile was still here and not half a mile away at his younger brother's house for the night. She hated to think what might have happened if the sound of him thundering up the stairs had not scared the man off. Better not be wistful about having such a strong protector always on hand but Lady Drace was a fool to turn him away. She obviously had no idea of the dangers ahead of a lone woman with a tiny and dependent child.

No point in her howling for the moon, though. She couldn't take a lover when she had a son to make it impossible. She managed not to trip over her own feet as she went downstairs and refused to let Toby see how frightened she was. He was virtually asleep when Magnus shook his head at Peg and Cook, waiting at the bottom of the stairs to fight off the world with skillets and carving knives. Hetta hastily gathered cushions and made an improvised bed on the *chaise* in the little sitting room so Magnus could lay Toby down. She covered her son with her best cashmere shawl and he sighed and stuck his thumb in his mouth and fell asleep. She hoped nobody had noticed the tear that slipped down her cheek.

'Trust Peg to watch over him, Mrs Champion,' Magnus said softly, as if he knew she wanted to sit by him all night. 'I will sleep for an hour or so, then take over, so she can get her beauty sleep.'

'I'll not let any harm come to him, missus, so you go and talk to Mr Magnus. We'll both be here when you get back.'

'Thank you,' Hetta whispered and knew it made sense to talk elsewhere, but leaving Toby was so hard. 'I must not tie him to my apron strings,' she said after she followed Magnus out of the room to whisper in private. 'There's no surer way to make him rebel, but I don't want whoever was here tonight near him ever again.'

'No sign of him now, Mr Magnus,' Jem said as he heard them speaking even this softly and popped his head out of the kitchen door.

'Nothing more to be done tonight, then, but can you sleep here and leave my brother's house to look after itself for once?'

'Aye, it'll be safe enough. I'd back Ma to see off a troop of cracksmen and she don't hold with fresh air, so they won't find a way in even if she don't shoot them before they get close enough to try their luck.'

'As well I'm staying here, then. I don't want to boil or be shot by mistake.'

'Aye, and it's dandy here now,' Jem said and went off to find a chair to doze in with one eye open. Hetta wouldn't want to be the one to try to pass such a tough and knowing young man by as well as Magnus Haile. Toby was safe as he could be anywhere.

'You didn't argue about me staying here,' Magnus said when they were alone.

'I am always willing to let propriety go hang if my son's welfare is in the balance. He is far more important than such empty nonsense.'

'Not nonsense. You know as well as I do we are not to be trusted alone together for very long.'

'Don't worry, I won't tell anyone about our kiss, so your reputation is safe.'

'You know that's not what I meant,' he said and sounded annoyed she was refusing to take his scruples seriously.

'What I mean is I love my son, Mr Haile.'

'Of course you do, but what about your good name?'

'What about it? Do you seriously think I worry much about it after travelling halfway around the Continent when Toby was a baby?'

'No, I suspect you did that to make certain

your father could not send you back to your grandmother.'

Hmm, that stopped her in her tracks for a moment. Of course, she had, but not many people saw past her supposed impulsiveness and she wished he hadn't either. Even her father had never actually asked why she set off alone except for her baby. 'Do you, Mr Haile?' she said coolly enough, but he was even more dangerous than she thought now he added acute understanding to the dark good looks.

'Yes, I do. Don't forget I have kissed you, Mrs Champion, so I know how much of a disguise you wear to fool the world. You are nothing like the sober and timid little mouse you pretend to be on the inside, are you?'

'No, I would probably be dead by now if I was,' she said soberly as all the times when it was best to go unnoticed piled up to say she had been right then, but somehow she didn't want to be plain and unmemorable Mrs Champion any more. Not here and not with him.

'You are a redoubtable lioness instead, then?'

'Indeed, and you know what they say about them and their cubs, don't you?' she said proudly and felt as if the battle going on under their words could be more painful than the wildest fight with Bran in the old days.

'You are unsafe, then?'

'Do I look as if I am?' she demanded, standing with her hands on her hips and her spectacles firmly in place again.

'Yes. You look like more temptation than you will ever know,' he said huskily, but how could she believe him when he had obviously been so besotted with a beauty like Lady Drace that he had thrown caution to the four winds? 'But I am very wary of females with hidden depths nowadays,' he added bitterly and of course he was, so why was she bothering to pretend it didn't matter if he liked or loathed her?

Because she didn't want to care too much and she had Toby to put first—oh, and she had wed Bran in a fine romantic haze of hopes and dreams and they all fell flat on their shiny little faces.

'Good. I am wary of males with any depth at all. Now I have a boy to watch over, sir, if you will excuse me?'

So he did, the great fool.

Chapter Ten

Hetta thanked Peg for watching over Toby, then stared down at her son as soon as they were alone again, her brooding gaze softened on his sleeping face. He was worth it, this boy of hers. Worth being lonely for, worth being awkward and angry with Magnus Haile when she didn't really want to be either deep down. Truth to tell she longed for comfort, longed for him and his strong arms around her that would feel like a taste of heaven at this moment. Instead she sat lonely and shaken and uncertain and gazed at her son as if to say she was sorry she had taken her eyes off him long enough to notice what a fine man Magnus Haile was. The memory of his kiss haunted her, though. She shifted uneasily in her chair, then stilled when it seemed as if Toby might wake for a moment. No, he murmured in his sleep and turned over as if her intent gaze disturbed him. Hearing him sigh and drop back to sleep, she told herself nothing mattered if he was safe.

She thought about tonight again. How well had the attempt to snatch Toby been planned? It felt desperate and impulsive, yet whoever made it must know there was no dog nearby tonight to warn a stranger was lurking in the shadows. And she and Toby would have been alone in the house but for Cook and Peg, if not for Magnus Haile's solitary drunken-spree misery, and who would have had the foresight to plan for that? Neither he nor Jem Caudle would have been here to scare off a kidnapper if not for the man's secret love affair with a brandy bottle. Hetta felt suspicious of everyone she had met since they'd landed in England but the ones under this roof right now. Oh, and Lady Aline—she trusted her almost by instinct—just as she trusted Magnus not to play both sides against the middle. He was here by accident tonight and would keep his despair to himself. Had Magnus and Jem Caudle spoilt a daring attempt to snatch Sir Hadrian Porter's grandson and get the King's Bloodhound off a murderer's tail tonight? If they had, someone had not been clever enough to spy out the land first or he would have seen Magnus through the open windows before a furtive entry at the back of the house where Toby's nightlight gave away which room he was sleeping in.

Too restless now to be still, she adjourned to a section of hallway where she could watch Toby's makeshift bed while she paced softly enough not to disturb him. The most obvious person to take advantage of a situation was the one who had created it. She couldn't let her dislike of Lord Carrowe for making love to the young girl Lady Drace must have been ten years ago, then casting her aside for richer pickings, blind her. But even after what had happened Hetta was glad to be away from Carrowe House. She paused in her pacing to wrap her arms about her body. She felt cold even thinking about that sad old place where questions about a brutal murder seemed to haunt every dusty corner.

'Here.' Magnus's voice was soft enough, but the sound of it still made her jump. Her heart raced in what she told herself was shock at his sudden appearance, not wild excitement he was here in the almost darkness with her, which suddenly felt rich with possibilities. 'You gave Toby your shawl and one of the girls must have left this one behind.'

'Thank you,' she said. 'I am sorry,' she whispered as she wrapped the soft shawl around her, noticing vaguely that it was far less fine than her own. She felt restive and hard done by at her own father's benign neglect at times, but the Haile girls had been through so much hardship thanks to their father that she was ashamed of herself for complaining about Sir Hadrian's far lesser sins.

'You are tired and worried and have been shunted from pillar to post ever since you got home, Mrs Champion,' he said in such a neutral voice she decided she preferred him being brusque and frowning. '*I* am sorry there is no better gentleman present to help you tonight,' he said stiffly.

'I will take any help I can get to keep Toby safe,' she said lightly, but it wouldn't do, she simply didn't have enough lightness in her after such a day.

'Even mine?'

'Especially yours,' she said with a great sigh as she let herself soften at last and nearly stumbled with weariness. All the steel being a mother had put in her spine threatened to melt at his soft question, so she met the glint of his dark eyes in the near darkness and refused to pretend any more.

'Why?' he asked rather huskily, as if he felt a touch overwhelmed she might trust him when she knew too much about him.

'You are a protector, not a destroyer.'

'How can you say so? You know how I was that day at Dover and when you got here today.'

'Yes, you were frustrated and out of temper. If you don't think I have seen such things before, but with added venom, you have a very rosy view of my life so far, Mr Haile. Even when you are grim and moody and in your cups there's no malice in you and if you truly didn't care what anyone thought you would worry less.'

'I might not if I was a pompous ass like my brother Gresley,' he said absently, as if he was flattered she thought him a better drunk than Bran and was trying not to admit it.

Hetta was too busy wondering if his brother was quite as self-satisfied as he liked to pretend, to wonder about the insecurities life and

Lady Drace had put in such a well-born and physically powerful man as Magnus Haile. She would keep that thought to puzzle over later, when she couldn't sleep as she sat by Toby's side and worried about him and the future. 'He is an earl, though, isn't he?' she said and hoped there was no hint of her unlikely suspicion his own brother knew a lot more about his father's murder than the Earl was ever likely to admit. 'Perhaps noblemen don't need to worry about good manners and propriety as we mere mortals do.'

'I thought you didn't anyway, but I need my beauty sleep now even if you do not. Might I suggest we continue this conversation tomorrow when we are a little more refreshed?' he said as if they were saying polite farewells at a *ton* party.

Hetta let him guide her back to her seat as if it was in a box at the opera because she was so tired she was almost aching with it and she probably wouldn't sleep, but he didn't need to know. 'Goodnight,' she murmured softly enough not to wake Toby.

'Goodnight,' he whispered and bent so unexpectedly close he had snatched a kiss from her undefended mouth before she could even think about moving or glaring at him. Now she would not sleep for missing the feel of him against her. She cast a brooding look at the seat he must have taken up in the hallway to watch over her as she watched over Toby. She wondered if Jem Caudle was sitting in a shadowy corner with a green baize door propped open to furtively watch Magnus watch her watch Toby, or if Peg was doing the same to him. Her thoughts got so tangled as she thought out the chances anyone but Toby would get a wink of sleep tonight she lost the thread altogether.

She awoke among a luxury of cushions in her absent hostess's favourite armchair to another glowing morning after her best sleep in months. She frowned at the thought of Magnus being able to watch her sleep for the second time in a day and waited for her son to leap out of his makeshift bed, as impatient for this day as he had been for all the others in his short life so far.

Magnus was less sanguine about the day ahead by the time they all had breakfast and

Wulf walked over from his house with the dogs who were already in a state of high excitement after being parted from him for a whole day and night. Toby was happy to promise not to leave the ground and stay in sight if he could run round the gardens with two overgrown puppies and tumble in the sun until it was hard to tell where boy left off and two black and white dogs of uncertain ancestry began.

'Did you get any sleep at all, then?' Wulf asked after Magnus told him about the events of the night.

'Jem and I kept watch by rote,' he said and frowned at the horizon as if it must be guilty of something.

'So you had all that time to sit and think, or was your poor head still aching?'

'No, sorry, little brother, I got off lightly.'

'Shame.'

'Yes, I suppose I ought to be.'

'No, you should be glad it's over. Lady Drace was right to make a new start and at least she left you free to do the same.'

'Yes, she did,' Magnus agreed and was surprised not to feel any of the hollow fury that had dogged him since Delphi had refused to wed him after admitting the child she carried was his and not her late husband's. Mrs Champion had broken the cycle of depression and self-reproach for him somehow and he'd kissed her as if they were important, and yet he still didn't know her first name. He really must find out what it was. Although she seemed to have decided to put all her energies into her boy and to the devil with all Hailes, he could hardly go about lusting for a lady he could only call by another man's name even in his head.

'Having established that mercy, we can get back to last night's circus? You have someone in mind as the cause of it all, don't you?'

'Yes, but I can't tell you until I'm sure. I need to catch him at it and I must speak to Sir Hadrian Porter before anyone goes anywhere.'

'Where are you thinking of going, then?'

'I don't know yet, but we need to keep a watch on Mrs Champion and her boy and I'm none too happy about Mama and the girls living in a hired house in a seaside town where too many people come and go for strangers to stand out.'

'There's no real threat to them, though, is

there?' Wulf asked, and the idea seemed to jolt him out of his light-hearted mood.

'Not as far as I know. They lived in a ruinous old barn where anyone with a mania against us Hailes could snatch one of them if they wanted to and nothing happened. So, no, if you ask me this has to do with Sir Hadrian Porter and his reputation for succeeding at impossible tasks.'

'Do you think he would take risks with his daughter and grandson's safety?'

'I think he's done everything he can to minimise the risk to them, but he can't be in half-a-dozen places at once, so I intend to see to their safety myself. Perhaps you and Isabella could join Mama and the twins in Worthing for a week or two in case they need watching over as well?'

'Isabella is going back to Wychwood with her sister Miranda and Carnwood. Even though we are out of the worst of the heat and smoke most of the time here, Derbyshire air is cleaner and apparently it's a lot safer there as well.'

'The great lovers have had a spat, have they?' Magnus teased and was surprised to see his brother blush.

'No, but I have to work and I can write in

Worthing and still get my copy to the printers in time, then check the proofs, I suppose.'

'Can you really?' Magnus eyed his brother sceptically as he recalled how restless he was when Isabella was not nearby nowadays. Suddenly a very good reason why Isabella might agree to be fussed over by her elder sister occurred to him. 'Well, well, Papa Wulf,' he drawled with a mocking grin as he saw the truth in his brother's refusal to meet his eyes. 'You must be cursing your profession for keeping you apart right now.'

'Don't. She didn't want to go, but she is so ill of a morning the thought of being cosseted by Miranda was too tempting in the end, the poor darling. As soon as this book is finished and at the printer's I can gallop to Wychwood to join her in approved Haile style, so you had best get this business of yours wrapped up faster than I can wield a pen,' Wulf said as if trying to get his old cynical air back, but the joy of being loved and the prospect of a child didn't leave room for any.

'Isabella is healthy as a horse,' Magnus said to reassure his brother. 'Although you two could have waited a little longer before making me an uncle again, if you ask me.'

'I love her too much to be careful,' Wulf admitted shortly.

'I did notice. Jem and I are hoarse from shouting greetings at one another under your bedchamber windows, so you can get out of bed and say hello to your family once in a while.'

'Is that what you were doing? We thought you must be going deaf.'

'Did you, now? Well, congratulations anyway, little brother,' Magnus said and slapped Wulf on the back. He was glad Wulf could shout his delight from the rooftops as soon as he knew Isabella was safe after the birth. 'I hope it's not twins,' he added absently.

'Oh, Lord, I hadn't thought of that,' his brother said with a dazed look in his eyes at the idea of two babies instead of the standard one. Wulf had gone from lone wolf to devoted husband and father very suddenly, so no wonder he was shaking his head as if he couldn't quite believe it.

Magnus wondered about a very different future from the one he thought he'd wanted for himself even a week ago. Wulf was living proof a man's life could change between one second and the next, wasn't he? But, no, that wasn't going to happen to him. Mrs Champion wouldn't want to be landed with a shop-soiled fool like him after marrying a very different one last time.

'Twins,' Wulf said in a dazzled voice.

'Come on, Romeo. There's a book for you to finish and felons to catch before you take that idea to Derbyshire and break it to Isabella as gently as you can.'

'It might not be,' Wulf said as if he was reassuring himself.

'Of course not. Mama had five of us before the twins came along. But you had best go and tell Peg your news while I watch Master Tobias and your misbegotten hounds for you because she will never forgive you if you leave her out.'

Chapter Eleven

Hetta heard exclamations of boyish joy and happy yips and barks coming from the kitchen garden where she was picking blackcurrants for Cook in an attempt to make herself useful. She would have to trust Magnus to keep an eye on Toby and what sounded more like half-a-dozen dogs than two. This was a family home and she should not be here, but she didn't want to leave what felt like the peace and safety of Develin House, despite last night's events. A kidnapper might be lying in wait for them out in the real world and her lovely confidence in her ability to protect her son was draining away by the moment. Of course, she had slept with a pistol under her pillow plenty of times when Toby was a tiny, vulnerable little being with only her between him and disaster. How she had cursed herself for ever setting out with him on her own with the benefit of hindsight as she searched for her father in recently war-torn lands. Too late to go back by the time she fully took in the risk she was running, but she hated herself for putting her precious baby through so much because she didn't have the courage to stand up to her formidable grandmother and bring up her baby her own way.

Now she could afford to travel in style whenever she did so without her father. She could pay for secure places to stay and reliable guards and outriders whenever she thought they were needed, but this was different. They were in England now and should be safe, but instead she felt as if someone had kicked the legs out from under her. The temptation to cling to the nearest solid object was nigh overwhelming, especially when he happened to be Magnus Haile and she wanted to cling to him anyway.

Even as her fingers picked steadily and the bowl grew full of the rich fruits of high summer, she had to stop herself tipping up the stool and running to reassure herself Toby was safe. She had to trust Magnus and his younger brother to keep him within sight and safety. If she got so anxious she refused to let her son out of her sight, trouble would follow as surely as night followed day as Toby grew more and more restless at such a restriction on his freedom. She dreaded the thought of trying to track down a runaway son before a kidnapper could catch Toby. So, what on earth *was* she going to do? The thought of lodgings somewhere quiet felt like sitting waiting for an enemy to pick them off now and she tried not to let the fact she might never see Magnus Haile again weigh in the balance.

'There you are,' the man himself said as if she was hiding, which she had been, so he was right in a way, wasn't he?

'Yes, here I am,' she said brightly.

'We need to talk about the future, Mrs Champion.'

'Do we? Then I foresee a blackcurrant tart quite soon,' she said nonchalantly, wondering where this particular Haile was proposing to bundle her off to next.

'Could be messy,' he said casually and even a night half-asleep in a chair had left him a very different man from the wounded drunkard she encountered yesterday.

An image of dark, sweet juice slipping from

her lips as she gazed at him spellbound, so it could be licked away by a lover before it got anywhere dangerous, was enough to make her avoid his acute gaze as she tried to dampen the heat at the heart of her and slow her breathing to normal. What on earth was the matter with her? Her imagination had never been so racy and louche before and she was nearly sure she didn't like it.

'We had best make sure Cook doesn't press one on us when we leave,' she said as if worrying about the upholstery of a hired coach was her biggest concern.

'Speaking of leaving, Wulf and I have a plan for that.'

'How ingenious of you,' she said, stung that he seemed so keen to get rid of her.

'Now don't be like that, Mrs Champion,' he said as if she was being sweetly unreasonable, but here she was having fantasies about him while he only wanted to see the back of her as fast as possible, so why shouldn't she be?

'Call me Hetta, for goodness' sake,' she corrected him sharply, as if he was being wilfully formal by calling her that when he had no idea what her first name was.

'At least I can now, when we are alone.'

'We are about to part very likely for good, so it won't cost you much effort.'

'No, we are not.'

'Are *you* going to kidnap us as well, then?'

'If I have to.'

'Why would you take so much interest in a pair of strangers?'

'Because you don't feel like one and you seem to be in danger because of our family muddles. Wulf and I have decided he will stay in Worthing to make sure our mother and little sisters are safe and I will remain here with you. It's the only way to stop any risk of last night's villain being able to threaten your father's investigation of our father's murder.'

'I thought you didn't much care if he was caught or not and what right have you or your brother got to dictate where I go and what I do?'

'We don't, but the world will point a finger at Mama and the girls if Sir Hadrian does not find either of us guilty. Even the thought of such a future for them makes me determined to find out who really did it. As for dictating to you,

I hope common sense will argue it is the best idea, but perhaps I overestimate you.'

'Why would it?' she said scornfully because she knew about this sneaky longing she had to cling to him like a limpet and, hopefully, he did not.

'If you set off in a hired coach with only your son for company you could be waylaid wherever this abductor chooses. Whoever tried to take your son last night might pay a coachman to take you straight to him or choose to drive the thing himself and how would you stop him?'

'With ball and powder and any other means to hand,' she said with pretend confidence, because he was right, of course, but that didn't make being told what to do any less irritating somehow.

'This isn't bandit country, Hetta. Shooting any stray man who decides to ride up close to your coach in order to ogle you is frowned upon by the justices here.'

'I only shoot out-and-out villains,' she said with a very straight look to tell him he had best be glad she didn't have a pistol in her hand right now.

'Have you ever done so?' he said, sounding intrigued, and why did he have to possess a sense of humour as well as all that arrogant glamour? It really was most annoying of him to disarm her with it at the wrong moment.

'I fired wide, because even you must know how inaccurate a small gun is and I didn't want him bleeding all over the place,' she said casually, although the idea of putting a bullet in any living creature still filled her with horror.

'I hope you have a pair of them, then, or did you make him wait to be shot while you reloaded a lone one?'

'Never you mind. What have you and your brother decided I am to do next even if I can defend myself?'

'Shooting anyone who looks at you the wrong way is not classed as defending yourself under British law and I only meant to make a suggestion of what we might do to stop you having to shoot anyone before you decide I'm next.'

An idea he intended she would go along with if his arrogant certainty had anything to do with it. 'I will be certain to let you know if you ever get me angry enough for that, but kindly explain this notion of yours, since I cannot go armed to the teeth.'

'Hetta the Bandit Queen fills me with terror,' he said with a hot look to give his words the lie.

'As well I left her on the other side of the Channel, then,' she told him with a very straight look to say, *Stop trying to seduce me with words. I still want to know what you are up to.* The trouble was he might manage it if she let him, even out here in broad daylight with the kitchen windows close by and her knowing better.

'Did you, now?' he asked, with a faraway look in his eyes at the very thought of such a mythical version of her it made her want to snatch off her sun hat and wave it in front of her hot face.

'Stop it,' she ordered him as brusquely as she could when her voice sounded husky and sun warmed even to her own ears. 'Your plans for my immediate future, if you please, Mr Haile?' she demanded and heard the disastrous half-promise of seeing about that bandit version of herself after all this was over beneath the anger.

He grinned as if he heard it, too. 'I have four sisters, Hetta. The eldest has a gift for lofty scorn you would envy. You should compare notes.'

'Why would we trouble ourselves to do such a thing?'

'Nicely done, but Lady Mary would add a steely hauteur I don't think you will learn if you live out your century and Norfolk is a little out of the way for us this time.'

'Out of the way of what?'

'Intrigued?'

'No, annoyed,' she lied.

'You like my next sister Aline, though, don't you? Toby does nothing but sing her praises as a far more learned and much cleverer person than I am. He is right, of course, but she would make an ideal companion on your journey, if we can persuade my mother to spare her to us.'

'What journey, you annoying man?'

'Definitely intrigued.'

'No, just furious and about to throw a basket of blackcurrants at you.'

'You couldn't reach me from there,' he argued.

'Maybe not, but your snowy shirt and that lovely waistcoat would be ruined by any strays that hit you.'

'Lovely?' he asked with a revolted look, as if the very idea was unmanly.

'Well, it is *very* fine,' she said with a mocking look. She admired the way the silk back moulded to his leanly muscular body and the stiffer brocade outlined his front and was secretly glad it was too hot for him to wear a coat around his own home on a day like this, but she was hardly going to tell him so, was she?

'Behave yourself,' he drawled as if he knew she was distracted by his manly physique, even when she was trying so hard to be angry with him for making plans behind her back and once being Lady Drace's lover.

'I don't know what you mean.'

'Oh, I think you do, Hetta.'

'I wish I'd never told you my name now,' she said as she felt a blush give her away.

'I can't let you dash round the country falling into scrapes while I stay here and wait for you and your son to be kidnapped,' he said, quite serious at last. 'Think how desperate this man who came after Toby last night must be if he was the one who murdered my father, Hetta. He knows he will swing for it if he's caught, so there's no barrier left for him to cross that will make him hesitate before he defends himself by whatever means come to hand. He has nothing left to lose by doing all he can to keep your father off his scent because once his actions come to light he will be a dead man anyway.'

'And for his sake I lose my freedom?' Hetta agreed wearily.

'Nobody said it was just, but you can have it back as soon as he is safely in jail, or wherever else your father and his masters choose to put him, but for now, please will you go along with my plan and give us some chance of catching him.'

'Am I to be a moving target to make that more likely, then?'

'No, that's the very last thing I want.'

'Tell me what it is,' she said with a sigh.

'You agree?' Magnus sounded incredulous when she nodded after he outlined his plan for her and Toby to tour whichever parts of the south and west took their fancy. With Lady Aline and Peg for company and propriety and him and Jem as a discreetly armed and very watchful escort.

'It will serve as well as any scheme I can come up with for the next few weeks and would get us safely away from London. You are right—any houses for hire for the summer will be of poor quality if they are still vacant by now. Playing the tourist is as good a way as any for us to pass the time until we can go back to real travelling.'

'Real travelling?' he echoed as if she had insulted his country.

She ought to be more tactful about a place she would probably have to live in while Toby went to school, but she wasn't ready to tell him all her intentions quite yet. She needed to remember she was an independent woman and he would walk away from her as soon as his father's murderer was caught.

'That was badly said,' she said with another sigh. 'Although I will admit the Heath has been a pleasant surprise to me, despite all the dramas.'

'I shall nobly ignore that sneaky caveat and there's a great deal more of your homeland for you to see yet and I have never been bored by travelling around it. To walk from one new wonder to another and linger where I fancy is my idea of heaven, especially during a summer like this one when any sane body would choose to be out of London.'

'You sound as if you do so quite often,' she said, intrigued by that glimpse of a very different man to the Honourable Magnus under the skin.

'I like to walk and it is a good way to avoid summer house parties and overcrowded fashionable resorts. One set of people believe I am with the other and vice versa, so I can please myself for weeks on end with nobody much the wiser.'

'You should be a poet,' she pretended to mock him, but deep down she wondered if he wasn't ideally suited to the task, with those brooding looks and hints of a tragic past to gild him even more in the eyes of his besotted female fans.

'Maybe I should, if I had any talent for versifying. I could stride about the hills and dales brooding about my sins instead of doing it in my mother's dining room.'

'And get fresh air and exercise while you are about it,' she suggested, picturing him doing it anyway and feeling that wicked tug of attraction as she decided the role would become him even if he wasn't a poet.

'To get back to the subject we are meant to be talking about, you don't object to my company on your journey, then?'

'Why should I? To paraphrase your words to Toby, you don't smell and you are good enough company and might even frighten off a potential attacker with one of your frowns, so why turn down such a stalwart escort when I need one?'

'Because I feel as if you are on the edge of rebelling against your father's ordering of your life and might think I want to walk in his footsteps.'

'No, you are a very different man and I never was one to cut off my nose to spite my face. My son has been a target for ruthless men who want to frustrate my father's work since the day he was born and it has made a realist out of me whether I like it or not.'

'I am sure Sir Hadrian is concerned about your welfare as well as his grandson's safety and well-being.'

'Maybe, but Toby is the joker in his pack. Papa knows he only has to play it and I will agree to whatever he decides will keep Toby safe from his enemies this time.'

'And if not for your responsibility to him you would dive head first into any mystery that intrigued you without a second thought, wouldn't you?' he challenged her disguise of the meek daughter and he really was dangerous, wasn't he?

'Possibly,' she replied with a thoughtful sideways look to wonder how he knew there was a daredevil streak in dull and respectable Mrs Champion she managed to hide from everyone else, even after that epic trek to catch up with her father when Toby was a baby because she refused to be taken over by her grandmother or her late husband's relatives and told what to do for the rest of her life. 'If not for him, my whole life would be different, but so much *less.*'

'So, you would stay out of your father's darker projects for your son's sake, even if he did not blackmail you into it then, wouldn't you?'

'Yes,' she agreed, surprised he already knew her so much better than her father seemed to. 'I married Brandon Champion because I wanted a life of seagoing adventure, but he only wanted a domesticated little sparrow who would stay quietly out of the way while he got on with real life. Now there's no Bran to tell me what to do or where to go, he has left me with the biggest reason I could ever have not to take part in Papa's adventures even if I have been able to live in countries most ladies can only imagine and Toby has a broader view of the world than most schoolboys can even dream about. How Bran would laugh and say it served me right for not being the grateful little miss he thought I was when he married me if he had known my father would hobble me with a promise I made to him when I was desperate to escape from England. But you are right. I shall always put Toby first and he will be safer and happier touring your precious country than he would be in some shabby lodging in a quiet town with not very much for him to do except long for this puppy he is so obsessed with.'

While I try to find a place to live while he's at school that doesn't fill me with dread for the boredom and misery of being without him for at least five days out of every seven with nothing much to do to fill the time with, she added in her head.

She would not confide in him how she hated the idea of living for any weekends her son wanted to spend with her as Toby got more and more absorbed with new friends and adventures she truly wanted him to have.

'As well Champion is not here, then, as I would bloody his nose for being so harsh to a wife he obviously didn't even try to understand. I never liked him much and I'm sorry he led you such a dance, but I wish you would make peace with his brother, Hetta. Marcus isn't in the least bit like his younger brother under those gilded Champion looks that must have made you think he was the next pea in the pod. Mark and his wife are fine people and well worth knowing and it would be good for Toby to know they are very ready to welcome you both.'

'They were not very eager to meet me when Bran was still alive.'

'And I know how sad they were his wife refused to meet the rest of the family. Mark thought Brandon must have set his bride against them since he was always so jealous of Mark inheriting the title and estate when neither of them could help the order they were born in.'

'Bran said the Champions could never forgive me for eloping with him when they had a much more suitable bride picked out for him.

He said his family and the girl he was meant to marry were furious with me.' Hetta paused for a moment, thinking of all the untruths Bran had told and wishing he had been different. He was frail and all too human under those angelic looks and easy smiles. Best if she refused to dwell on his sins now he would never have a chance to make up for them. 'Are you telling me about them to distract me from the journey you seem to have been planning all night?'

'No, and if we do set out it will be in your hands where we go and what we do next. Please don't say the prospect of even that much freedom isn't tempting you because I will know you're lying and it's really my company you can't stomach.'

Yet he is the most tempting part of this scheme and never mind freedom to go where I want and the open road, wicked Hetta whispered in Mrs Champion's ear.

'It seems an appealing idea to wander wherever the fancy takes us,' respectable Mrs Champion admitted warily and ignored her inner fool as best she could.

'I hope you will see the true beauty of your own country without either your grandmother or your late husband pushing you from pillar to post and not consulting you about any of it,' he said, tactfully leaving out Papa's ordering of things ever since she'd tracked him down in Spain all those years ago.

'You make me sound as if I don't have a mind of my own, Mr Haile.'

'Heaven forbid, Mrs Champion,' he said with a wry smile. 'You must have a will of iron to have managed to get your Toby this far in relative safety.'

'That's not what you said at Dover,' she reminded him lest she get too giddy about his backhanded compliment.

'I said a lot of stupid things that day,' he said gruffly.

She hoped, for his sake, that he meant he was ready to go on with his life now Lady Drace had set him free to be his own man again, but from the familiar frown she suspected his thoughts were with his child again and that was a loss he would never quite put behind him. He would be a lesser man if he could and she didn't want him to be one of those, so any woman who wanted to love him would have to love that part of him as well, she supposed. Luckily, she didn't want to love him, so that wasn't a problem for her to solve.

Chapter Twelve

'I am not complaining, you understand, but I still don't quite know how this happened,' Hetta said to Lady Aline Haile two days later as their comfortable travelling carriage pulled away from the latest stop to change horses and Peg was already nodding in her corner of the carriage.

'I am not quite sure either, but at least Master Tobias here is an improvement on the pampered darlings Lady Warner thought I could make into young ladies without any effort on their part. He is objectionable in his own right, of course, but he doesn't want to paint fans or cover the land in whitework,' her new friend said and at least the reason for her brief stay at Carrowe House to meet a potential employer was out in the open now and Aline seemed happy with Toby as an alternative pupil to Lady Warner and her fluffy-minded daughters.

'I don't suppose the Misses Warner do either,' Hetta pointed out even so.

'Maybe not, but I never did have any patience with useless so-called accomplishments, so I do not know how to do any of them, even if I wanted to teach them to anyone else.'

'Then I cannot imagine why you wanted to be a governess in the first place! You are far better off with us. I can safely promise my son isn't the least bit interested in ladylike skills and preoccupations. Toby, get your head back in here and out of the way this instant, before it gets chopped clean off by one of those shop signs,' she ordered her son, who was busy gawping at the narrow streets and perilously overhanging buildings of the ancient city they were passing through.

'The builders would have to know how much load and counterweight was safe for those floors to carry them that far out into the streets, Mama. One inch further and the whole lot would have ended up falling down on top of passers-by. I wish I could meet one of them and find out how they did it and if they planned it that way or just learned how from trial and error.'

'Considering the carpenters and masons have been several hundred years in their graves by now, I can't say I share that wish, my son.'

'I expect there are apprenticeship records and guild standards, so we could look them up when we are in London next time,' Aline offered as if she was every bit as interested in such details as Toby. 'Of course, they might not have survived the Great Fire since the Guilds suffered so badly. A good many of them lost everything and had to begin again as best they could,' she added, and the two of them discussed air currents and wind directions and flashovers and who saw what when during that terrible time and invented all sorts of intriguing details of a huge blaze that had, thankfully, been over for nearly a hundred and sixty years.

Hetta sat back to watch the town thin out into mellow countryside and was glad she didn't have to imagine the terror of watching so much of the old city being eaten up by fire for Toby this time when the loss of life and homes filled her with horror. Hiring Lady Aline as her companion and Toby's teacher for the summer had been right for all three of them, but it was still annoying for her to have to admit two Haile men were right at the same time. At least she had insisted on visiting Lady Carrowe and her youngest daughters before they went on to find grander and more remote scenery further along the southern coast of England. She wanted to thank the lady for letting her stay at Develin House and reassure her she intended to treat Lady Aline as a friend and travelling companion rather than a paid employee. And they all needed to prove to managing Haile males that ladies were not a set of puppets to be moved about at will.

I have missed my chance to secure the package you speak of and agree it would make it far easier to control our man and scotch this enterprise before it gets out of hand.

The carefully worded letter read as if the sender was half-expecting a third party to read and puzzle over it before it reached its addressee, or a very wary person indeed. The recipient frowned at the dull and dusty landscape beyond the open window and tapped restless fingers on the desk. This place was halfway between nowhere in particular and somewhere else, but at least it had seen a mop and broom in the last month or so.

M. has put himself in the way all the time since then and keeps the package very close indeed. I will watch and wait, but there may not be another chance to secure the parcel.

I intend to find another way to control the hunt, but I cannot follow that particular avenue without giving away my intentions to scotch this business for good.

'Fool,' the reader murmured into the sticky air. 'Must I always think for you and do everything myself?'

Even Toby had seemed overawed by the scale and atmosphere of the ancient cathedral at Winchester. Hetta had felt her feet complaining about the acres of stone floors she seemed to have walked over already, so she was glad to stand and gaze at the brightly painted round table said to have belonged to Arthur and his Knights. She had wondered if it was such a good idea someone insisted it was repainted thirty-odd years ago and if they had blotted out an ancient past by making it more pristine for the modern age. They had a stimulating argument about whether Arthur and his Round Table existed outside legend over an excellent dinner that night, before Hetta felt oppressed by the silliness of the gossips when Magnus pretended to leave for a night at another inn, lest anyone think poorly of Mrs Champion for not employing an older chaperone than his sister to keep them quiet about this stately progress along the south coast. She fumed every night as they made their way through Hampshire and Dorset and the pretence continued and he really spent every night in the stables or some barn nearby where he could catch out any stealthy predators on their tail and keep her coolly respectable at the same time. Her wicked thoughts about all the mischief she might like to get up to with him, if only he would let her, were private and nothing to do with anyone else.

Apart from that burr in her boots, this leisurely exploration of her native land was far more interesting than she feared it might be when they set out to hide in plain sight. She was beginning to be convinced by the age and interest and sheer beauty of this generous country. The sky might be grey and the sea as muddy looking as a town puddle now and again, but then the clouds or sea mist would disperse, and the sun shone, and she didn't think she had ever seen the sky as clear and washed as clean a blue as it was here on the best of summer days. She watched and listened for the rush of speed and sharp wings as swifts flew over their heads, squealing with the joy of going where no man could and all the while martins and swallows swirled for insects as if their faster cousins were not even there. There were flowers of such minute and delicate beauty they seemed even more of a marvel than their lush cousins further south. Magnus Haile even knew where to look for the last of the orchids to show Toby their exquisite and sometimes quirky beauty. Then there were lush valleys where the buzz of bees and less welcome, but at least not deadly, insects gave away the quieter blossoms of the hedgerows now the full rush of spring was apparently over.

Even the towns in this part of the world

seemed to have dreamed their way through what seemed more like thousands than hundreds of years with history undisturbed in their cellars and attics. Except apparently this whole coast had been deep in the smuggling trade for almost as long, so it wasn't quite as peaceful and innocent as it seemed even now. Among sheep-cropped cliffs and sturdy cattle in their lush pasture, Magnus said there were hidden ways so deep and out of the way lines of pack ponies could work their way through them in broad daylight and a stranger would never be any the wiser. Best not to go looking for them, he warned Toby as interest sparked in his bright blue gaze and, to Hetta's amazement, her son nodded and looked manly, as if keeping her out of trouble was his life's work instead of the other way around.

Toby loved the odd and sometimes eerie Chesil Beach under a summer fog near the inn they were very comfortable in for nearly a week, even as his mother felt a prickle of unease walking out on the flat expanse of pebbles as if she was being watched again by unseen eyes. When the mist cleared to reveal another beautiful sunny day, her son ran whooping with

joy across the wide sands at Weymouth beach
and out into the sea without even bothering
to take off most of his clothes. Glad to shake
off the odd mood of this morning, now such
fancies seemed folly in the brilliant sunlight,
Hetta stood by and smiled to see her son so
carefree and full of excitement and told herself it didn't matter if Mr Magnus Haile was
as benignly detached from her as if he really
was only here to keep a watch out for villains
and other hazards. So, they meandered along
the coast at a leisurely pace, and apart from
her ridiculous awareness of Magnus Haile at
every second step, she began to see what he
meant about their native land. This land was
green and beautiful under the summer sun—
how could she have dismissed it as grey and
dull when she lived in London, then Lyme? She
supposed grief for her mother and her lonely
life under Lady Porter's stern roof was followed
by the gradual realisation she had made a huge
mistake in eloping with Bran, which explained
a lot, she allowed, as she let her much younger
self off one or two idiocies.

At least now she was falling in love with her
own country and it wasn't because she saw it

through Magnus's eyes when he pointed out this landmark or that hidden beauty spot to Toby or Aline.

Their journey rumbled on into August and the heat built a little higher, but she and Toby were used to far hotter summers than this one and now even the servants seemed to be in a holiday mood. Peg grudgingly agreed it was quite nice to be rambling along like this when it was warm and fine and if she didn't have to harry laundry maids about the right way to remove stains from the fine muslins that were all Hetta and Aline could endure on the hottest days. Insisting on mending Toby's linen and making him new shirts as he wore them out or carried on growing like a weed gave Hetta an excuse to sit sewing by Peg and listen to her tales of the Hailes as children and pretend it didn't matter Magnus was avoiding her. Just as well he was, she decided. He was an impecunious gentleman with very little inclination to be a fortune hunter, despite his late father's blackmailing efforts in that direction. He might have felt a few moments of hot desire for a willing woman, but it had obviously been no more than that. Those kisses at Develin House stole her breath even now when she let herself dream about them, so she pushed them to the back of her mind and tried to concentrate on her needlework. She whipped stitches into a parade-ground neat line as even the shade grew sticky and a little bit trying, and Peg dozed. No, if he wanted her he would have to prove it, then catch her as if he meant to. She would not make it easy for him.

'The landlady has sent out some small beer straight from the cellar for Peg, but Ally insisted you would prefer tea, Mrs Champion,' the man she had been trying so hard not to think about said from behind her, so no wonder Hetta jumped as if she had been stung.

'Oh, thank you—and your sister is quite right, of course,' she made herself say as coolly and distantly as he seemed to want her to be, once they had set out on this frustrating but at the same time rather wonderful tour.

'You always seem busy,' he said with a nod at her neglected sewing.

Hetta hastily picked it up again and set a stitch or two before she realised he wasn't going to put down the tray and lope off as if he was far too busy to spare any time for her today. 'I sometimes think Toby grows between one day and the next,' she said nonchalantly. He could hardly expect her to be openly delighted to see him after weeks of pretending she only existed as Toby's mother and Aline's new friend, not as a still fairly interesting and desirable female.

'Boys his age are full of so much hope and hunger for the future it seems as if they are trying to get to maturity by willpower alone,' he told her as if he had thought long and hard about Toby's rush to grow up and thought she might like his opinion. She might, but she liked a great deal about him that he didn't altogether want her to as well.

'Girls are quieter about it, but much the same underneath, except we are taught to be more diffident and self-contained.'

'Is that what you learned at your mother's knee, then? I admit to being surprised if it was. Katherine, Lady Porter's *Letters* form a fascinating little book Wulf drew my attention to before we left Hampstead and he even managed to track down a copy. He sent it on to enliven my nights in various different hiding places and I have to say she doesn't sound like a conventional lady to me.'

'No, she wasn't,' Hetta said with a fond smile as she refused to wonder why he had taken so much trouble to read an obscure book not many people had noticed when Papa had the less personal passages from her mother's letters collected and bound as a public memorial to such an extraordinary woman. 'You will already know she corresponded with some of the most radical thinkers of her day, but took her own path. Luckily for me she did not share the Godwins' ideas about rearing daughters or Rousseau's theories about children raising themselves on wild instinct and navy beans.'

'You were lucky indeed, then,' he said with a grimace.

'Yes, but she was extraordinary enough to keep me with her even when Papa thought I should be packed off to school in England.'

'Perhaps your hurt and grief when she died would have been less acute if you had already been parted,' he said as if he recalled quite a bit about that sense of loss of at least one caring parent from his own schooldays.

'And perhaps I had the best possible time with

her as I could, while I could,' she said fiercely, because grief for her mother was always waiting to trip her up even now and she wouldn't cry in front of him. 'Boys are different,' she said with a gesture of her hand to admit it was a lazy argument. 'Toby has lived in the world as it is, rather than the way I would prefer it to be, so he must learn to be self-sufficient as well. I know I cannot tie him to my apron strings.'

'He's such a bright and happy lad I don't think you have even tried to,' he said gently and she looked directly at him for the first time and saw everything she had longed for all these lonely nights in his dark brown eyes.

Warmth and understanding and something a lot more exciting seemed to look watchfully back at her and she sighed for the scruples and protectiveness that had made him sleep in a stable while she enjoyed a restless, if virtuous, night's sleep in the innkeepers' best bedchambers. It was what she told him she wanted. No, what she knew she must not have however much she wanted it. So, he was right. They had to avoid any more long nights in the same place, like the one at Develin House that seemed like long months instead of a couple of weeks ago now. She felt the heaviness of longing in her supple spine and shoulders as she unconsciously bent towards him as if he was magnetic and she couldn't help herself. Straightening hastily in her chair, she shot him a sidelong look to see if he had noticed the wanton creature she wanted to be.

Either he was pretending he hadn't or he truly had no idea what was going on in her wicked thoughts and all-too-willing body. 'You set him up as best you can for life, Hetta,' he reassured her. 'Toby knows he is the centre of your world and you would go to the ends of the earth for him if he needed you to. It will do him very well in life, I promise you.'

'How do you know?'

'Because it is what our mother did for us— well, all of us except Gresley,' he added as if he had to be strictly honest with her now they had let some feelings through the pretence they were little more than chance travelling companions. 'Our father doted on his heir, but my mother was less loving with him than the rest of us for some reason. Gres is the most like the old man out of the seven of us and I suppose that did him no favours with her as soon as he was old enough to follow the Earl about as if he was a demigod.'

'Poor little boy,' she said and Magnus seemed to think harder about that statement and he nodded slowly as if realising his eldest brother hadn't been so lucky to be the firstborn son after all.

'Indeed, and he has grown up a disappointed man somehow,' he said and didn't meet her eyes this time.

Was Magnus Haile going to follow in his elder brother's footsteps in that much at least? They had loved and lost the same woman. Well, Gresley had cast her aside, turning his back on his lover for money, but would both brothers end up less than life intended them to be because of Lady Drace? She hoped not. The new Earl must have repented his wild ways when he wed his lady, or she would have heard whispers of scandal about him by now. Maybe he would even be remembered one day as the man who had saved his family estates from ruin after sacrificing his real love for them. And as for Magnus Haile, what would his salvation prove to be? Not loving Mrs Hetta Champion, obviously, but if ever a man needed a purpose it was this one. He had so much promise of goodness and happiness in him he deserved better than drinking his life away and idling about town because he refused to leave his mother and sisters to his father's mercy. That was it, wasn't it? The great fool had put aside his own need to make something of his life as a second son to stay at Carrowe House and soften the blows for the members of his family he loved so deeply. Now the old Earl was dead he could be free to find his own way and she wondered when it would occur to him he was able to do what he wanted now, without them suffering for it behind his back.

'Oh, there you are, Master Magnus,' Peg said as she broke out of sleep with a little snort and a startled look so they all pretended she had been awake all along.

'Yes, here I am, my lovely. So, when are you going to make me a happy man and marry me at long last?' he teased her with a wicked smile.

'Never, my handsome lad, and you should be fixing those dark eyes of yours on a fine young woman like this one here instead of plaguing the life out of old Peg.'

'Poor old Peg, my foot,' he said as if he would

like to challenge her for being devious and saying things he preferred unspoken, but that was not in the rules of the game, whatever this game they were all playing was.

Chapter Thirteen

Exeter was a fine and handsome city with a magnificent old cathedral and a generous scatter of ancient inns and posting houses Mr Haile could pretend to retire to for the night, once he was certain his charges were safely tucked up somewhere else. Did he and Jem take it in turns to slip back and watch the inns where she and Toby and Aline stayed all night? Hetta wondered. Perhaps Magnus spent the rest of his evenings when Jem was on duty drinking and dancing and enjoying the company of less respectable women. Maybe he whirled a different laughing, dizzy, obliging female about every other night of the week. He sometimes looked as if he hadn't had much sleep, but if he was haunted by images of him and her wanton self undone in the intimate darkness together as well, there was no sign of it in his relentlessly polite greeting for her every morning and very frustrating it was, too. Soon her father would solve his father's murder and she and Toby would either return to their wandering existence again without even a hint of Mr Magnus Haile in their lives to make the sunlight seem brighter and the road ahead less dusty and tedious, or she would find a place she could tolerate living in for him to avoid as if he didn't want to encourage her fantasies about him sharing it with her.

The day they'd landed in England she would happily have turned about and faced the sea again to get away from it, but now she hated the idea of leaving the white cliffs at Dover behind once again because of him. It felt almost as if this country could really be her home in the right company and he was wilfully denying it to her. Then she stood on her first Cornish cliff and stared down at a clear turquoise sea with the sun dancing on its waves and fell in love with it for its own sake. Even with the memory of all the clear and perfect seas and sunny and cloudless days in the sun of an African or French or Italian sky in her mind she could not fetch out a brighter, clearer image than this. She could live here, winter or summer, and never tire of the moods of sea and sky, but the idea still didn't bring the pleasure it should because if ever a place called out for the right company it was this and he would be far away, chasing rainbows for a very different woman than Mrs Hetta Champion.

Magnus thought he was doing well at staying close to his charges, but also keeping his distance from them until they got to Cornwall. Hetta and his sister seemed to throw off another layer of caution and propriety in this clear and sunny weather on the most beautiful of coasts he had ever come across. He only had himself to blame for suggesting they come here to this place he had always loved, winter or summer. The sun was hot on another cloudless day and the air seemed as if it had been washed and ironed on its long journey across the Atlantic Ocean. He gazed at the incredible clarity of a sea where waves were barely a light silver glint over clear turquoise and an even deeper blue further out. On such a day he wished he could paint himself a reminder of a perfect day to keep with him for the rest of his time on this earth. He desperately wished for a picture of Hetta Champion so he could linger over might-have-beens even more reverently as he got older and heard tales of her dashing re-marriage to some exotic foreign nobleman who was going to appreciate her as extravagantly as she deserved. He was far too flawed and shop-soiled to deserve to even try to cut the damned caper merchant out, he reminded himself, even if he had been rich enough to make an attempt at blinding her to the sterling character of her imaginary suitor. She would give him a thun-dering scold and bid him a hasty goodbye if he let himself say out loud even one or two of the impulses and needs in his heart and head he knew he should not have. Until they knew who this elusive rogue on her and Toby's tail was, he couldn't say a word out of place to her for fear she would banish him and be left with only Jem and his brave and rather reckless sis-ter Aline for protection. He could creep around the neighbourhood and perhaps beat the dratted hedge creeper at his own game if Hetta ever re-alised how base his thoughts were and banished him from her presence, but this was far better. He was close enough to her to be able to scare the villain away, but far enough away to live with his own conscience and not ruin another woman's life with his hot and hasty passions and this headlong need of her that sometimes felt too mighty to ignore.

Virtually penniless as he was, he could not marry her even if she would let him. And he wouldn't wed a woman who only wanted to *let* him wed her after Delphi anyway. Only her raw need and deep and abiding love in return would get him to propose marriage to any female ever again and this one would reject him even if he did. At Develin House she might have said yes, but now she would dismiss him as a woolly-minded idiot who didn't know his own mind. Because he had held himself on such a tight rein with all the miles they had put in he must seem like a tin soldier rather than a real man to her by now.

Ironic, wasn't it? Here he was, learning to want and need her more and more the deeper they got into his favourite county, and his careful avoidance of even a touch or a whisper of desire between them was driving her ever further away from him. Now he had seen her defended and undefended, generous and free as well as tightly buttoned up and wary, and every day seemed to gift him more revelations about her true self. She had a deep character and hers was a slow beauty a man had to look at twice to truly appreciate. He could wind himself up in finding out more and more about her with every day they spent together for the rest of his life, if only he was worthy of sharing it with her in the first place.

'You could swim, too, Mr Haile,' Toby danced up the beach on the hot sand to tell Magnus, so he had to give him a proper hearing since the eager boy had distracted him from dreaming of impossible things.

'Now I am officially grown up, I cannot strip off every stitch I have on as freely as you do, Master Champion,' he replied with a gloomy glance down at the lightest trousers he had left in a once extensive wardrobe.

'Why not?'

'Because I am a man and grown men cannot disport themselves thus in the presence of a lady. It is simply not done, Master Tobias.'

'We should make them go away, then. You must be devilish hot in all those clothes.'

Magnus was startled into laughter at this sudden transformation from small excited boy to miniature young man. 'Devilishly so, old chap, but it would not be very gentlemanly to banish your mother and my sister to the inn so I can take to the sea as well as you, Master Neptune.'

'I can swim like a fish, can't I? Mama taught me as soon as I could stand upright without toppling over. She says I took to it like a little eel.'

'She is quite right, as usual,' Magnus replied more soberly as he forced his brooding gaze away from the women on the shoreline and out to sea.

It did him little good. His imagination had already removed every single one of Mrs Hetta Champion's light draperies and watched her dive into the deliciously cool waves naked as Aphrodite. For her son to swim as surely and strongly as he did, Magnus doubted she could have stayed primly on the shore and kept all her stays and drawers and petticoats on while she taught him to swim as little more than a baby. He just hoped Sir Hadrian had the sense to make sure no man was close enough to watch his daughter naked as the day she was born while she did so. Magnus Haile should be the only man who ever saw Hetta so sensually and gloriously nude and he added the fantasy to the ones already haunting him.

'She usually is, but don't tell her I said so,' his companion said with such a solemn and confidential look Magnus had to bite back another bark of laughter. Bless the boy for giving his thoughts a less carnal turn again and making him laugh. 'She learned to swim when she was a baby herself,' Toby went on with no idea any mention of his mother and swimming so fluidly put Magnus in a fine pother again. 'Her mama taught her because they lived such a wandering life she needed to know Mama would stay alive until she could be rescued if she ever fell in. I'm glad I didn't fall into the Channel on the way over here, though. The sea was far too cold and wild even for a man to swim against it that day. It doesn't look anything like it was then today, does it?'

'No, but I am ashamed to say I don't know where the Channel stops and the great Atlantic begins,' Magnus replied absently, the pain of bidding goodbye to his own child gnawing at him with that reminder. This time he felt another pang at the idea of this one leaving for other countries as well. Caring was the very devil, wasn't it? He had never wanted to be cold and unloving like his father, so he was fated to do it even so. Somehow, he would bid goodbye to the boy and his mother with better grace, so they wouldn't know it hurt.

'This could be a proper ocean, then?' Toby interrupted his gloomy thoughts.

'It could.'

'I never swam in one before. Do you think it's colder or harder to swim against than the Channel? I was too little when we were in Spain and Portugal to find out. Mama won't talk about it and I don't remember being there at all.'

'How disappointing for you,' Magnus said and stored up the knowledge the boy's mother must have tracked down his grandfather in those far-off lands for it to have been so long ago. He recalled tales of guerrilla bands and unrest lingering in both countries after the Great War. Magnus shivered even in this heat to think of Hetta going so far with a babe in arms and more or less alone. No wonder Sir Hadrian tried to keep her out of his adventures. He must have been horrified by all she risked to find him once her husband died and Toby was safely born.

'Yes, it was. Italy is on the Adriatic and Greece on the Aegean, or at least the bits of it we went to are, and oceans are vast, aren't they? My papa sailed them from the time he was eight or nine, but I think I would be bored when it took so long to cross them. Mama says Papa was at sea for months on end.'

'I have never sailed one myself, so I have no idea if the roll and thunder and all the strange sights sailors report make it seem worthwhile. You must ask my brother Wulf next time we meet, since he sailed the Atlantic twice over.'

Magnus's little brother had made that impulsive and thankless journey to a new world to escape falling in love with Isabella, as if Wulf could escape loving the woman he was obviously born to love, Magnus thought scornfully. Then he felt uneasy because he might be doing exactly the same himself. It made him think about instincts and attractions even a strong man could not fight and Magnus didn't have enough willpower to stop his gaze lingering on Hetta Champion's svelte but curvaceous figure even with that tale of passion and pig-headed stubbornness in his head. She was outlined by the light breeze he was so glad of until it shaped her thin muslin gown and lawn summer petticoat so close to her body it was as if even the wind loved the feel of her body under its stroking caress.

His inner demon lingered appreciatively on the view of *Hetta, As Outlined by Zephyr* and wished he could paint again. A glowing renaissance nude with the luminous light and tender brushstrokes of a master like Titian, perhaps? No, that was far too much temptation to even think about with the model for it so near and her son watching the scene around him with eager eyes as he dried off in the sun. All the secrets of the earth seemed open to Toby's wondering gaze right now and Magnus didn't want him learning too much about how a grown man reacted to a very grown-up woman and he would if Magnus didn't get a better grip on his baser impulses before they gave him away.

Hadn't the kick of nausea in his belly when he recalled the hollow feeling of dread and misery the day he bid farewell to his daughter been enough to remind him what came of immoderate and unthinking desire? Even if Hetta wanted him in return, he couldn't risk making another child who might grow up fatherless. And she showed no sign of being as tortured by longing for the ultimate release with him as he was for her. As well for both of them if she was immune to his so-called charms, then. They did enough harm with Delphi to last a lifetime of penitence and regret.

'You will burn if you sit around in the sun for much longer, Tobias,' he said and gestured towards the clothes the boy had thrown off on his way to the sea. 'Don't expect me to pick up after you. Your legs are younger and you stripped your clothes off as if you were being filleted on your way to the sea of your own accord.'

The boy laughed and Magnus felt a lesser version of that pang stab at his heart. He couldn't afford to love this bright, wondering and sometimes too-trusting boy. It would do neither of them any good to let a bond grow, then break it when this journey was over and done with, so he frowned at the untidy array of boy's clothes scattered about and turned his back on their owner as if he disapproved.

But turning round left him staring straight at

Hetta as she laughed with his sister and sheltered her eyes with a raised hand to peer at something interesting on the horizon. It took him a while to wrench his gaze away from her to find out what she was watching. Ah, yes, a couple of seals were lying back in the water, looking as if they were lazily laughing. She was close enough now for him to see her mouth round in an 'Ooh' of wonder as the slick, sleek creatures almost seemed to wave back at them in the crystal clear, sun-warmed waters of this wild coast at such a languid hour of day.

Having seen seals dream before, he was more fascinated by Mrs Hetta Champion as nature intended her to be. Here in this wild land so far away from the controls and prejudices of the *ton*, she was relaxed and light-hearted as he would never have dreamed she could be that first day at Dover in those fearsome spectacles and a deplorable gown and shabby cloak. Now he could see the slender, eager girl she must have been when reckless and ambitious Brandon Champion courted her in secret like the rogue he was. Behind the strict-with-herself woman she became when her husband disappointed her, she was a warm and complicated siren. Or she would be if she ever felt the power of her femininity with the man who would truly show her how much he appreciated her in their bedchamber as he made love to his wife as often as he could for the rest of their lives.

No, he wasn't marriage material. Nor was Champion, he reminded himself as a distraction from wanting her even more, if that was possible. Recalling the selfish, brash and ruthlessly charming lad he'd never liked half as well as his elder brother, he thought it very likely her husband bent the girl this woman was then out of shape. He had to admire her for keeping the girl alive under the guard she raised against the world when Champion failed her. The real Hetta was light-hearted and merry with her son in a way Magnus wished his own mother could have been with her children. He shivered despite the hot sun. No muffled giggle or moment of furtive humour with his mother and younger brother and sisters had gone unpunished by his late father if they dared have a life apart from him and he caught them at it.

Magnus tried to reassemble the uninterest he tried to feel for Hetta that first day at Dover, but it let him down. It was not uninterest even then. He had been bitter. No, that wasn't right either. He had been more bitter than usual when a shabby young woman stepped forward to challenge him over her son. The light in those acute grey eyes of hers behind the ridiculous glasses hinted at depths well worth guarding from the likes of him as he verbally lashed out at her from the depths of his agony. An agony confused and burnt about the edges now he looked back. Fury at Delphi's refusal to see sense had goaded him as much as love by the time he got to Dover but, whatever it was, it was toxic. Hetta's love for her child seemed to show him all the things he could never have as he had bid farewell to his little girl. Delphi had been close to fainting at the very sight of him, now he'd served his purpose and had made the child she must have longed for all through her empty, self-inflicted marriage to Drace. Clearly Delphi still longed for Gresley even when he'd wed another woman for money. He wished she'd had the strength of mind Hetta did and had turned her back on a man so unworthy of her. Magnus snapped back to now and realised he must look so grim it was little wonder Toby had cast him a puzzled glance, then run off to find his mother.

'Mama, Mama, it's just like Greece, isn't it? I swam with fishes and the water is almost warm and there are seals and Mr Haile says sometimes you can even see dolphins from here if you are very lucky. I love Cornwall—can we stay for ever?'

Magnus swallowed another dose of bile at the thought he should be teaching his own child to swim and bask in the English sun one day. He needed to cut himself off from the grieving father inside himself to stay sane. It was hard to live with this hollow at the heart of him, but he was weary of the constant ache of it, so goodness knew what the rest of the world thought of him. On such a day he contrasted a sun-bronzed, quicksilver boy with the hesitant shadow Delphi could easily make of their daughter. It wasn't fair on Delphi to make the comparison, but he met his sister's complicated brown and moss-green eyes and saw compassion and too much understanding looking back at him. He managed a rueful grin, to tell her he would get over his grief for his own child now he knew what it was. There would always be sadness for his child growing up puzzled and hesitant about her supposed-to-be-dead father, but it was time to stop wearing his woes like a badge and get on with life. And to get his hot, guilty and deeply covetous thoughts away from Mrs Henrietta Champion before he ruined another woman's life with lust-driven need.

'I doubt it's quite this hot and lovely here all the year round, my darling,' Hetta told her excited son, and her smile held such love Magnus felt his eyes threaten to water, so he looked away.

'It isn't,' he said and, stiffening his sinews, even managed to turn and smile like a polite friend. 'I think it is still majestic in winter, when fog makes the whole place feel eerie and a little bit brooding, or the sea beats at the coast as if it wants to knock it down. I could live here with the thunder of the sea as a rough lullaby if only I could find work to keep me, but this is a hard land to live off, Toby, so I should scrub out any dreams of going out with the fishing boats or joining a smugglers' gang if I were you. Your poor mama will take to lying on a sofa with a vinaigrette all day long if you so much as look as if you might do anything of the sort and quite right, too. Fishermen and smugglers are more or less the same around here and a tougher band of rogues you won't find. The last thing they want aboard is a curious boy who can't keep his eyes to himself or a still tongue in his head.'

'I can,' Toby argued, looking injured. His mother raised her eyebrows and challenged that assertion. Toby kept up the act of misunderstood angel for a while, then shrugged and grinned. 'I can't, can I? But I so badly want to know things that I can't help asking questions.'

'And I want you safe while you find out, my Toby. Then perhaps you can be my older and wiser son who finds a way to live here one day. You can look after your white-haired mother when I am in my dotage and nobody else wants me.'

Toby looked back with mischief dancing in his blue eyes that were so like his father's surely even Brandon Champion would have found enough room in his heart for his son if he had lived long enough to meet him.

'Don't tell me you won't do it, Tobias, my love. I might decide it's high time we moved on and I should tear you away from this fine beach and Mr Haile in order to do some packing if you refuse to look after me one day as I have you for all these weary years,' she teased her son.

Magnus almost laughed because she looked like a girl herself today and far too young to have a seven-year-old son. She had let the mischievous breeze tease through her loosened hair and vitality seemed to shine off both Champions as they took in the wonder of this world beyond the world.

'You won't, though. You love it here, too, Mama.'

'I do, but I won't if you stow away on a fishing boat or sneak out at night to secrete yourself aboard for a smuggling run.'

'Mr Haile says they don't do it much since the Great War ended. It wouldn't be half as much fun as when duties were so high they hid goods in the church and ran cargoes in under the Revenue cutters' noses either.'

Magnus felt his heart swell at the very idea he could have all this for himself, if he was idealistic or good enough to plunge head first into Mrs Hetta Champion's unusual life and convince her they were fated to live together for life. She felt like his guilty hope—this girl-woman and her beloved boy. He couldn't allow himself to truly feel the tug of such a dream, so he distracted himself from the yearning that shook him by holding his hand out for his sister Aline's sketchbook with a brotherly grin of invitation.

'No, Magnus, I need to work them up before they are fit to be seen. You know how I hate anyone else seeing my work until it's in a far more finished state.'

'I know you hate anyone to see it, full stop, since it has never been deemed good enough to be viewed at all.'

'Then pay me the courtesy of not expecting to see them until and unless I am satisfied they are ready to be seen.'

'No, I am your brother—I have a right to be obnoxious for your own good. It's what I was born for,' he argued and snatched the book from her slack hold before she could whisk it behind her back and refuse to display her work yet again.

'There are times, Master Tobias Champion, when it is not as wonderful to have brothers and sisters and be an adult as you believe,' Aline told Toby as if he was the only person on this beach she could speak to at the moment. Hetta was holding her hand out for the sketchbook when Magnus had finished looking at it and Aline probably couldn't even begin to say what she really wanted to in front of a relatively innocent boy.

'Why not?' Toby demanded with a frown to say she should try being seven and three-quarters and this short and on his own.

'Because you cannot do as instinct dictates and thump your brother hard in the stomach, then reclaim your property while he is lying groaning at your feet.'

'I suppose not,' he said with a regretful glance from Aline to said brother as if he'd like to see it done.

Magnus sent his sister a superior look to argue it was unlikely, since he was far more muscular and wary than he was last time she'd tried it. Then he truly looked at the fine watercolour sketches in the book his sister usually managed to close when anyone was close enough to be curious about it. 'These are superb, Ally. Why on earth do you insist on keeping them to yourself?'

'Any competent drawing master would tear them to pieces.'

'Nonsense. I always knew you could draw, but now I can see you have true talent for it as well as watercolour painting. These colour washes are exquisite and the sea creatures look as if they were just this minute plucked from the sea. As for this study of our young man here bending over his net to trawl some unsuspecting rock pool, I defy anyone else to catch his absolute concentration half as well as you have.'

'You do get so intent when something fascinates you,' Aline explained to Toby as if she should apologise for drawing him so truly his vibrant energy seemed to come off the page.

'Can I see?' Hetta asked with a politely long-suffering look Magnus didn't believe in any more than her discarded glasses.

She was a very determined lady, Mrs Henrietta Champion. He suspected she got her way more often than not, even if her son and father did manage to frustrate her before she had time to summon her best arguments. He flicked through the remaining pages Aline had filled with such skill and energy he marvelled that he'd never noticed how good she was until now and passed it on with an almost apologetic look at his sister. This must be how she coped with a life so limited by poverty and scandal until their father died. He should have known about her secret life and all the energy and hope she put on paper when there seemed to be so little room for it in her everyday life. Somehow, he hadn't even noticed a hint of such refined skill and talent until now, so he had been wilfully blind about her as well as the woman he once thought he loved.

Remember that resolution you made to pull yourself together, Magnus Haile, and don't put on another hair shirt until you've washed the last one and handed it back to its real owner.

It was hard work not hating himself for neglecting his little sisters while he lived the idle life of a half-hearted dandy about town once he came down from Oxford. He had danced and boxed and enjoyed being the spare and not the heir, with the odd fantasy about Delphi being free and realising what a fine lover he would make to enliven his useless existence. He should have realised how badly the scandal the old man made up about their mother had hit his sisters' prospects. And why *did* the old devil do it? Was it because the old Earl sensed his wife had stopped loving him, if she ever had? Or did he find out she loved a younger, better man, even if she refused to break her marriage vows? Who knew what went on in the old man's head? Magnus was very glad not to know because if he didn't understand he couldn't be like him, could he?

'What about me?' Toby demanded, glaring up at the neat little sketchbook his mother was so deeply absorbed in when he could only see the plain covers and had no hope of looking over her shoulder.

Hetta gave Aline a questioning look as if to ask permission to lower herself to her son's height and show him. Wise not to trust him with the book, given his usual impatience with finding out about the next item on his list, but when Aline nodded resigned agreement the lad was so open-mouthed with awe at the paintings in front of him Magnus took his opinion back. Toby had the making of a true observer of wonders and his usual brash curiosity masked a true respect for the extraordinary and wonderful.

'Will you teach me?' the boy said breathily as he stared at the image of a piece of seaweed and some driftwood with the slick sea still shiny on it as the tide went out.

'Hmm, maybe one day. For all your quickness at other things I have yet to see any sign of great talent in your drawing, young man.'

'I never knew paint could do this,' he explained earnestly. 'Mama and Grandpapa took me to see some fusty old paintings in Florence and Paris, but that was all saints and martyrs and silly-looking women with no clothes on.'

Magnus couldn't hold back a bark of laughter at Toby's scathing description of some of the finest paintings the world had ever seen, if excited reports of fabulous collections of old masters in both cities were even close to the truth. 'Please promise me you will never aspire to be a diplomat or politician, Toby,' he managed to say as soon as he could get a word out without recalling the expression on the boy's face at his revolted description of them.

'Why would I want to be either?'

'I can see no reason at all, or why anyone would expect such feats of self-restraint, my son,' his mother said with a smile that lit sparks of gold and turquoise at the heart of her grey irises. Magnus wished she wouldn't do that. It made her gaze all the more fascinating without the disfiguring glasses even she seemed to realise weren't doing their job and were getting between her and this beautiful country.

The genuine warmth under all those layers of armour and her joy in her extraordinary son made Hetta Champion look the very opposite of the woman he first took her for. She was so close to being beautiful in a light muslin gown thankfully devoid of the ruffles and half the petticoats designed to bell the skirts out now fashion said ladies could almost have waists again. Nowadays he preferred simplicity and her natural good taste to the extremes of fashion. On the way here, her disguises seemed to have peeled away layer by layer in the warmth of high summer.

Now sunlight picked out dark fire in her chestnut hair and made him wonder why he ever thought her plain under the fearsome cap and bonnet she wore the first day. The heat and her own inclination to be less buttoned up and guarded meant her hair was dressed loosely today, and the faint breeze from the sea tugged playfully at a thick tress that had worked its way out from under her hat and lay like a glowing wonder full of life and colour against her pale neck and downwards where he dare not let his fascinated gaze drift and make himself visibly aroused once again. Heat seemed to glow out of that fiery dark lock, though, and he wondered if it felt as hot to the touch as it looked from here. He began to raise his hand to find out and shook his fingers out impatiently before tucking his hand behind his back as if he was ashamed of it. He *was* ashamed of his masculine impulse to explore and familiarise himself with this very feminine woman who was somehow all the more appealing to the hunter in him because she usually hid feminine vulnerability behind a shield of brusque motherly efficiency and plain clothes.

'I'm hungry,' Aline said and sent Magnus a steady look to say she saw that betraying gesture and could read him like a book.

'Me, too,' Toby agreed eagerly. Magnus couldn't let himself be sorry his sister distracted them from her beautifully observed sketches of life and the natural world, because she did it for him as well.

'Know exactly what you wish for before you jump this time, big brother,' Aline muttered as she moved past him to pick up a stray item of her pupil's clothing Toby hadn't even thought about putting back on when he hastily dressed himself. 'A true gentleman never throws his drawers into the sea,' she told Toby with a severe look she used to disguise her true self as well now Magnus came to think about it.

'More than that, a gentleman actually wears his drawers, instead of throwing them where they might get washed away,' Magnus said with mock solemnity.

'It's too hot to wear anything you don't have to,' Toby claimed airily, but Magnus was glad of every layer between him and Mrs Hetta Champion as he turned to watch the sea while they walked away from it and he muttered something about seeing them all later.

Chapter Fourteen

It was the middle of August before the Champions and Hailes were back in Devon. Magnus frowned at the road ahead and decided to forget a fantasy of Hetta always at his side to tease and plague him for his own good. He squared his shoulders and rode in the dust kicked up by the carriage horses for a few moments before dropping further back to cast a brooding gaze over the gentler curves of the south Devon landscape and calculate how long it would take to reach Isabella's small estate in this lush county. Aline had passed on the fact Isabella had one here and felt guilty she had never visited it. Then his sister insisted they owed it to Isabella to go there and report back as they would only need to go a few miles out of their way. He would have preferred to leave them in safe lodgings and come alone, but they would not be left behind, so he supposed this was better than two stubborn women setting out alone.

'That will teach me to use logic on a pair of females determined not to be logical,' he told the moody-looking sky. His horse twitched its ears as if to say *For goodness' sake get on with this daft journey or take me to the nearest stable and forget about it.*

Of course, he was delighted Aline and Hetta had taken to one another. He reminded himself to be pleased about it when he rode past the carriage and they didn't even notice he was going ahead to escape swallowing Devon dust whenever he breathed in. Aline and Hetta had a habit of presenting him with *fait accompli* and he was certainly not happy about them. First there was a letter from Isabella asking him to visit tin mines and copper barons to find out if there were fortunes lying about for her children's trustees to invest in. No, he could have told her so without all that effort— everything that could be got out of the land was already being wrenched away, but he knew it was only an excuse for them to stay longer when he wasted time and energy compiling a report for her.

Now Isabella obliged Hetta and his sister by agreeing he should inspect Abrah House, the small estate her brother-in-law bought when he was her guardian and trustee, if that wasn't too much trouble? He sighed and shook his head at their blatant scheming and wondered if Hetta had any idea Aline and Isabella were doing everything they could to throw them together. If they only knew how hard it was for him to act the gentleman with this constant grind of wanting keeping him awake night after night, they might let him return to London and hand the task of guarding Master Champion and his mother back to Sir Hadrian Porter. They might, but he shook his head as he reached the conclusion, no, they would not do so *especially* if they knew about his driven passion for a woman who obviously didn't want another husband, or she would have one by now. And how could Aline not know he was close to breaking point? The tension in the air when he and Hetta were even in the same room felt almost touchable to him now and he got more besotted with the glorious, complicated, somehow rather innocent, woman with every mile they travelled together, confound it.

It *was* time they moved on. It had been getting even more difficult to resist Hetta's subtle appeal as she explored rugged shores and green and fertile valleys, bleak moorland and ancient villages that seemed to have grown in their hollows rather than been built there by human hands. She was open and joyous in Cornwall, and the more he saw of the real Hetta under her shabby disguise, the deeper he fell under her spell and she didn't even know. At least now she was wearing a grey cotton gown for travelling—given the dust and tedium, muslin was impractical—but it was best not to think about his appalling physical state whenever he saw her fine feminine figure outlined by the wretched stuff now. These hills meant the younger passengers got out of the coach to walk while it laboured uphill with Peg and the luggage, so Hetta and Aline had to dress more practically. Magnus didn't want Hetta gloriously unbuttoned for any stray traveller to gawk at, so he blessed the grey cambric and hoped it would rain when they reached their destination, so she would wrap herself in the deplorable cloak she had on when he'd first set eyes on her. Even that day his inner rake had enjoyed the contrast of the hidden with the obvious as Delphi had ruled the dock with the confidence of an established beauty and he'd felt guilty about noting another woman's attractions while he tried to plead for a part in his daughter's life.

He shivered and eyed the road ahead as he thought how far he had come since then. His attention sharpened on here and now as he saw the road narrow and deepen ahead of them. Trees grew so thickly all of a sudden that they almost touched overhead and shadows lay in gloomy pockets on the road. The suggestion of a breeze was rustling leaves and whispering of unseen eyes and waking ancient fears that prickled the hairs at the back of his neck. They were vulnerable here. He remembered the night at Hampstead when some felon had tried to steal Toby away and shivered despite the sticky heat of the enclosed valley.

Magnus had put his confidence in Sir Hadrian Porter's talents for untangling knots that looked impossible and left him to worry about the last Earl of Carrowe's murderer. His task was to keep Hetta and Toby, Aline and Peg safe, so he could put all this frustrated passion into making sure nobody got close enough to catch any of them and prevent Sir Hadrian doing his job. He let his thoughts linger for a snatched moment on the suspicion that his elder brother was deeper in this dark business than he wanted him to be. A cold shiver ran down his back and he was glad this wasn't the time or place to wonder why the suspicion had haunted him all the way to Cornwall and back again. He had been avoiding the issue since they left Hampstead, but he must confront it soon although he had more important people to worry about right now.

Magnus had kept an eye out for signs they were being followed or watched when they were busy being tourists. Instinct whispered they were scrutinised by unseen eyes on Chesil Beach, but the feeling went as soon as it washed over him that foggy and uncanny seeming day and he had dismissed it as fanciful. He had no suspicion stealthy eyes were watching again until they made their way through shadowy woodland and it intensified as they went down the deeply carved road. He held his horse steady with willpower and his knees and tied a Belcher neckcloth over his mouth and nose, then slipped back into the dust behind the carriage so he would be close enough to fight an attacker off in this confounded rat run. His sharpened senses heard the jingle of a harness and a few murmured words from coachman to guard and he knew they were uneasy as well. Jem winked at him from the roof and at least Magnus could trust him to keep a sharp eye out if he was blinded by dust.

'You look like a highwayman, Mr Haile,' Hetta told him when the road widened and he could ride alongside the carriage again.

'I look a fool, Mrs Champion.' He lowered the mask enough to speak, since most of the dust they were kicking up was behind them in a greyish cloud that could warn anyone they were coming if the trees were not so thick here they absorbed it.

'If you ride ahead, you could avoid the dust,' she said as if she had no idea why he was staying close. He knew from her steady gaze and refusal to show fear in front of her child she was conscious how vulnerable they were.

'I don't think my horse is a natural leader,'

he explained as if he only came to exchange polite nothings.

'How frustrating for you, Mr Haile.' So, she thought he was more inclined to lead than follow, did she?

Magnus sat taller in his saddle until he remembered how he'd drifted through life since coming down from Oxford. 'He suits me well enough,' he said and endured another ten minutes in the dust.

'Poor horse,' the lady murmured when he rode back to her side of the coach when those minutes were up and they were still not clear of heavily wooded land.

'I am quite sure he would prefer a nice cool stable and his oats, but if he had showed more spirit early in his life he would not be a nag for hire now.'

'He seems well enough to me,' she said as if there were double meanings behind her words as well. Did he? Was he a good enough gentleman when he forgot the sins and clumsy omissions of the past? 'You would not have accepted him when the ostler brought him out if he didn't have the power and endurance for a long ride.'

'No, he has plenty of staying power and a good eye.'

'There you are, then. Or rather here *we* are— nearly at the end of this gloomy wood at long last.'

'Indeed,' he said with a swift look round and an uneasy shiver. He could almost feel intent eyes on them as they ambled along at a pace meant to ensure this team of horses could stay the journey, since there was nothing much between them and their destination now but woods, moors and sheep.

'I shall be very glad when we reach Abrah House,' Aline confided from the seat with her back to the horses that she and Hetta took by rote with Peg because Toby was carriage sick if he sat that way round.

Magnus opened his mouth to say they should have let him come alone again when a shot rang out like the crack of doom. There was a startled silence and for a moment he could hear nothing at all. Then pigeons flapped into frantic flight and a pheasant exploded out of the undergrowth, squawking and scolding and threatening to push the already skittish horses into a blind panic. Even Magnus's steady mount danced under him as time started up again. He asserted control over the spooked animal and blessed its steady common sense, but curses rang out as the coachman fought to control the panicked carriage horses. Jem and the guard glared into the thinning woodland with their guns cocked and ready to blast away at the shooter if he was reckless enough to show his face. At last Magnus had time to feel a numb sting in his upper arm and dismissed it as a pinprick. He knew how lucky he was the bullet scorched along his skin instead of finding a truer mark. It felt urgent to get them all out of this wretched wood as fast as possible and never mind worrying about the hot sting of pain until there was time to see how much damage the rogue had done. Stay around here much longer and the villain would have time to reload or aim a second weapon.

'Whip up,' he barked at the coachman. 'Nothing more than a scratch,' he reassured the man impatiently when he seemed to hesitate and wonder if Magnus was capable of following them if he did as he was bid. Magnus urged his own mount to canter and make it harder for whoever had tried to kill or maim him to try again. He hoped he was right about it being only one attacker, because if there were enough of them to be so bold a fresher horse could soon outrun a heavy travelling carriage drawn by a team picked for endurance not speed.

'Now do you see why I wanted to come alone?' he shouted at Hetta as they tore out of that damned valley as fast as they could go and she seemed determined to keep watching out of the window instead of crouching down to avoid being injured in their dash to safety or shot at by unseen attackers. It felt to Magnus as if the whole of nature let out a sigh of relief as well when they were over the hill and out into fresh air and moorland.

'So, whoever that was could pick you off then come after us?' Hetta yelled back as if she was furious with him for being out in the open when that was simply where he had to be. Hetta waved imperiously at his injured arm, as if she didn't have the right words to scold him for getting shot. He tried not to be flattered by the fear in her eyes as she ran them over him to check he was not concealing a dreadful injury under the long tear on his sleeve and a faint stain of blood.

'Best let them get their breath back,' Magnus told the coachman now there was hardly enough cover for a lost sheep, let alone a hurrying assassin. 'Take a few minutes to settle them while I see if I can spot him.'

Jem tied the reins of Magnus's horse to the back of the carriage and insisted on scrambling after Magnus when he climbed the high bank to survey the scene behind them with a fine telescope he'd once borrowed from Hetta and conveniently forgot to return.

'Wulf will have my hide if the rogue shoots you,' he grumbled at Jem while he focused the powerful glass on the distant trees.

'Not even a rifleman could get me from that far away and Mr Wulf will have mine if I let you get shot again.'

'No need. He's gone,' Magnus said.

Through the scope he found a beaten-down nest of greenery, but it was empty and the oppressive feeling of invisible evil had gone as well. The wood was just a peaceful place to shade weary travellers on a hot afternoon. A few yards further on and the shooter would have been visible from horseback or the roof of a carriage. Further back the shadows would be too dark and shifting to hit a target. The villain had time to find the right spot to shoot, then melt away, and that spoke of planning as well as a ruthless sense of purpose. Magnus could count the number of people who knew where they were bound on the fingers of one hand. So, what good would killing Magnus Haile do the last Earl of Carrowe's murderer? Deflection, he decided grimly, shutting the telescope and slipping it back into his pocket. Somebody wanted to get Sir Hadrian away from London and the scene of the crime. Magnus's scowl went grim as he went through a mental list of who might know their destination and be desperate enough to lie in wait to kill again if it would save his own neck. A common-or-garden villain would have cut his losses and run when Sir Hadrian Porter came home, but an *uncommon* one might have too much to lose.

'Travelling together was supposed to bring us safety in numbers,' his sister told him when he and Jem had scrambled back down to the road.

'Not a very successful strategy as it turned out,' Magnus replied. Remembered shock in her eyes and a total lack of colour in her cheeks told him she knew how close he had been to disaster in that shadowy hollow. 'You would have been safer in Exeter while I came here alone.'

'You could have lain in a ditch for days before anyone found you in such a remote spot and what would become of us then?' Hetta argued.

'I dare say you would manage,' he said and had enough sense to hide a grin when she raised her eyes to the heavens and held up her hands in despair.

'Now *I* would like you to ride while Mr Haile comes with us, so we can attend to his arm, Jem. Lady Aline and I will feel better when we have dressed his wound and, as we will be the ones who end up nursing him if he neglects it, please ignore his protests,' Hetta said before Magnus could reclaim his horse.

Jem grinned and Magnus realised it was quicker to do as she wanted than argue. 'This is ridiculous,' he protested as he was pitched forward when the driver set his horses as headlong a pace as they would go on this last stretch of road.

'As ridiculous as pretending you are not hurt, then falling off your horse when you lose so much blood you pass out?' Hetta challenged briskly.

Aline was waving Peg's sewing scissors about with such intent Magnus hastily shrugged off his coat before she could ruin it completely and he didn't have many left. 'It's hardly big enough to call a flesh wound,' he grumbled as the graze along his forearm refused to bleed again for his would-be nurses, but still ached like hell. Peg nodded and left Aline and Hetta to it while she listened to Toby's list of possible ways for a person to die of even the smallest wound, as if fascinated.

'Next you will try to tell us someone thought you were a deer,' Hetta challenged briskly, yet Magnus thought there were traces of shock and anger and something a little more encouraging haunting her fine eyes as she defied him to make light of this even for her son's sake.

'Of course not. That would be absurd,' he countered partly to distract himself as Aline ruthlessly rolled up his shirtsleeve and peered at the graze. 'Ouch!' he exclaimed when his sister prodded the wound ruthlessly, then took the tweezers Peg produced from her vast bag. Magnus wondered if Peg had the contents of

Pandora's box inside it to distract himself from what his sister was doing.

'Hold still, you great baby,' Aline told him as she carefully removed a couple of strands of fine linen thread from the wound and he flinched as it throbbed anew.

'No man is a hero to his own sister,' he explained wryly to Toby. They exchanged manly glances and Magnus was relieved to see colour back in the boy's cheeks. Magnus wanted to reassure him no harm would come to him or his mother while he had breath in his body to prevent it, but he didn't have the confidence to after this latest attack. At last Aline and Hetta were satisfied he really wasn't badly injured and agreed the wound was best left to heal in the fresh air rather than being wrapped in a bandage as if Magnus had no say in the matter. Half his attention had been outside the vehicle all the while and he was relieved when the road dipped down again to see a more generous countryside with fertile fields and only scattered trees to give shelter to neat cottages and farms. Not much risk of someone creeping around this landscape unseen and he guessed not many strangers passed this way when their now very dusty carriage and four was greeted with such wide-mouthed astonishment.

'We're there. It says Abrah on that old stone,' Toby informed them.

Magnus was glad, first that they were indeed about to turn between two ancient stone gate-posts with gates that did not look as if they had been shut since the Civil War and on to a well-kept drive. Second that the boy's mangling of the English language diverted Aline from fussing over him.

'Please don't think I have forgotten what happened, Mr Haile. I am not a fool and I know that was no wild shot from a local poacher or a footpad taking a holiday in the country, so don't you dare lie to me,' Hetta told him very softly as he sat back to let Toby and the ladies descend first, despite his gentlemanly duty to hand them down on to the swept gravel in front of the venerable old oak door.

'As if I would dare,' he murmured when he was finally allowed to clamber out of the vehicle like an invalid and could look for any suspicious pockets of cover nearby. Not much chance of an attacker slipping in here with so many servants milling about the place, Magnus was surprised there had not been several collisions already in their hurry to greet the visitors. Either Isabella was being very badly served by whoever managed the estate now, or Sir Hadrian had decided it was time he stepped in to protect his family a little too late in the day.

'You would dare anything if you thought it would help keep us safe,' Hetta told him not very admiringly. He shrugged under her critical gaze, then flinched when the movement jarred his wound.

'A suspiciously large staff for a house empty for the last decade, don't you think?' Aline observed when brother and sister were left in the hallway while Hetta and Peg bore a protesting Toby off to be washed and settled in a room running off his mother's and already marked out for them before they got here.

'Sir Hadrian is a step ahead of would-be assassins keen for more Haile blood this time. I wonder how many gardeners and grooms the old place really needs to keep it in perfect order.'

'Dozens, I expect,' Aline said as if she didn't think so either.

Magnus wondered if she had anything to do with this vast staff being here to care for the needs of a small party on an informal tour of the West Country and looking to stay in one place for a week or so. She'd seemed uneasy on that day at Chesil Beach as well, but if she'd written to him it had taken Sir Hadrian a long time to put plans for their greater safety in place. Magnus frowned and felt the idea of a wild card slip into his head, someone Sir Hadrian did not have a stealthy watch on. He suspected the man was not wrong-footed like this very often and someone had managed it this afternoon despite all his best-laid plans.

'They will fall over one another looking for something to do before long,' he said as he glanced out of a side window and saw gardeners scything a lawn that had already had enough attention to make it forget years of being grazed short by livestock instead of manicured within an inch of its life.

At least he could let himself feel weary and even a little bit shocked now they were here and all exits and entrances covered. He had already watched the coach dragged into the long-disused coach house by enough grooms to staff a racing yard and the coachman and guard greeted by a head groom more like a retired prize-fighter than a son of the turf. His would-be assassin would be caught if he tried to get anywhere near the place to try again, but the nagging worry he was someone too close for comfort haunted Magnus. He felt the heaviness of suspecting Gresley could be behind this latest attempt to draw Sir Hadrian away from Carrowe House. All the sleepless hours he had spent on guard against this very outcome and trying to keep lustful thoughts of Hetta at bay stacked up on him all of a sudden and he stumbled over his own feet. It only took that misstep for his sister to get on the other side from his injured arm and try to support him up the stairs when she was almost a foot shorter.

'I dare say Jem will soon be up to unpack and set this already immaculate room to rights, so I suggest you wash off the dust and grime with his help, then rest for an hour or so, big brother,' Aline said after nodding approval of the cool and inviting bedchamber made ready for him.

'Maybe,' he conceded with a longing glance at the wide and comfortable-looking feather bed, wishing he was clean enough to sprawl across it straight away and fall into dreamland. 'I don't get shot at every day,' he added with a wry smile. She shook her head, murmured something unladylike and left him in peace.

Chapter Fifteen

It was very early the next morning by the time Magnus woke with a curse, glad he had at least bathed and shaved before he'd fallen so heavily asleep he missed dinner and another evening of trying not to lust after Hetta too openly. He shook himself like a great dog, discovered his arm felt almost as good as new and threw on the clothes Jem had laid out for him last night. Raiding the silent and for once empty kitchen for a large slice of pork pie to calm at least one ravenous appetite, Magnus let himself out of a side door and trod softly over newly pampered lawn until he was far enough away from the house to stride out through the stir and sleepy twitters of predawn lightness. Going upwards almost by instinct, he stood just below the summit of the hill above Abrah House, so he wasn't outlined on the horizon, to survey the generous valley below. Hugged by the hillside and protected from harsh winds coming in off the not-so-very faraway sea, Magnus could easily see why Lord Carnwood had bought this neat estate and fine old house when Isabella was his ward. Rich pasture for cattle and fine summer grazing on the surrounding hills for sheep would mean a good return for tenant farmers and landowner alike.

He frowned down at the stone-tiled roof of the gracious old house as a glimmer of rising sun picked out details in the landscape. Lovely though the place was, it did not seem secure enough to offer a safe haven for Hetta and Toby once the staff were whittled to a simple enough household to see to the needs of a couple of ladies and one boy, when Toby was not busy elsewhere. He thought Isabella was about to offer this place to Hetta to live in while Toby was at school, but it was a devilish long way from London with thick and dangerous woods all along the only road out. He let out a huge sigh and reminded himself it was none of his business where Hetta chose to live in future.

Now he was still supposed to be responsible for hers and Toby's safety, he should be watching for stealthy enemies, not dreaming in the soft light of dawn or speculating on Hetta's future. At least here there was no prickling sense of danger to raise hairs on the back of his neck. Instead a familiar warmth and heightened awareness whispered Hetta was close even before he saw her standing under a nearby tree watching him watch the empty and still-dreaming valley for invisible enemies.

'You seemed very preoccupied by your thoughts,' she said when he was close enough for them to speak and not disturb the peace.

'I wanted to be sure all was well, considering I slept so long I should resign from the Watchman's Guild before they throw me out,' he said lightly even as awareness tingled along every nerve and it seemed as if they were the only two people in the world awake so early in the day.

'Is that what you are, our watchman?' she asked huskily, almost as if she shared the feeling they could be so much more than this if things were different.

'Not a very good one,' he said gloomily.

'On the contrary, we are all alive and safe and you were the only one who got hurt yesterday.'

'I can hardly feel it now,' he said, trying to appreciate the way the rising sun picked out more and more detail of the fine valley below them when all he could think of was her.

'Yet you seem to think I don't know that bullet was inches from killing you yesterday. And do you think I am too stupid to realise the scoundrel could have been aiming at me when you got in the way?' she demanded as if it was his fault.

'I don't think you stupid at all,' he said, pretending he was watching a couple of farm servants fetch in the cows for milking at the farm down the valley.

'Then at least look at me while I thank you for saving my life,' she demanded with an exasperated sigh.

'You have no idea how hard it is for me *not* to look at you, Mrs Champion,' he told her dourly.

She had brooded about his injury all yesterday evening, stayed awake for most of the night and woken up from an appalling nightmare where the bullet had hit him somewhere vital and he'd done the unthinkable and died on her. Died on *her*, not on his sisters or his mother or his brothers or anyone else. She noted her very specific description of the terror that woke her up gasping and on the edge of screaming until she recalled herself back to reality. Fortunately, Toby slept as if it was his life's work and was still blissfully unaware in the adjacent chamber when she checked on him.

She let her eyes rove greedily over Magnus while he was looking the other way, to be sure it really was a nightmare and he wasn't concealing some huge hurt not obvious at first glance. She had jumped out of bed with that last appalling dream still in her head and knew she must wait for Magnus to wake up before she could check he was really and truly still alive and her appalling dream only the work of a horrified imagination. So, she washed hastily, bundled into underpinnings and her favourite muslin gown, dashed a brush through her rebelliously curling hair and crept out here to wait for him to wake up. Except he was already out here, already busy about what he thought of as his duty to protect her and Toby from his father's murderer.

'Hetta,' she corrected huskily, then wondered if it was best if Mrs Champion faced him today. She was a little stiffer and more correct, maybe even more sure of herself than Hetta. Mrs Champion knew what she wanted out of life, but Hetta struggled with needs and desires Mrs Champion did not want to hear of.

'You should have brought a shawl, Hetta,' he told her when she shivered at the thought of some of those needs and this terrible temptation to find out if he could fulfil them more richly than Bran ever had, even when he was still trying to be her ideal husband and win her family over to a hasty marriage over the anvil.

'I am not cold,' she murmured, wilfully playing with fire.

'I like you covered up,' he said as if the words were forced out of him.

'Oh, really?' she asked coolly, stung because he looked as if he wished she had stayed away and waited for the world to wake up as well, so he could hope they would be interrupted.

'No, I like you any way you care to be, but it won't do, Mrs Champion.'

'No, it won't. I am sorry. I should not have come outside at such an hour and ought to have gone away until the world is awake when I saw you standing so intent and alone.'

'You should,' he said austerely, but his deliciously intense dark brown eyes were saying something very different and Hetta badly wanted to read their message instead of listening to the wise words coming out of his mouth.

'I still have to thank you for saving my life yesterday,' she argued as she held his gaze, and most of her breath, and wished she could tell him how terrible that moment had felt when the shot rang out and she felt him flinch at her side. The noise of it had haunted her ever since. Maybe he would be embarrassed if she poured all that out as if they mattered uniquely to one another. He had another woman fixed in his heart and a very different child he wished he could be father to than her beloved Toby.

'An exaggeration,' he dismissed her words impatiently and he didn't think nearly enough of himself, whomever he loved.

'No, the truth,' she argued and cursed Lady Drace for making him doubt the deep-down strength and integrity of the Honourable Magnus Haile.

'The truth is I would rather die myself than live with the memory of seeing life seep out of you in front of me, but we two cannot afford to deal in truths, Mrs Champion.'

'Oh, for heaven's sake, stop calling me so,' she said impatiently and defied him with a challenging gaze to rival his. The ever-present temptation of being more than two polite strangers travelling together argued with the caution his mouth was saying while his eyes agreed it was a waste not to give in.

'Your father will be on his way soon, eager to get to the end of this sordid little mystery and relieve me of my task of protecting you and your son. If I do not address you in the proper form, I expect he will have me sent to the colonies in chains for disrespecting his daughter,' he said, almost as if he thought it was a joke she would laugh at lightly, then trip off to breakfast, as if he wasn't out here making every other prospect but him dull and lifeless.

'You had best kiss me now, then, had you not? While we still have a chance of not being found out,' wicked Hetta whispered and leaned back against her tree to squint up at him as the steadily rising sun got in her eyes.

'I am only human,' he muttered almost to himself before he blotted out the sun for her and who cared if it was dark or light, sunny or stormy, when he was close enough to touch?

He was here. His breath was short and fast as he gazed at her mouth so hungrily she slicked it with her tongue and let out a little gasp of half-nerves, half-eagerness for his kiss, his touch, anything and everything about him, and Hetta really was a bad woman, wasn't she? 'I love human,' she whispered.

'Fool,' he chided her even as he bent his head that last delicious inch and there was nothing guarded or hesitant about his kiss. It *was* full of pent-up frustration and heat and as intense as the late summer sun she could feel warming his back when she wound her arms round there and added to the heat of Magnus Haile's desire for her, for her—not Lady Drace or some other, more convenient, female, but her, Hetta Porter, the real, wanting woman who lived behind Mrs Champion's disfiguring glasses and dull plumage because she was so scared of trusting the fire and need inside her with a man like this one. No, not one *like* him, only this one. There were no more like him. Never mind his brothers and all the other Haile cousins and uncles who apparently resembled one another as if marked out as a tribe. None of them had his strength and sensitivity and character because none of them was him.

And he felt as if he had been guarding this headlong need since they last kissed at Develin House all those long and frustrating weeks ago. Even as she bent into his passionate kiss, let him know how urgently she wanted him back, she soothed his tense and pent-up muscles, caressed her way down the supple line of his spine and secretly chided him for being too strong. If only he was a weaker man he would have kissed her again in every inn she had slept in along the south coast this summer, made those nights magical and gloated over instead of stark and often sleepless without him. If he wasn't Magnus Haile he could have been her summer lover all this time and to hell with murder and mayhem and the risk of making a noble bastard.

Hetta spared a second from being hot and far too happy about being kissed again by this unique man, and desperate for more, to worry at the idea. Heat blossomed at the heart of her and a poignant shard of something wistful stoked it at the thought of carrying his child there, deep inside and secure as its father adored the little thing and lavished even more sensual attention on its proud mama than usual. It didn't seem impossible standing here, but it was. He was who he was and she dreaded the captivity of another marriage based on necessity and not love. A child in need of a name would be a very different necessity from Bran's wild ambition to be an admiral before he was forty, or her own desperation to get away from the Dowager Lady Porter's relentless drive to get her unsatisfactory only grandchild married to rank and fortune. It would still be a marriage made because Magnus refused to have another child of his called by another man's name. Some of the magic fell off her cloud of bliss at the thought the beautiful Lady Drace had been his last lover and now he was kissing plain and impulsive Hetta instead. Maybe he felt her withhold some crucial part of herself and wanted to lure her back. Anyway, he inflamed the heat between them by pulling her away from the hardness of the hoary old tree, so she could be closer to the hardness of his powerful and vigorous body. A body she was eager for in every pore and sensitive inch of her, she reminded herself as she luxuriated in being so wanted, so deeply needed the urgency of it all, she was goading them both to let it take over the world and never mind the day gradually waking up around them.

'We can't,' he murmured after a tortured groan, but he still held her so close she could feel every rigid and tightened inch of him.

His gloriously taut muscles trembled like a racehorse eager for speed, or a man desperate for his lover. Her breasts were tight and almost painful against his sober summer waistcoat and all that delicious manly haste and quickened breathing she had caused. Her nipples tightened and hardened even more as she brushed closer to him and bent a little further back against his arms to stare up at him with a wordless challenge. Yes, there was heat and ravenous hunger battling with cool sense and wariness in his dark eyes. She felt tears threaten as the reality of who they were rushed back and put caution in his gaze.

'I admit we can, but it's not enough for you,' he said as if the words hurt, but he was going to say them anyway.

'No,' she said bleakly. Toby's existence meant

it could not be and so did his little Angela, in her very different way.

Magnus felt agony drive through his heart as if another bullet had slammed into him to smash it to eternity and made himself let go of another lot of hopes and dreams and step away from her. She didn't love him and why should she? What was there to love about a man who'd deluded himself he loved Delphi for all the hopeless years she was wed to Drace? Then he let the confounded woman use him like a naive boy instead of a man who thought he knew enough to pave the world before Lady Drace taught him otherwise. He recalled the agony of knowing the woman he thought he loved was growing his child in her belly and refused to admit he had anything to do with her. And then she had taken his baby away.

No, there was nothing to love about him, so no wonder Hetta was refusing to even look at him. She'd suppressed passionate, unconventional Hetta for far too long behind her son's needs and her own caution. Champion had treated her like an object to be collected, then discarded, instead of a person with needs and hopes Champion had never come close to ful-filling. Of course, the real woman behind all that caution was eager to be free, to explore who she really was and what she wanted to do with a personable enough man who ap-pealed on some level to the lovely female she was under layers of caution and lack of confi-dence. He was still vain enough to know there was a surface gloss to him, now he was back to his usual rude health and burnished by the summer sun. He had a vigour and youth that called to the vigour and youth in her and made her vulnerable to purely sexual attraction be-cause she had kept it clamped down deep inside her for so long it was rebellious and looking for mischief.

Lucky she was standing on the little hillock beyond the cover of the trees where he stood, watching her like a hungry watchdog eyeing a juicy bone it knew it could not have, when Jem tracked them both down and did his best to pretend they were not even a little bit un-done by passion. Magnus noted the slight slip of fine muslin that only vaguely masked her rosy-skinned shoulders underneath it. There was a button he must have undone and she fumbled it back into place as soon as she re-alised she looked loose and lovely and there was a lad approaching with his best imitation of an elephant to give her time to be her proper self again. Magnus felt something twist in his belly as he recalled his own amusement when Jem had used that tactic on Wulf and Isabella to divert them from loving one another long enough to pay attention to some visitor or an urgent message he could not put off giving them any longer.

He didn't feel very amused now, not with Hetta looking flustered and shamed at being caught all the way out here at this hour of the day with a man who must look as if he had been ruffled by the north wind. He remem-bered how her hands had caressed his hair and shyly undid his shirt to find out if his mascu-line nipples were echoing her much richer fem-inine ones and why wouldn't they when every inch of him was hard with wanting her? The memory made him smile, despite this hollow ache inside him and the dread of never being able to watch her looking slightly undone and so utterly beautiful to a would-be lover ever again. She had her back to him now, but didn't she realise how supple and feminine and ridiculously arousing it was? Morning sun was lighting fire in her rich chestnut hair and the lightest of breezes had sprung up when the dawn was a fading memory and it was playing among the folds of her softly clinging gown as if that was all it was born for.

He gloated over the memory of her every hesitant touch and murmur of feminine appreciation as she let her hands rove over his body. At least he was fit and well muscled again after a summer of riding and self-denial.

No, remember how she flinched when you called a halt, Magnus, and of course she doesn't love you.

He shifted away from the tree he had been leaning against, smoothed his hair and straightened his waistcoat, then buttoned his shirt far enough to nigh strangle him. He hated the confinement of a stock and cravat now, after years of believing they were an uncomfortable necessity for a man of fashion. In many ways he was a changed man, but how dearly he wished he had changed in time to win the respect of a woman he wanted to love. She would wave it away as the easy words of a man of light mind and elastic conscience and she had already wed one rogue, so why would she waste the pent-up passion and glory of the real Hetta on another?

'Sir Hadrian Porter has sent a messenger,' Jem explained rather breathlessly, his eyes on the horizon in case they had not finished being embarrassed by the sensual tension Magnus could almost taste in the air.

'What did he say?' Magnus asked wearily, turning his back on the temptation of Hetta standing not ten yards away so he could at least try to think about someone else.

'To expect three for lunch in the parlour and a dozen or more in the kitchen,' Jem told him concisely. Sir Hadrian must have decided to bring this business to a head even before the attack on the way here, then. He could not know about their latest near-disaster yet, could he?

'We had better not waste any time in making the house fit to welcome more visitors even if he brings a murderer with him. I can see no other reason for Papa to come here except to tell us who killed your father,' Hetta told Magnus coolly.

He would argue, if only Sir Hadrian appreciated what a unique daughter he had and valued her properly. The man had abandoned her to his stony mother when she was grieving for her own mother, then manipulated Hetta when she'd tracked him down with Toby still a babe in arms. Magnus felt his fists tighten and ordered himself to relax and let the mature and headstrong Hetta order her own future. He had no right to snatch a part in it. 'I don't know why he had to drag whoever did it all this way,' he said.

'And I don't want you caught up in your father's murder again,' she said as if he was yet another of her responsibilities.

'Afraid I killed my father in my sleep?' he drawled, but he had to divert her somehow.

'No, but you were there that night and I don't want you accused by mistake,' she disarmed him by admitting.

'I thought you trusted your father to get to the truth?'

'I do, but I don't trust those who employ him not to do what is expedient rather than what is right if he doesn't find it soon enough—they are politicians after all.'

'Your father will drive them to wherever he wants them to go.'

'All right, then, be stubborn. Put all your faith in him. But don't expect me to break you out of jail if you turn out to be wrong.'

'Don't you fancy being a criminal's moll, then, Mrs Champion?'

'No, I don't have any acting talent.'

'Flaunt that figure you take such pains to hide and my jailers will be putty in your hands,' he told her with a leer to demonstrate he had noticed every one of her feminine assets.

'You can get on and rescue yourself for that, Magnus Haile.'

'They will have to catch me first,' he said modestly and grinned as if he was still his old carefree self and his heart wasn't aching at the gap between her and her father, but at least she forgot to worry about him in her haste to get everything perfect for Sir Hadrian's visit and whatever strange visitors he brought with him.

She marched back to the house with Jem in tow to organise hospitality for an unknown mix of visitors plus one murderer. She cared enough to want him safe and that counted for something. Perhaps he wasn't as hopeless as he thought and the dangerous tug of her one day seeing past his affair with Delphi and lack of any noticeable purpose in life before his father's death whispered there might be hope for him after all. One day, if he worked hard enough.

Chapter Sixteen

Despite staff falling over one another all morning to make the old house even more immaculate and ready for visitors than usual, nothing prepared Magnus for the sight of his elder sister-in-law's ponderous travelling carriage lumbering up the drive. Constance, Lady Carrowe, had brought three grooms and half-a-dozen outriders with her, but Magnus thought a highwayman watching for a chance to rob would be more intimidated by the closed coach with some very alert guards that followed her swaying monstrosity up the long drive. Sir Hadrian waited until Connie had gone in, amid as much fuss as she could make to remind the world she was a reigning countess, then jumped down from the anonymous-looking vehicle to bustle a cloaked and hooded figure inside before anyone could see more.

'I refuse to be put off or left behind or lied to one more time,' Connie told whoever was listening with a stubborn tilt to her chin as she swept into the drawing room as if she owned it.

'But you could easily have miscarried, jaunting about the country for days on end to find me, my love,' Gresley protested weakly.

'I am perfectly well, despite the fact you are always dashing about the country and not telling me why and that would wear on any wife's nerves, let alone mine. I know you have a mistress, Gresley, so don't try to deny it. When I think of all the reasons you came up with why I could not go to London or Leicestershire with you, or the times you stopped away without saying where you were going, I would be a fool not to realise. I won't be made a mockery of any longer.'

'Dash it, no. That's not why I...' Gresley's voice tailed off and he looked so hunted Magnus almost felt sorry for him, then recalled his suspicion Gresley was wrapped up in their father's murder and doing his best to deflect blame and hardened his heart.

'While I have to wish her ladyship had not come so far in her condition, I have to agree it is high time your wife knew the truth, Lord Carrowe,' Sir Hadrian said sternly.

'Thank you, sir,' Connie said as if she really meant it. 'This latest disappearance was the final straw and I refuse to be kept in the dark any longer.'

'I think you showed great strength of character to come all this way in a delicate state of health, your ladyship,' Hetta intervened before Connie had hysterics.

'I am quite robust after the first few months,' she admitted, and since his sister-in-law usually played on her sufferings for the Haile succession, Magnus knew she was truly anxious about what Gresley had been up to behind her back this time.

'You must have had a long and weary journey and even the most robust of us get tired at times like this.'

'Thank you, Mrs Champion. My husband wants me to turn round and go home, but I must know what has been going on.'

'I agree, but why not let me call for your maid to accompany you to a quiet room I prepared for visitors to wash off their dust and maybe even change into a fresh gown after such a tedious journey? You will feel so much better and I will make sure the gentlemen do not begin without you.'

'Thank you,' Connie said as if she was truly grateful.

'She would come,' Gresley said helplessly when even the sound of his wife's silk skirts was lost behind a stout oak door.

'She *is* your wife, Gres. Her father-in-law met a grisly end and she has a right to hear the truth,' Magnus told him and wondered who Sir Hadrian was hiding behind another door along that hallway guarded by two of the armed men.

Gresley looked unconvinced. 'Why?'

'We can't hold the line as a family if she doesn't know where it is,' Magnus said impatiently. Had his elder brother always been this irritating?

'Why is Mrs Champion here, then?' Gres objected as if she could not hear a few feet away in a room that suddenly felt small with so many uneasy people in it.

'Speaking for myself, as I am wont to do nowadays, my lord, I believe I need to hear this tale since someone has chosen to involve me in it whether I want to be or not,' Hetta told him with a challenge in her steady gaze he did not meet for long.

'Sir Hadrian has come to give his conclusions about the old Earl's murder, so you had best not be rude to Mrs Champion if you want to know what they are,' Magnus told his brother severely, and Gres could hardly admit the last thing he wanted was the truth coming out, so he subsided into sulky silence.

Connie bustled back into the room and, since Magnus had never known her to change in less than an hour, at least she was eager to hear the truth. 'You can have the joint stool, Gresley. We can't wait while you send for a seat more befitting an earl,' she told her husband when he stood up to give her his chair, then looked round for something more suitable for his lordly backside.

'You like me to consider my state,' he protested as he lowered himself in more ways than one.

'Not today,' his wife snapped. Magnus wondered if she shared his suspicions about Gres and pitied her if they were right.

'If we can proceed?' Sir Hadrian queried mildly.

'Not much choice,' Magnus thought he heard Gresley mutter into his wine.

'Be quiet, Gresley,' his wife ordered sharply.

'It seemed better to meet here rather than in London,' Sir Hadrian went on, 'but we have a deal to do next, so I shall be brief.'

'Good. Need to get back to Exeter in time for dinner,' Gresley grumbled as if food was the most important thing on his mind. Magnus doubted it from the hunted look he cast about the room as if looking for possible lines of escape.

'Then first I must say the last Lord Carrowe's murder could have been solved straight away if I could have visited the scene before it was cleaned. Still, at least I was given a good description of it by Dowager Lady Carrowe's housekeeper.'

'Peg insisted on cleaning the Red Room herself,' Magnus explained to Hetta. 'She said the girls should not have to and I was miles away and ill. She would not allow an outsider in to gossip about the horror of it to anyone who would listen, so we Hailes owe her a great deal.'

'I don't see why. She is only a servant,' Connie said haughtily and reminded Magnus he didn't like her.

'It was a great help to hear a concise and intelligent description of how the room was before she cleaned,' Sir Hadrian said. 'And a drawing of his late lordship's wounds was made by the Coroner's Clerk, so it was clear from the outset two people were involved.'

Connie gasped at the thought of two murderers running wild in a house her husband now owned, however little she intended setting foot in it. Magnus recalled finding the old man's bloody corpse and wondered if he would ever get the image of his father lying in his chair horribly murdered out of his nightmares.

'I believe the late Earl may have already been dead when the second actor arrived and attempted to confuse the issue,' Sir Hadrian continued.

'I didn't know,' Connie whispered as if news of that second person confirmed her worst fears and Magnus hoped that was all he was. He preferred Gres as sideshow rather than the main act.

'Why should you, my lady? But now we must

establish the order of things before I propose a logical solution to your family mystery.'

'It was footpads. Any fool in London could have broken in and killed him,' Connie insisted as if she suddenly didn't want to know the truth after all.

'Yet any fool in London would know there was nothing left worth killing for, as the last Earl of Carrowe had sold it before they got there.'

'There are a lot of fools in London,' she insisted doggedly and Magnus pitied her for the long, shocked stare she gave Gresley's now ashen face.

'Not many who would break into a ruinous old house in the little hours for not much return, Lady Carrowe, and it must have been hard for a lady to go there at dead of night.'

'Ridiculous. A woman would not have the strength for such a vile act,' Connie insisted as if she might be accused of doing it herself if she didn't find good reasons why not.

Magnus supposed anyone who lacked this horrible whisper of suspicion he had might suspect Connie of enough ruthless ambition to kill her father-in-law before he landed the earldom in such debt even her vast fortune could not pull them out of River Tick. He might think so even now if she was a good enough actor to disguise her guilt if she stole down to London one dark night to stick a knife in the man who stood between her and a countess's coronet.

'You would be surprised what a lady can do if she is driven hard enough, Lady Carrowe,' Sir Hadrian said coolly. 'But it is high time you knew who did it,' he added and went to the door to signal his taciturn henchmen to bring in the prisoner.

'Delphi?' Magnus's exclamation was drowned out by Gresley's moan of protest and Connie's gasp of horror.

'Careless of you to get caught,' Hetta said as if she wasn't surprised.

Lady Drace looked as coolly composed and pointed at Connie. 'She wanted to be a countess so badly she would have killed her own mother. I don't know why any of you are looking at me as if I did it.'

'You know perfectly well Lady Carrowe did not kill the late Earl,' Sir Hadrian told her sternly. 'You have had plenty of time to consider your position on the way back here, Lady

Drace. Do you really think there is any point in this charade?'

'Your pride will not allow you to admit you failed, Sir Hadrian, so any poor creature will do for you to land a dreadful crime on and you prove it by picking on me.'

'No, I seek the truth.'

'Then don't look at me,' Delphi said and Magnus groaned on her behalf because she didn't seem able to hear the double meaning in her own words even now she had said them.

'Did you leave the country to evade justice?' he asked and, since she refused to meet his gaze, he concluded she did. 'Then what possessed you to return?' he added when her silence gave her away.

'I thought I was lonely here, but it was nothing compared to being so far away from…' Delphi let her voice tail off and for a dreadful moment Magnus thought she was about to say she found life impossible without *him*. It showed how far he had come when relief nearly felled him as Delphi's gaze went past him to fix on Gresley instead. 'Him,' she continued as if she couldn't help herself.

'Was anything you ever said or did true?' Magnus had to ask.

'Yes, *he* was,' she said, her eyes wild and all the pent-up passion in her finally flying free and a bit terrifying. 'I loved him when I was little more than a girl and he loved me back, but he had to marry *you* for money,' she said, pointing at poor, shocked Connie as if she hated her.

'I…well, I can't believe it, even of you,' Constance said and Gresley stood speechless and watched Delphi as if he longed for and feared her at the same time.

'I would have walked through hell for him, and lived in a hovel on nothing a year—but, oh, no, *you* wanted his title and Haile Carr to queen it over and the vile Earl of Carrowe coveted your dowry to pay for his sordid pleasures. So Gresley was sold to you like a chest full of tea or a slave from one of your father's plantations and I wed Drace, because what did it matter who my husband was when I could not have yours? I got a husk of a man nobody else wanted despite all his wealth and ancient, if puny, title. You had everything I ever wanted,' Delphi raged as if she had to get all she had kept quiet for a decade out in the open. She looked as if she truly hated Connie, when the late Earl of Carrowe was the one who'd caused such grief and fury, not poor plain, ambitious Connie. 'You wed my only love for the sake of a *title*. I loved him even after he left me to live half a life without him, just so you could preen yourself on becoming a countess one day.'

Delphi turned her eyes away from her rival as if she could not endure the sight of her open-mouthed and silenced. Her gaze lit on Gresley and softened, as if only for him could she be as nature probably intended her to be. 'That wicked old man told me he had threatened to have me killed if you refused to marry his fat little heiress,' she told him sadly.

'That's true,' Gresley muttered.

'So, when he tried to blackmail me about the true parentage of my child I had to make him understand I am not a terrified girl anyone can brush aside like a fly now...' Delphi paused and her eyes were on Magnus. 'Didn't you realise he would turn on me when you refused to wed a fortune?' she challenged as if this was his fault.

'I thought he might blackmail his friends or maybe the King, since he knew far too much about them all, but I never dreamed he would turn on you.'

'He already knew too much about *me*, though, didn't he? I suppose you didn't know it wasn't his first scheme to sell an unwilling son to the highest bidder.'

'And *you* took me to bed in lieu of my brother,' he said because he could not let her shuffle off the blame on everyone else for her crimes any longer.

'Yes, you *are* better in bed than Drace and it was time I had a proper lover again. My husband didn't even realise I was not a virgin on our wedding night,' she said, her eyes on Gresley again, as if she forgot everyone else when he was near—even if she almost hated him for it at times.

Poor Gres seemed almost in agony. By loving the girl Delphi was then too much to leave her be, he must have felt weighed down by guilt ever since he married poor rich Constance instead of his young lover.

'My father ruined everything he touched, including me. I was never strong enough to fight back like you and Wulf did, Magnus,' Gresley admitted bleakly.

'You knew what the Earl was doing to squeeze more money out of me last year, though, didn't you?' Magnus asked him bitterly. 'You stood by with your hands in your pockets and whistled while he tried to push me into a marriage of convenience as well. You did not protect Delphi and her child when he wanted to use them to get his greedy hands on a share of the Drace fortune from the sounds of it either.'

'And at least Magnus had the grace to want to marry me,' Delphi added as if she regretted having turned him down. Magnus shot Hetta a desperate look to plead for rescue. Even having to think about asking Delphi to wed him for the sake of their child felt hellish now. 'Although I suspect he doesn't want to now,' Delphi added with a long look at Hetta and a shrug to say, *He's yours. I never wanted him anyway.*

'Our daughter is the only good thing to come of this foul mess,' Magnus said austerely.

'And that devil threatened to expose her secret when he failed to push you into a rich marriage. He had already borrowed against Miss Alstone's dowry, you see?' Delphi explained, as if anything *could* explain what she had done.

Magnus heard steel in her voice and thought

his father had been even more of a fool than usual to risk goading her when her child was all she truly had to show for the heartache and denial of ten long years without her lover, or for most of them, if the guilty look Gres cast her, then his wife, now was anything to go by. After Angela was conceived, when Delphi had turned a hard face on Magnus and refused to wed him, they must have resumed their passionate affair. No wonder she'd turned down every impassioned plea he made her to let his child be born legitimate. Maybe Gres found out what she'd done when he stayed away too long after Drace died and that was the goad that finally stoked Gresley's pent-up desire for her to breaking point. He might even feel sorry for them, if his child wasn't in the middle of the havoc they'd created.

'I should have realised he would turn on you when he failed with me,' Magnus reproached himself even so.

'You don't think like your father or brother or Lady Drace,' Hetta said and came to stand by him, as if she had been trying not to intrude on family business until now, but this was too much for her to be silent about.

'He nearly spoilt Isabella's life by forcing me to offer for her or blight my daughter's life before it had hardly begun and I sat around feeling sorry for myself while you had to face him alone.' Magnus found he could apologise to Delphi with Hetta's hand in his.

'Not entirely,' Delphi argued.

'No, you had a confederate that night and afterwards.'

Delphi sighed as if she was glad to tell her secrets even with Sir Hadrian looking on as if none surprised him. 'Gresley showed me a secret entrance and guided me through a musty old hidden passage to the Earl's private sitting room that everyone else had forgotten about,' she admitted recklessly. 'And I made him stay outside to be sure nobody disturbed me. I told the old man he could tell the world and if I had to wed you he would not get a penny by revealing our secret. He sat there and laughed at me. He slouched in his worn-out old chair with a chipped old wine glass in his hand and jeered as if I was nothing and my daughter did not matter a snap of his fingers. I took a stiletto dagger my father brought back from Italy with me to make me feel braver as I crept through that old ruin in the dark. I never intended to stab him, but he said such terrible things the knife was out and in him before I even knew it was in my hand. It went in so easily I could not even believe I had actually done it until he slumped back in his chair and swore I had done for him and was even more damned than he was now. He didn't even bleed until I pulled the knife out, so I only had to wipe it on his sleeve to get clean away, and I could hardly raise an outcry or be found there by some unlucky chance, so I ran back through that dreadful passage and out into the night and I didn't stop running until I got back to our lodgings in Chelsea.'

'Was that where you lived with my elder brother whenever you could steal away to meet him?' Magnus asked.

'Never you mind,' Gresley said curtly.

'I *knew* you were not in Leicestershire when you got the terrible news the old man was murdered,' Connie said furiously. 'You were so furtive about the accident you claimed you had out hunting I knew you were lying. I thought you were with your mistress when he died and you were, but not quite in the way I imagined.'

'He was dead by the time I realised Delphi was long gone. I admit I tried to make it look as if a thief broke in and killed him when there was nothing left worth stealing. Then I took off every stitch I had on, bundled the bloody rags together under my arm and crept up to my old room by another passage for a change of clothes, before I left secretly as I got in. Nobody else realised there was a warren of passages behind all that rotten wainscoting and I could not be seen at Carrowe House. I took away every sign I could find that we had ever been there and went off to get the full story of what happened from Delphi and burn my bloody clothes.'

'I thought the late Lord Carrowe was already dead when the second attacker struck him to confuse the magistrates,' Sir Hadrian said coolly.

'Maybe his heart gave out. The wound didn't look deep enough to kill him and Delphi hasn't strength enough to drive a knife far into a man's chest.'

'Unless Lady Drace was very lucky, or unlucky, where she stuck her knife. It would take considerable strength or expert knowledge to get through his ribs to his heart,' Sir Hadrian said as if weighing up their story. 'If the wound was not severe enough to kill him, the blows to the head certainly were, so the Coroner would not look for signs of apoplexy with so many signs of violence on his body. You could have hung the very person you wanted to protect, Carrowe.'

'You can't hang her, Papa,' Hetta said and what a moment for Magnus to finally realise how much he loved her. He wanted her to love him back so much he squeezed her fingers too hard and she shot him a startled look. He eased the pressure, but the truth was he never wanted to let her go again.

'The Hailes will be dogged by rumour and suspicion for the rest of their lives if we let her get off scot-free,' Sir Hadrian objected.

'And before we go any further I would like to know which of you shot me yesterday,' Magnus put in with a hard look for his brother, so at least he knew how startled Gresley was that anyone had shot at him.

He had his answer. Hard to know a woman he once made love with so passionately could aim a shot at his heart. What a fool he had been

not to see there was a vixen hidden under all
that blonde beauty years ago. He would have
saved the agony of the past eighteen months if
he was a more perceptive man, but then there
would be no Angela and he refused to regret
her for a second.

'Obviously she must go to Bedlam,' Connie said as if that shot was the final proof she
needed that her enemy was mad. Magnus
warmed to his sister-in-law again but shook
his head in denial.

'She is not mad, just obsessed with Gres.
I almost feel sorry for you,' he told his elder
brother truthfully as all Delphi had done for
frustrated and twisted-up love of him ever
since he married Connie looked as if it now
sat like lead on Gres's shoulders.

'So do I,' his brother said with a twist of saving humour that almost disarmed Magnus, now
he knew the great fool had not lain in wait to
kill him yesterday after all.

'Distraction,' he confirmed for his own sat-
isfaction, although that was the wrong word.
She had meant to kill or maim him in order
to draw Sir Hadrian out of London and away
from Gresley and all those panicked attempts

he had made to drag the King's Bloodhound away from his lover's trail.

'I was close to finding the secrets built into Carrowe House when you wrote to your lover, was I not, my lord? I believe you were supposed to wait for him in some quiet French or Italian city where nobody would know Lord Carrowe from Adam, Lady Drace. You did not stay away very long, though, did you? I admit you are the wild card I did not allow for when I let my daughter leave London with you, Mr Haile. I had a watch put on you, Carrowe, after the bumbling attempt at snatching my grandson failed as you probably meant it to. The idea was to shock me into defending my family so I did not go after any of yours.'

'I thought you would abandon the case and go away,' Gresley confessed with a shamefaced look at Hetta. He avoided Connie's gaze altogether.

'At least you lack the ruthlessness of a true villain,' Magnus said as if he could comfort his big brother for being such a bumbling great fool when he had made such a mess of so many lives by not standing up to their father and walking away with Delphi when he should have done all those years ago.

'Unlike her,' Connie said, pointing at her rival like an avenging angel.

'You are the expert, Papa. You can decide what to do with them,' Hetta said with a revolted look of her own at Delphi. Magnus hoped that was for his sake and decided it would take the judgement of Solomon.

Chapter Seventeen

'It took me far too long to find the passages
built into Carrowe House so cleverly you hardly
believe they are there even when you know
the secret of them,' Sir Hadrian told Hetta and
Magnus while they were waiting for the horses
to be harnessed to his carriage a few hours
later. 'I thought that a canny man who survived
the Civil War with his fortune increased tenfold
would be sure to have a way ready to hand if he
ever needed to leave stealthily when the country rebelled against another king. Someone was
certainly coming and going at Carrowe House
at will and listening in places they should not
be able to listen, but it was Lord Carrowe's fury
when Toby got too close to one of the entrances
to those hidden ways by a chimney in the old-
est part of the house that finally put me on the
right track. Until then I thought I might have

to have the house taken down stone by stone to get at the truth of what happened that night.'

'You knew someone could go wherever they wanted in the awful old house, yet you let me stay there with Toby?' Hetta said sternly.

'Yes, but I allowed you to go to Hampstead, then dash about the country with Lady Aline and Mr Magnus Haile when my grandson's usual curiosity had served its purpose. I knew you were a lot safer with them than with their elder brother and from the day I arrived in London I realised Lord Carrowe was trying to bend his family to his will. I took exception when he tried to manipulate mine as well and put a constant but very discreet watch on his movements to make sure he could not come after you again without me knowing about it.'

'I don't know how he intended to have the house demolished without those passages even I had no idea were there coming to light,' Magnus said hastily to avert the argument Hetta had to have with her father in private to make herself feel better about having it.

'Carrowe House is as rotten as a pear and tinder dry,' Sir Hadrian said with a shrug to say who would care if it burned to the ground so long as nobody was hurt?

'You are going to be busy, Papa,' Hetta said rather ironically. 'What with fetching Mr Haile's daughter home and working out the most effective way of committing arson so every trace of old secrets are obliterated before you go. I dare say you will not have enough time left to order my life as well as everyone else's any longer,' she ended and neatly stepped around that argument.

'Are you not capable of ordering it yourself, then?' he asked as if he had not interfered in his daughter's life before and after he extracted that promise from her when Toby was a baby. Magnus felt his fingers tighten to a fist and made them relax when Hetta shook her head at her father as if she had already wriggled out from under his thumb and had no intention of ever going back there, so it did not matter what he thought she could or could not do.

'Of course. I shall make Mrs Wulfric Haile a fair offer for this house and estate, and if she refuses, I will find somewhere else to make Toby a home for the next ten years or so,' she said calmly.

Magnus's heart sank at the discovery she had a large enough fortune to buy such a place outright, rather than rent it as he had supposed she might until she found a smaller, neater and more convenient place closer to London. *Once a fortune hunter, always a fortune hunter*, he could almost hear the gossips whispering eagerly if Hetta was ever foolish enough to marry him.

'What busy folk we promise to be,' Magnus said heavily and left them to bid one another farewell.

'What will you do now?' Hetta asked after her father's carriage rumbled away with Lady Drace on board again, bound for yet another and more lasting new life. As soon as the last echo of their going had died away, the Abrah Valley was so quiet it was almost as if they had imagined all the upheaval.

'Work and raise my daughter,' Magnus said. 'What about you?'

'I intend to become a staid and settled Englishwoman after all. Papa is off to chase rainbows for the King somewhere even more exotic than usual and you have taught me to love my own country, so I shall stay here and let him do so without me. With a few sturdy servants and your sister's excellent company, if she will agree to lend it to me, we will be very comfortable here or in some other fine house even nearer to the sea if your sister-in-law does not wish to sell Abrah House.'

'Live with me instead, Hetta?' he said recklessly.

'Why?'

'I know I must look a bad risk, but please take it with me anyway. I am all yours.' He ran his fingers through his hair and left it wild again. Time to set caution aside and dare to hope, he decided, as the prospect of life without her seemed bleak indeed. 'Be my first and last true love, Mrs Champion. I would love to try to be Toby's father to the best of my ability and however many children of our own we might have as well as my Angela. Can you trust me enough to be the best reason I breathe, Hetta?'

'How am I to do that when Lady Drace was at the centre of your world for so long? How can I be sure I am there now instead? You yearned for her all those years, then made a child with her, Magnus. How can I ever lie next to you and listen to you call out her name in your dreams? Marrying Brandon was foolish of me, but wedding Lady Drace's lover would be like promising to walk on hot coals for the rest of my life.'

'I'm not that bad and I don't love Delphi. I love you. No, don't wave the word aside as if you can't or won't believe me because I once mistook something else for love. I did not say it a few hours ago when you might have believed me, but you said you didn't want me, so how could I?'

'I didn't—when did I say that?'

'You said no when I asked if there was any hope for me.'

'I did?'

'You agreed I was not enough for you,' he said.

'Not as a furtive lover,' she said as if he was a fool to misunderstand. 'I have Toby and you are going to get your daughter back to make it impossible as well. Being the best parent you can be reshapes the whole world.'

'I know,' he said, the one certainty in his life at the moment being the complete love he felt for his little girl the instant he laid eyes on her in her mother's arms and Delphi would not even let him hold the little mite. 'I admit I fought against the attraction I feel towards you because whatever I mistook for love twisted me in knots and now you don't believe me.'

'I am plain and already a mother, so I could be a good enough wife for your good enough life.'

'You are not plain, very far from it. I won't let even you call yourself so. Champion made you think so to keep the wolves away when he was at sea, but you are so far from plain I have to wonder about your eyesight after all, Henrietta. Now *I* love your witchy eyes behind the schoolteacher spectacles you hide behind, so keep them on if you really need them and look in the next mirror you come across with their help and see what I see. Your hair is rich and hot and wonderful as well, and as for that mouth, madam, it is a snare for any unwary male who looks at you as if you are much like any other woman, then longs to feel it move under his until he can hardly sleep of a night. Your trouble is you listen to those who don't adore the look of you and take the word of a fool who doesn't as if every word Champion said was gospel. I think the obvious gets less wonderful with time, but I could look at you for a lifetime and never be bored. No, don't turn your head away and refuse to listen to me. We matter, Hetta. *You* matter. At least listen to me while I try to convince you I shall love you until my dying day whether you want me or not. I know you wed Brandon Champion far too young to realise he could never make you happy, but he has bent you out of shape as a woman. That is not my fault, so please don't punish me for his sins as well as my own. At least you have had appalling taste in husbands until now, so I won't have to fight the memory of him to get to your heart. I curse the fates for landing you in the man's lap when he could never deserve you if he lived to be an ancient admiral and gave up chasing other women the day you married him, but at least he will never be much of a rival for the prize of your best husband.'

'I don't think Bran was capable of being faithful, but I shall not marry again,' Hetta told him with a snap.

'Why not? Champion was too deeply in love with himself to love you with all his heart and soul, but you cannot dismiss love and marriage because he was a fool.'

'And you are not?' she said with irony so bitter she was surprised there wasn't a breakaway Hetta wilting on a sofa or beating her fists on a wall.

'Maybe I am, but I still love you,' he argued with the frown that did things to her insides she didn't want to think about right now. 'Only a striving, restless, bad-tempered and independent-minded female will do for me, so isn't it lucky I found enough sense to fall in love with you at last, Mrs Henrietta Champion?'

'Hetta,' she corrected absently and saw hope spark to life in his dark Haile eyes that she couldn't quite let him believe in yet. 'And you are right about one thing. I never loved Bran as a wife should love her husband. I have held back from living my best life because I was so afraid of making another huge mistake, but I still won't wake up tomorrow morning looking lovely as the dawn. I cannot endure seeing your disappointment every time you open your eyes to find me in your bed instead of a beauty like Lady Drace.' She saw him flinch and it looked like confirmation she was right. 'I don't want to hurt you, Magnus, but it would be foolish of me to jump into another hasty marriage and end up even more disillusioned.'

'No, don't put me in the same category as Champion. I won't sit on his shelf, preening myself for being so handsome and splendid. This feeling I have for you is so different I refuse to rank it with anything I felt for Delphi. I love my child, Hetta, but Delphi's stony face when I was pleading with her to marry me forced me to see what a fool I was to think she had loved or ever even truly wanted me as a man. It hurt like hell at the time, but I am glad she did refuse me now because I would hate to be married to her and longing for you instead. I don't care about your fortune either, despite what the gossips will say when you marry me.'

'I have not said I will do anything of the sort and you are not in the least bit humble deep down, are you?' Hetta protested.

'I am trying,' he argued ruefully. 'I suppose I must learn if I am going to work for my living.'

'I don't care how rich or poor you are. I will not marry you without a very compelling reason to risk tying myself to a tyrant in breeches.'

'Isn't love enough?'

'I don't know,' she said truthfully and he didn't exactly look delighted about a not-quite dismissal if he really did love her. The thought of him as her lover thrilled every part of her, but she wasn't ready to admit it until she felt a lot more certain of herself and him. 'And don't glare at me. I won't let you bully me into saying yes,' she told him bluntly.

'Want to lay a bet on how long you can resist?' he asked with an edge of temper in his deep brown eyes. He stopped pacing to glare a challenge that sent her heart leaping into her mouth and made her breathing come fast and shallow.

'How much?' she countered recklessly.

'A chance. If you won't say yes to me, then don't say no either. Give me space and time enough to convince you I will be your best and last husband.'

'Modest,' she said with rather flippant irony, but from the spark of devilment and hope in his eyes he knew as well as she did it wasn't an outright no this time and hope was fluttering to life deep inside her. 'And Bran was not exactly stiff competition for the title.'

'Whereas being wed to you would be the biggest challenge of my life, Hetta. I would feel blessed every day I woke up with you in my bed, glaring back and letting me know I must still work to convince you we did the right thing by saying yes for a lifetime. Make no mistake about it—I want you at the heart of my life. I want you pretending to be grumpy and too engrossed in our vast tribe of offspring to hammer me into the shape you want me to be. I want to refuse to be hammered and relish every battle and skirmish while I seduce you into believing in who you really are and, speaking of seduction, I want you right here and right now. I have wanted to get past those spectacles and kiss you insensible since the second time we met. You should be careful how you provoke me now it's not only a want, but a driving need.'

'I am not the provoking one. You are,' she grumbled even as the heat in his gaze made her knees weak and her heart beat thunderously.

'Want to bet?' he asked softly again and bent his head to meet her eager lips and put a stop to all this talk with a searingly hot kiss.

Everyone for several miles around ought to feel such an earthquake happening nearby,

Hetta decided hazily. *A kiss never felt like this with Bran, though, did it?* she heard her inner Hetta remark pointedly, as she reached up an unsteady hand to caress the back of his neck as she had longed to on the way here. He groaned about that frustration and her own heartbeat galloped. Her hands were busy among his sooty curls and why should she hold back now she had the springy gloss of them under her fingers? Here were strong bands of muscle at the joint of head and neck that felt so vulnerable when he was bent over to seduce her with this sweet madness. His hands went places guaranteed to awaken sensuous possibilities. Had Magnus ever stroked and worshipped his Delphi's curves and slenderness as eagerly as he was seducing hers? The throaty purr of content about to let him know this was wondrous stuttered into a sigh of regret.

'Stop thinking of them,' he murmured in her other ear and she reluctantly opened her eyes.

'I can't. They are always with us,' she whispered. 'Your Delphi had so much of you, how can I forget her?'

'Because she didn't want me and I never

knew her. Losing you because of her seems so appalling I refuse to even consider it.'

'Lady Drace has gone, so what do you have to lose?'

'You can say that, held in my arms, seeing what you do to me?'

'Yes. I think I must have learned too much about passion and not enough about love from Bran to believe I could outshine such a natural beauty in your bed.'

'Then you are right, Mrs Champion,' he said bleakly.

'I told you I was,' she said numbly.

'Not about us, about them,' he told her so furiously she had to believe he meant it. 'Lady Drace allowed me to batter against her chilly loveliness for years to get back at my elder brother. Brandon Champion showed you a shallow rake will grab what he wants like a greedy child, then make a woman feel less for giving it to him. If we let them they will destroy our future as well.'

'I thought you said you didn't have the words?' she said as that version of them made her shiver at all the lost chances she might be whistling down the wind if he was right.

'They have not convinced you yet, though, have they?' he said and sounded so flat about it she could not lie.

'Not yet, no,' she admitted. 'I want to stay here in your arms and be seduced into knowing we can make a real marriage out of this fascination, Magnus, but I am not sure I can yet. Perhaps I need to believe in me before I can believe in us.'

'Don't wrap it up in kind words, Hetta. You don't trust me to love you back with all I am. It hurts like hell, but I will prove to you I mean it if it takes the rest of my life. Champion cozened you into leaping into marriage when you were too young to know your own mind and I cannot do the same, even if you are quite old enough to know your own mind this time.'

'You mean I am no longer seventeen and vulnerable.'

'I can tell,' he said and his velvet-dark eyes went dreamy and intense and she must be mad to resist this temptation to get to the nearest bed and be very busy about bonding with him as lovers.

'Then we could...' Hetta let her voice tail off

as she saw his eyes go stern, then soften with wicked laughter.

'Oh, we most definitely *could*, Mrs Champion,' he murmured as the promise of him being her lover was very real between their eagerly curious bodies. 'But if there is to be no wedding, then there is no bedding for me either,' he said as if he was the king of the virtues, not wild Magnus Haile striving to win over his last lover.

'If my husband had been cold and distant in the marriage bed, I could trust passion more, Magnus,' she said earnestly, and somehow, she had to convince him it really was a problem. The easy words and kind acts of love had melted away like ice in the July sun as soon as Bran got bored and marriage meant they could not walk away and say, *Well, that was a mistake. Let us forget we ever met and both move on to try it again with a new lover.*

'It can be a snare for a man as well, don't forget,' he said rather bleakly and she felt the wrongness of putting memories of Lady Drace using him for her own ends in his eyes again. 'And don't expect me to watch another woman sail away with another child of mine I am forbidden to see,' he said bleakly.

'Oh, I see what you mean,' she said, her suddenly chilled hands covering her cheeks because she did and she really would not do that to him. 'I would never walk away from you if we made a child, Magnus. I could not be so cruel to either of you.'

'How flattering you will only agree to wed me for the sake of a child we might make,' he said flatly, as if the words tasted vile on his tongue.

'There is no satisfying you, is there?' she snapped, then realised the double meaning in her question as his rigid frustration made an unmistakable fact of his mighty self-control. Bran would have had her on the nearest flat surface by now and never mind who might come upon them while he satisfied himself. She flushed at the thought of sharing headlong passion with a lover like Magnus, glad he could not know how much heat there was in her belly at even the thought of a child of theirs growing inside it. 'It would not be the only reason I agreed,' she said carefully.

'Then marry me, Hetta. Let me teach you

about loving by practice instead of all this end-less theory. You will know the difference be-cause I never felt a tithe of this desperation in my heart and soul for another woman. At least Champion was a good enough lover to make sure you will feel the contrast between lust and love.'

'Not yet. I want to know we are right for one another before we make a family.'

She wondered at herself for not tipping straight into loving him, but the mirage of it hurt so much last time she did not dare. It had hurt when her heady romance with Bran fell into ashes, but if she made such a mistake with Magnus it would destroy parts of her Bran had never been able to reach. She simply could not push herself over the last barrier and admit how deeply she longed for Magnus Haile until she believed him wholeheartedly.

'I will never sneak into your bed by night and leave in the dawn, Hetta. It has to be daylight and every day for me from now on.'

'Will you wait for me to know if I can offer you all that?'

'Do you think I flit from one woman to the next like a bee after pollen, Hetta?' he demanded so harshly she had to look him in the eye when she answered or be a coward.

'No.'

'But?'

'But I was so convinced I was doing the right thing last time, Magnus.'

He sighed and looked furious and frustrated and as broodingly, hastily magnificent as the first time she laid eyes on him, so she knew she had won some time or he would not be so angry about it. She cursed Bran for easy loving and hard living and hesitated, the grind of unsatisfied desire tearing at her as if her own body was crying out how wrong she was to send him away when she was so raw with wanting him back. No, she could not tell him how much she longed for the fact and fury and sheer male beauty of him in her bed and not trust him to love her for the rest of their lives, so she could not have him until she did.

'I would never act the great lover, then run when our marriage wasn't what I expected like Champion did, but what's the point in wasting breath when you don't believe me? Please go and ask Jem to pack for me and order my horse to be saddled, before I beg or lose control of myself, and we start another darling little one because I got out of control and you lost all your choices after all. I shall be along when I can take my leave without the world knowing I am your very frustrated suitor,' he said tightly. 'So please go now, Hetta, while I can still listen to my inner gentleman and let you be, but promise not to forget me while you work out your new life.'

'As if I could,' she said and felt the fury of frustrated desire inside her as he turned away as if he could not wait to leave. This could be the biggest mistake she had ever made, she decided as she left him standing stiff and solitary and gazing at the road out of the Abrah Valley as if he had already begun to leave her.

Chapter Eighteen

A fortnight later her own words echoed in Hetta's mind like a sentence handed down by a judge. As if she *could* forget the man. She eyed the unopened letter on her writing slope and thought it typical of him to send it off with such strong strokes of the pen she could see where he'd had to mend it even when he was addressing it to her. She knew without lifting the seal that he was angry with her for the heartache and loneliness of them being apart like this. Fury seemed to glower off the hot-pressed paper and she picked it up, then dropped it as if it might bite.

'Come on, Hetta. Open the dratted thing,' she chided herself.

She slipped the paper knife under his seal and smiled at the arrogance of it as she decided he must have had his seal made before he became a working man. 'M.H.' sat proudly with his mother's personal arms and only included his father's as hers had when she married him. Love for his mother and younger siblings must have been all that stopped him cutting himself off from the Earl and striking out alone years ago.

Never mind that now. The sooner this first letter was read the sooner they could get his first blasts of fury out of the way.

Mrs Champion, it began, so she was right.

How can I call you anything else when you will not commit any of yourself to me?

He seemed to argue as if he had heard her thoughts. It was all right for her to smile dreamily into the middle distance as she read his impatient words because nobody was here to see her doing it.

So far the only effect of your embargo is frustration and sleepless nights for me and who knows what for you. I am intrigued to hear if you are heartsore and weary, too, since it seems unfair I suffer alone.

At least I am a dedicated and industrious

*employee, because I have to do something
with all this time and pent-up emotion.
My sister-in-law and even her formidable
brother-in-law Carnwood are so impressed
I shall be a legend in the city by the time
you decide to relent.*
Your faithful, reluctantly obedient servant,
Magnus Haile

Hetta eyed his first missive with an exasperated scowl. How could she call it a love letter?
Yet she had to smile, despite him making her
wait so long for so little. She could picture him
writing it with his dark brows almost knit in a
dark and furious frown at her for putting them
through this separation. She badly wanted to
be the last love of his life, though—no chance
of being the first when his precious Delphi had
sat on that throne in all her expensive glory for
so long. If he was to persuade Henrietta Champion he really did love her, then being so typically Magnus and furious about it might be his
best strategy yet.

His words made him seem so vitally present
and real he could be in another room refusing
to speak to her, or a town not a half-an-hour's

ride away being stubborn, instead of a hundred miles distant or more. Hetta looked over her shoulder to make sure he had not brought the message himself and sighed with disappointment when no trace of him lurked in a dark corner, glaring back at her for making him stay away all this time for no rational reason at all as far as he could fathom. She could hear Toby in the next room asking Lady Aline a spate of eager questions now he was home from his small but scholarly prep school for the weekend, so she frowned, mended her pen and found an equally small piece of paper to write on and make Magnus curse her conciseness as well.

Mr Haile,
How refreshingly brief your first ever letter to me proved to be.

I trust you are well and suppose you must be, since you have so much energy to spend on your work you do not have time for more than a few gruff lines.

I will not be any man's second-rate wife, least of all yours. Nothing I read today makes me think again about your flatter-

*ing offer, so you will have to try harder to
convince me of your sincere regard.*

*Lady Aline is going to write by this same
post, so I shall not include any details of
our lives. She is sure to confide them to
you, so we need not repeat ourselves.*
I wish you a good day, sir,
Yours etc.,
Mrs H. Champion

That ought to make him think harder about
sending more of himself next time, if he didn't
give up altogether. If he was going to, she
would rather he got on with it, and it wasn't as
if she wanted outpourings of impassioned po-
etry or wild promises of undying love until the
end of time, but this was meant to be a wooing,
wasn't it? She already knew he was morose and
contrary as well as funny, loyal and strong as
steel. It was the everyday intimacy of his love
she wanted convincing of.

She sat chewing on the other end of her quill
and wondered if that was her problem instead
of his. If he truly did love her, perhaps that was
why he sent such a brief and cross-grained letter. If he was missing her so much he could not

get smooth words and gallant phrases down on the page, he might deserve more than the same in return. She could not manage to rip her letter up and send a sweet and conciliatory one instead, though, so she let it stand and resigned herself to another few weeks of painful suspense.

Either he loved her, or he didn't. Their game of pit-pat would resolve if he shrugged and went on with his life without such a difficult female, but she desperately hoped he wouldn't.

Dear Mrs Champion,
Is that better? Neither stiffly formal nor mawkishly loverlike, so you will not need to hide my letter if someone comes in and catches you reading it.

I do hope you are going to read it, by the way? Imagine my chagrin if you throw it in a corner for a servant to puzzle over later.

As for my lack of persuasive powers and inability to hide my fury, you already know I am no poet. My brother Wulf got all the eloquence in the family.

I am glad Aline is coming into her own as a companion of precocious young gentle-

men and finicky ladies, but I could do with some of her patience and Wulf's way with words right now.

Since I lack words I shall borrow a few from the hero of one of my favourite novels by the late Miss Austen and tell you that if I loved you less I might be able to talk about it more.

At least rereading Emma *helps me understand complicated, opinionated and managing females. Since I had the stupidity to fall in love with one of those I feel for poor Knightley more than ever.*

I do hope you have not taken up matchmaking to relieve your boredom, by the way? I have no wish to have Aline carried off by any of the local smuggler barons, and do not run away with the idea I will sit and twiddle my thumbs if you happen to be flirting with any of them yourself.

One word of any impassioned suitors will have me galloping to Devon in an even more furious frame of mind than when I left. I will come and find you, then make them regret their effrontery, Mrs H. Champion, so don't shake your head dismissively and frown. I don't care how powerful your father is. He won't keep me away if I need to come between you and another handsome liar.

Please be convinced soon, Hetta, because I am not a patient man and my new tailor is weary of taking inches out of my coats and breeches now I waste away for the lack of you in my life.

It has to be love, if you think about it, since neither of us would even think about facing a small riot over breakfast every morning for anything less when you consider how much havoc my daughter and your son will cause together.

I cannot say more now. The lack of you hurts too much to dwell on any longer and I should get some sleep before I am about Isabella and Wulf's business again in the morning and my little not-quite-an-angel runs poor Peg and my mother ragged as well as her father.

I love you—now and always, madam.

Be sure you come to Develin House soon and bring your infernal boy and my sister with you, because I miss them as well.

But most of all I miss you, my love.
Your Magnus

Hetta smiled dreamily at the view from the breakfast-room window and decided it would do very well as a summer residence when they were settled near Hampstead for the rest of the year. Even here autumn was nipping at the edges of summer, and if Magnus was to earn enough to support his family, he would need to spend most of the year near London or visiting Isabella's properties. Perhaps they had needed this time to find out how to be the very different people they were now, but she sighed and longed for him with a familiar gnawing ache that never seemed to go away. Physically she had longed for him as her lover ever since she laid eyes on him. She cursed Lady Drace for cutting him off from his little girl as she had and blessed her own father for making it the main condition of letting Lady Drace disappear into a new life on the other side of the world that she passed all care and legal responsibility for her daughter to the little girl's real father. Hetta had begun to believe Magnus was done with loving the woman and now his daughter could grow into a fine and hopeful young woman instead of sharing her mother's narrow and bitter life.

It was time for Hetta to accept she was well enough in her own way and at least she'd never killed anyone or used a good man's passion for her to make a baby she could pretend then to herself was his brother's begetting and not his.

So, was she guilty of pushing her own insecurities off on to Magnus? Yes, she decided. Did she love the man? Oh, yes, and after all these weeks of sleepless nights his impatient letters only confirmed it. 'I do. I love him,' she admitted to the lush hills and a long view to the far-distant sea and almost felt them shrug at such a tiny human pinprick in their ancient dreams. 'So why am I sitting dreaming about him while he is doing the same about me wherever he has gone off to this time?'

'Good question,' Aline put in from the doorway and made Hetta jump guiltily. 'What is the answer?'

Hetta hesitated for a moment between safety and risk and chose Magnus. 'I must go to London,' she said, jumping to her feet. Her world had turned the right way up again and it was going to stay this way for the rest of her life. 'I need to marry your brother.'

'Good, but there's no point in setting off without a spare petticoat and the rest of us in your hurry when you took so long to realise you want to marry him I was beginning to think you might never see sense.'

'Whose side are you on?'

'There are not going to be sides, are there? I truly hope not. I have had enough tantrums and arguments to last me a lifetime.'

'We are two very definite and argumentative people, Aline, but if you think a marriage between us will be anything like your parents' you ought to know better. And don't tell me your brother Wulf and his wife don't argue as passionately as I intend to argue with Magnus for the rest of our lives, because I won't believe you.'

'No, they argue all the time and make up so extravagantly we sometimes don't set eyes on them for days. It's embarrassing, but I suppose I shall have to get used to it since I love both of my younger brothers far too much to cut them out of my life and retire to a nunnery. At least you two have children to think about, so you can hardly pretend you both caught an illness that keeps you confined to your bed for days on end then miraculously wears off until next time you have a passionate falling-out.'

'Poor Lady Aline, you will have to find a lover of your own to fall out with at regular intervals,' Hetta told her friend with a dreamy look in her eyes as an image of Magnus vigorous and exasperated and intently passionate about her blotted out any images of Aline's potential lover from her head. 'I can't wait to get to mine now I know he really and truly loves me and I love him back.'

'I could have told you so before you sent him away.'

'Maybe, but being told something and believing it are two different things.'

'I suppose you did need time to get Lady Delphine out of your head, although I can't imagine why you thought he would want her once he'd met you. When I decide to marry I shall manage the whole business a lot more logically than you two or Wulf and Isabella. Only think of all the trouble and energy the rest of us wasted trying to make you realise Lady Drace should only have been a boyish infatuation. She used Magnus, Hetta. She kept him on a string and made him feel so guilty about deserting her that Magnus could never quite break free. All those years she danced him about to make Gresley jealous. Then she had the gall to use Magnus to get herself a child who looked like Gresley? Oh, for goodness' sake, Hetta, can't you see the woman has no taste? I don't know why you ever believed she was the love of his life.'

'Thank you,' Hetta said—what else could she say? Aline was right and when she chose to speak about personal matters she was sharply eloquent.

'You needed to learn what really mattered,' Aline said almost as if she could read Hetta's mind.

'Then I wish I was quicker on the uptake. I have missed him so much and it was cruel to both of us to send him away like that.'

'It was, but he understands you, so I dare say he will forgive you sooner or later. He needs you and Toby in his life as well as his own little Angela, Hetta. Don't doubt he has the space in his heart for all of you ever again and please don't let Lady Drace bend your view of him out of shape either. She doesn't deserve to have power over any of our lives after what she did to Magnus and even my father.'

'I pity the choices she made, but I hope she heeds *my* father's warning and stays out of England for the rest of her life, because if she doesn't I might be tempted to shoot her myself.'

'Oh, she will. I have no doubt your father has a way of reminding his enemies his reach is far longer than they would like it to be.'

'I suspect you are right,' Hetta said and spared a shiver for Lady Drace, if she ever dared to stretch Sir Hadrian's mercy and patience too far.

'You are late,' Hetta accused the darkly handsome, unshaven and arrogant male riding up the drive of Develin House as if the devil was on his heels.

'No, that would be you,' Magnus argued with a quirk of his dark eyebrows to let her know he was still in a temper with her and she had best not expect much quarter.

'We got here half an hour ago and have you any idea how hard it is to travel *ventre à terre* all the way from Devon to London?' she

asked him haughtily, even as her eyes ran slav-
ishly over him, looking for any little hurts and
changes to make up for the lost hours since the
last time she laid eyes on him.

'I got here as fast as I could,' he said and his
travel-worn state reminded her sharply of the
day they first met.

'So did I.'

'Not by any definition of *fast* I ever came
across,' he argued grumpily and she could see
from the strain in his tired eyes and the determined set of his mouth that he had driven himself as hard as he could to get here before she
changed her mind again. 'Are you really here
to marry me?'

'I hope so. Are you going to be more of a
gentleman than you were last time we were
here if I say yes?'

'I asked first,' he said and let her see the painful anxiety in his dear, darkest of brown eyes
and the hope underneath it that was probably
making this even more edgy and uncertain for
him than it felt for her.

'Yes,' she said and he stared at her for a long
moment as if he hardly dared to believe his
ears. 'Yes, I am going to marry you. Yes, I love

you. Yes, can we find the nearest inn with a clean bed in it and make love until I can't remember my name?'

'God, how I missed you, Hetta,' he told her, almost as close as the lover she wanted him to be, but he was not quite close enough yet. 'I'm filthy,' he said with a manly shrug.

She laughed. 'I do love you, Magnus,' she said in the most feeble, wobbly voice imaginable. 'There, I lost my words again,' she whispered as she broke first and launched herself at him, so he had to catch her or let her fall on the gravel.

'Those are the only ones that matter,' he murmured and kissed her with all the locked-up passion of too many weeks apart.

Hetta's legs felt boneless and she was melting with desire out here on his mother's drive where anyone could see them. She didn't care who knew how much she loved the man now. Anyone could know how deeply Henrietta Champion adored the Honourable Magnus Haile if they happened to be looking.

'Yuck!' Toby announced very loudly indeed from somewhere too close for his mother's dignity and peace of mind.

'I told you not to run ahead and look what happens when you disregard my advice, young man—you see things you did not want to.'

'They were kissing,' Toby told Aline with a sulky look.

'True.'

'Aline,' Hetta said reproachfully.

'Well, you were, but married people are allowed to hug and kiss, I fear, Toby, and your mama is going to marry my brother, so you will have to get used to it or go and live in another country with your grandfather.'

'No, he forgets about me all the time. I don't mind staying with him for a day or two, but I want to eat and sleep and do interesting things and he is always busy.'

'So?' Magnus said with that quirk of the eyebrow.

'Oh, very well, you can kiss her as long as I'm not looking.'

'Best look away now, then, lad, because I have waited six weeks for your mama to say yes to my proposal and I am not feeling patient.'

'You two are in the way of anyone who wants

to visit Lady Carrowe,' her son pointed out with such chilly dignity Hetta nearly applauded.

'He's right,' she told Magnus with an apologetic shrug.

Magnus blushed under all that intriguingly disreputable stubble and Hetta fell even deeper in love with him than ever. He did not step away from her as if he'd been caught doing something wrong and unmanly by her critical son. He kept his arm firmly round her waist as they followed Aline and Toby inside and insisted on keeping it there until Angela squealed with delight, struggled out of her grandmama's lap and toddled determinedly towards her father, holding up her arms to be picked up and hugged. Happy to be upstaged by the little girl who clearly adored her papa already, Hetta felt another anxiety soothe out and hope take its place. Angela was so much a Haile, how could she not love her? It would take time to win her over if the way the little minx was staring at her with a feminine challenge in her dark brown eyes was anything to go by, but Hetta was equal to it.

Chapter Nineteen

'My dears, I persuaded the girls to take Toby for a walk and Peg says it's time Angela had her nap, so I have you to myself at last. There is something I really must tell you before you go to see the vicar about your banns this afternoon.'

'We know marriage is a serious business and promise not to take it lightly, Mama,' Magnus said with one of the wicked, teasing smiles that made Hetta's knees wobble and he knew it, the rogue.

'I didn't go to all this trouble to get you two alone to tell you things you already know, my son,' the Dowager Lady Carrowe informed him in much the same tone as Hetta used when Toby was being exasperating.

Magnus fidgeted in a similar way to his step-son-to-be as well and Hetta's heart thumped another reminder of how much she loved this man. 'Why did you, then?' he asked.

'Because I must say things I don't want to before I lose courage,' her ladyship said a bit too seriously.

'Best get it out of the way, then, love, before Toby comes storming back in to try and catch me kissing his mother again and be suitably disgusted.'

'It concerns your father and elder brother,' Lady Carrowe said carefully and Hetta suddenly realised her future mother-in-law never called her eldest son by his given name unless she really had to and how odd that was in such a loving mother.

'The Earl is dead. Long live the Earl. High time we put the past behind us,' Magnus said, but he reached for Hetta's hand as if he felt a jag of anxiety as well.

'I wish I could, Magnus, but first I must tell you the truth. I managed not to reveal it when Wulf married Isabella, but he is my younger son, so it is not so important for him to know the true state of affairs.'

'The truth about what affairs?' he tried to

joke, but Hetta knew him well enough to sense his unease.

'Your elder brother is not my child,' Lady Carrowe finally managed to say as if she had to get the words out in a rush or not at all.

'He has Haile written all over him, Mama,' Magnus argued.

'Oh, yes, he is certainly his father's son—but not mine.'

'He must be. There's no other way for him to be Earl of Carrowe unless he is your son as well.'

'My son died, Magnus. No, don't try to tell me I am mistaken or feverish or out of my mind. Your father threatened me with all those alternatives if I dared speak up so often I cannot bear to hear them on your lips. My baby did not thrive and the Earl sent him to the country to be wet-nursed in good, clean air, but another child came back in his place, supposedly fully restored to health and thriving like a small miracle. I hoped against hope your father was right and my pale and tiny baby boy would grow strong at Haile Carr and I was too weak from the birth to argue. I was quite willing to take a risk and go with him, but the Earl found all sorts of reasons why I must remain in London while our baby breathed fresh country air and grew strong.'

'Gres has always been as strong as an ox, so it must have worked,' Magnus said stubbornly, but Hetta supposed this secret was a revolution for him, so she could understand his determination not to remake his life again without a fight.

'He is not *my* Gresley. Why do you think I cannot bring myself to call him by that name, Magnus? I felt so guilty when he came back and I felt nothing for him. Hetta—you will understand how I felt as a mother. You know every hurt they feel hurts us, too, every slight sting stings so sharply, but I felt as cold as ice about the boy Carrowe said was ours. For a while I thought I really was mad *not* to feel the bond I formed with him the instant he was laid in my arms rekindle the moment he was back.'

Hetta nodded, but Magnus wasn't ready to believe his ears yet. 'I have been told a difficult birth can make a mother feel oddly towards her child.'

'I told myself so for months, but then your sister Mary was born healthy and crying at the top of her voice most of the time, Magnus, and I loved her so much, yet still I could not make that bond with my eldest child. I tried to believe it was because my marriage soured after he was born and I was putting my unhappiness on to the baby because he looked so very much like his father.'

'What changed your mind?'

'His mother. She came to me when I was expecting you, Magnus, and explained that her son had been taken away from her and put in my Gresley's place. Now the Earl was refusing to pay her bills and her parents would not have her back under their roof even without her bastard child, so she came to Carrowe House when she knew your father was in the country. He had insisted the journey was too much for me in my condition and I learned later that he had got yet another mistress with child and might have been thinking of trying the same trick again, but she birthed a stillborn daughter and you were strong and healthy from first yell, so at least he had one legitimate heir.'

'Were you really so rudely healthy, my love?' Hetta said lightly, taking Magnus's strong hand in both of hers to lend him some of her heat and certainty, since she had felt him wince at the truth in his mother's voice and accept it at last. 'I shall be sure to remember when I am *enceinte* and will know to expect a prize-fighter to emerge shouting at the top of his voice.'

'As long as you are both safe he can yell until he's hoarse, as far as I am concerned,' he said rather hoarsely and squeezed her hand as if having his own boy one day might make the pains of the past seem as nothing in time.

'I had to tell you both the truth before you embark on marriage and a family.' His mother ploughed on with her story after so many years of uneasy secrecy. 'You are the rightful Earl of Carrowe, Magnus. Your elder brother is your half-brother by one of your father's mistresses, and a wide-eyed innocent she must have been to fall for his lies. Apparently, he wove a tale of his arranged marriage when he had to beg me to wed him. Why, he even threatened to shoot himself if I wouldn't give in and agree to marry him at the third of fourth time of asking.'

'Best not to try to understand how the old Earl's mind worked, love. Now he's dead, you need never listen to his lies again.'

'I know I should not agree the ending of any

life is a blessing, but that poor girl was driven too far and so was I. My husband was so eaten up by selfish wants he forgot to be the human being God probably meant him to be when he was born with talent and good looks as well as fine prospects and he wasted it all.'

'We could say the same about the King, but at least he can be kind as well as selfish and spoilt. Nothing can change history, Mama, and I could hardly prove I am the true Earl of Carrowe all these years later even if I wanted to,' Magnus said and Hetta let out a quiet sigh of relief. 'Gresley's wife's fortune is all that keeps Haile Carr and the rest of us afloat. Even if I wanted to be Earl of Carrowe, I would end up with an empty title, since the land and houses would all have to go to pay off the old man's debts, entail or no. What about you, Hetta? If you want to be a countess, I suppose I could try to supplant him.'

'I would rather live on the moon,' Hetta replied.

'We could be a bit cold, love,' he said with a look that said how much he loved her and how much he wanted to forget this in her arms as soon as they could carve out the privacy to be lovers at long last.

'Why did he do it, Lady Carrowe?' Hetta asked as Magnus didn't seem to want to.

'My father-in-law made a condition in his will my husband could not inherit the bulk of the Haile fortune until his own heir was six months old. No wonder Frederick laid siege to me and was very hot to beget an heir when I finally gave in and married him, but my poor little Gresley did not survive six weeks, let alone six months. By then your father owed thousands in debts of so-called honour and goodness knows what to the tradesmen, so he was desperate to get the rest of his father's fortune. When I challenged him with what he had done a few months after you were born, he finally admitted the truth as if he had not done wrong. The Earl of Carrowe should not have to wait for me to produce a healthy son when he had one so obviously a Haile ready and waiting to slip into his cradle when mine died. He even admitted he buried my baby in unhallowed ground so nobody would know the boy I got back was not mine. Except I knew he was the wrong child, and now the Earl is dead, I shall never find *my* Gresley and give him a proper burial. I hate to say your younger brother and sisters were born of hatred, but they were certainly not conceived in love. They had a hard start in life, but grew into admirable people, like you, my son,' she told Magnus, and it was true— her sons and daughters were all fine people.

Lady Carrowe was trying not to say her late husband's eldest surviving son followed his sire more truly than the rest of his children and never mind a physical likeness. Easy to think she would have snatched Mary and Magnus away and left the man after he revealed his wicked deception and downright fraud herself, Hetta decided. Difficult to actually do so when no court in the land would have granted her custody of her children, even if she managed to procure a legal separation from their father and prove she was a wronged woman. The silence lengthened as they thought through her ladyship's sad tale and impossible choices. There were no words to make a mother feel better about such a grievous loss and terrible betrayal, so Hetta did not offer them up.

'Well, I have to love Gres for standing between me and the title and saving me from having to make any of his choices, Mama,' Magnus said at last, with a wry shrug to tell her he really meant it. 'I don't want to be my lord or own a great barn of a house I lack funds to keep up. I certainly don't want a lifetime of duty and living in public with a wife who hates me.'

'I pity the current Lady Carrowe brazening out what she thought was a fine marriage to a man she now knows she cannot trust, although I don't think she quite hates him,' Hetta said. She even spared a pang for the Lady Drace she met that day at Dover before Magnus appeared. That lady seemed uncertain and a bit vulnerable, but Hetta recalled how Lady Drace had refused to let Magnus play even a walk-on part in his child's life and then tried to shoot him and quickly changed her mind.

'Aye, poor Connie, she made a bad bargain,' Magnus said.

'Marriage should never be about rank, money or financial gain,' the Dowager Countess said and shook her head sadly, as if she should have been able to stop that one even if Gresley was not her son. 'I am so glad you children have a chance to wed people who love and respect you.'

'But why did the Earl accuse you of being unfaithful when Wulf was born?' he asked his mother as if it was the mystery that had vexed him most about the late Lord Carrowe's unsatisfactory life.

'To make sure nobody would listen if I told them what he had done. I had sworn testimonies from the midwife who delivered his bastard son and the girl herself, you see? She gave them to me when I sold my diamond necklace so she could have enough money to leave the country and begin a new life. He was a fool not to keep paying her bills. If he had left her living quietly, knowing her child had a life she could not give him in her wildest dreams, she would never have told me.'

'Brave of you to confront him,' Magnus said grimly.

'Wulf paid dearly for it. The Earl used my baby's Develin looks to discredit us both and keep me quiet lest he did as he threatened to and take my baby and leave him somewhere I would never find him.'

'He bastardised his own son to stop you telling the truth?'

'Yes, and I still cannot bring myself to tell Wulf. I am such a coward.'

'Not you and what good would it do? Hard enough for me to meet Gres and pretend everything is as it always was without Wulf having to as well.'

'If I had only learned to love Gresley and never mind who really birthed him, he might not have been so easy to bend to his father's will, or Delphine Drace's, for that matter,' Dowager Lady Carrowe said with a pensive look. 'Being born in the wrong bed was not his fault, was it?'

They sat in silence and thought about the past for a few moments.

'Perhaps a little bit,' Magnus said with a grin at last. 'He should never have accrued his own debts and made love to a schoolgirl without marrying her. Even Brandon Champion didn't do that.'

Hetta hit his arm as he probably meant her to and the atmosphere in the Dowager Lady Carrowe's cosy sitting room seemed to warm and lighten as they forgot old sins for the joy of a very imminent wedding and Angela woke up anyway, so nobody could think about the past with that vital little mite determined to explore the rest of the world before bedtime.

Chapter Twenty

'What on earth are you doing?' Hetta gasped after being scurried along in the dark as if they had to win a race.

'Making sure you don't have to marry a lunatic.'

'I seem to be marrying one of those anyway,' she said and stood fast when he tried to tug her out of Lady Carrowe's shrubbery and on to the Heath, all silvered and tempting in the moonlight. 'Where are we going?'

'To Wulf's house,' he said as if the effort of getting even that many words out was so huge he had run out of them.

'Why?'

'Why do you think?'

'Oh, won't they be shocked if we turn up at their front door, then gallop off upstairs without so much as a by your leave?'

'No, they're not there.'

'And they are not coming back tonight?' she found enough breath to ask as he scurried her down the path the family had worn between Lady Carrowe's house and Wulf and Isabella's remoter one since her ladyship came home.

'No, they are busy being tactful in town with her sister.'

'Which one?'

'I don't care,' he said as if all that mattered was they were gone and he had waited far too long to be her lover. Which he had, of course, and so had she.

'Nor me,' she managed to say past the excitement scorching through her at the thought of a whole night together. 'What about Toby and Angela?' she asked, suddenly feeling guilty about sneaking off into the night and leaving the children behind.

'My mother and Peg are used to dealing with small and demanding girls and their big brothers, and Aline is there as well as the twins, if they wear out everyone else between the two of them. I think they can manage without us for one night, don't you?'

'They will know what we are up to?'

'I doubt it. Even Toby isn't quite that advanced and Angela loves all the attention too much to worry what her parents are up to.'

He had paused in the clear moonlight to stare down at her as if desperate for her to agree. He stood brooding about something and she guessed it was her maternal bond with her son and how far she was prepared to let it stretch as her boy grew into a man. Toby was nearly eight years old and growing like a weed and she had to allow him freedom to fall on his face now and again without hovering over him like a mother hen. It was going to be hard, but she had to do it.

'And now they have puppies, neither of them care very much where we are,' he added as if they had been his master stroke.

'Yes, and while we're on the subject of puppies, I almost hope he ends up sleeping in the stables with them tonight. I hate to think how many puddles there will be in his room by morning if he decides to smuggle them upstairs again because he thinks they might be lonely without him.'

'A boy needs a dog.'

'Maybe, but not two.'

'A girl needs one, then.'

'She is barely a year old, Magnus. She hardly needs a toy one, let alone one that is likely to end up bigger than she is.'

'They will be company for one another when he's at school,' Magnus said in a manly defensive sort of voice that said he wanted two pups of very mixed ancestry getting under their feet all the time almost as much as her son.

'Boy,' she accused him softly, the light of the full moon allowing her to see his one crooked eyebrow as he silently challenged her to think him anything of the sort. They were within touching distance of proving how much of a man he really was and she could hardly wait.

'I missed you so much,' she told him breathily.

'Then for goodness' sake get moving, woman, unless you want to be ravished out here, of course.'

'No, thank you. It might be a little chilly right now. Maybe next year, if your brother and sister-in-law happen to leave their love nest in the summer and we happen to be nearby to take advantage of it.'

'I shall have to make sure they do, then,'

he said, and Hetta was so intent on not stumbling in her haste to match him hurry for hurry she didn't even pick out spots ideal for loving outside on brief summer nights. Time, she decided with a delicious little sigh, she could spare some from scurrying back from Wulf's hideaway in the morning to worry about that.

'We have time, Magnus,' she said as if he ought to understand exactly what she meant from the joy in her voice.

'Then let's not waste any more of it. Ah, here we are at last. I hope Jem left the key in the right place because I'm probably not in the right frame of mind for picking locks tonight.'

'I'm marrying a criminal.'

'Wulf taught me and I expect Jem Caudle taught him. It is best not to enquire. Here, hold this,' he demanded as he reached for the tinder box and dark lantern the obliging Jem had left handy for them.

'Can't we feel our way?' she asked as he struck the flint a couple of times and she was moved by the way his hands shook so much he had to keep doing it to the accompaniment of a good many muttered curses she wasn't supposed to hear.

'Quicker if I find the lock and key first go,' he said between gritted teeth and at last the spark struck and was strong enough for the tinder to smoulder, then burn so he could light a taper, then the candle inside the lamp. She could hardly hold still for trying not to laugh.

'If we could see ourselves,' she said on another suppressed giggle as she trembled on the threshold of her future brother and sister-in-law's home and felt all the joy and nerves and longing building a wave inside her that might sweep them both away if they were not a lot more careful.

'I can see you and that's all that matters.'

'Stop talking. Get me upstairs,' she demanded.

'Who said anything about stairs?'

'Quick,' she urged as he fumbled getting the key from its hiding place, then into the lock, which seemed to challenge his suddenly clumsy fingers even more. 'Hurry,' she urged as she shivered with need and the chill of the frosty night.

'I'm going as fast as I can, woman.'

'My name is Hetta.'

'Do you think I don't know that?' he asked as he finally turned the key and pushed her inside

and had just enough presence of mind to remember to bring the key in with him and lock
the door behind them. 'At last,' he murmured as
he leaned back against the mighty oak planks
of it as if he couldn't walk another step.

'I love you, Magnus Haile,' she said so breathily she wondered if he would hear her past the
thunder of blood in his veins if the noise it was
making was anything like her racing heartbeat.

'And I love you, Hetta Champion. I must do
to have waited so long for you to make your
mind up and take a risk on me. Now be quiet
and let me show you.'

'Oh, yes, please,' she still managed to murmur before she was in his arms at last and everything made complete sense.

Hetta knew how it felt to be wanted and to
want her dashing lover back with a happy little hum deep inside to welcome his sensuous
attentions after all those months at sea. Bran
had been a passionate lover, so she expected
to be petted and praised before Magnus took
his pleasure and maybe she would even manage to join him, since she had spent so long
wanting him and pretending she didn't. But
she had no idea so much heat and pleasure and

love could take the breath out of her lungs and the thoughts out of her brain until she felt only Magnus with every one of her senses and had nothing left to spare for the rest of the world. It was urgent and primitive and hot, and she gloried in the feel of his hands running almost reverently down her back, then settling on her buttocks as if he did this every night in his wildest fantasies, so he knew exactly where to praise and urge and need her until the blaze was well and truly out of control.

His mouth was so emphatic on hers she wondered vaguely how they had ever managed to breathe without one another. She felt the groan in his hum of approval as she met him lip to lip and tongue to tongue and let her own hunger rage. Now his restless hands were exploring her supple backbone, up to a narrow ribcage that seemed to have the most delicious nerve ends where she had no idea nerve ends ought to be until this very moment. Closer, he wanted her closer.

Could they get any closer? a sceptical part of her asked.

Oh, yes, wanton Hetta replied and moved on to her toes to bend into his mighty body and stoke the fire even higher. He was so hot and right and hard against her, why on earth did they need all these clothes?

She must have said that last bit out loud because he smoothed his hands over the pelisse she had needed with frost forming outside on the dreaming Heath and a vixen shouting to her mate. It was almost as if he had forgotten what clothes were in his haste to be with Hetta. How could they stand so many sorts of separation? she wondered restlessly as the restriction of them chafed, but the fading warmth even in here whispered they needed them anyway.

'Never mind them. I want you,' she tore her mouth away from adoring his long enough to tell him.

'I'll never get us upstairs in time at this rate,' he said as if his tongue didn't quite know how words should feel.

The urgency in every inch of his body called out to the same in hers and agreed. 'Nakedness is overrated,' she told him as she tugged him close again with a laugh that forgot itself against the onslaught of his mouth as he scooped her in even closer and his absolute need was emphatic against her absolute need. So that was all very satisfactory, wasn't it?

A few fumbles with all this ridiculous finery and she was delighted when his bare hands got to her pantalettes and she blessed whoever invented them for leaving her free and him apparently very happy with the gap where they divided to make her life and his a lot simpler than it might have been. Easier to get to him, so she did and felt the absolute control he was having to clamp on his sex in the eager shaking of his body and the quiver of it as all the air sounded as if it was leaving his lungs when she spared a brief moment to admire him.

'Now,' she whispered, and that was enough to break the mighty shackles he must have been holding himself back with all this time. 'Oh, now, and now and *now*!' she gasped as he agreed and surged into the sweet hot heat at the heart of her, and he had made her feel so adored and crucial to him the newness of having the love of her life within and without didn't hurt as she had almost feared it might after so long.

He was here, her lover. Her only ever love. Her forever love. She squirmed delightedly to let him know how wondrous this was and felt him clamp some of those shackles back on his rampant manhood to stop himself finishing this right here and right now. Not that she would mind so very much if he had to, because she knew if she didn't get all the way to ecstasy this time there would be plenty of other chances and probably tonight, considering how much they wanted one another.

'We waited too long for that,' he argued rather shakily as he took a moment to clamp more chains on himself and wait for her to catch up.

'Can you read my mind?' she whispered, and perhaps this lovers' link of theirs was so strong he could right now. 'Then you know how much I want you,' she answered her own question and flexed the inner muscles that gloated all over again about how mighty he was so he moved with a moan of such acute pleasure that she did it again.

She reaped a whirlwind for it, she decided in a sensuous daze as he took over the race and carried her, connected so intimately her legs wrapped around his narrow flanks almost by instinct so they could get to the nearest flat surface and ride their wild gallop for the ultimate fulfilment she could feel beckoning, but could not quite reach yet. He changed the rhythm, deepened the intimacy and stared down at her by the dim light of that one small lantern still somewhere near enough to show them this much of one another at least.

'So beautiful,' he murmured. 'Keep your eyes open, love,' he urged hoarsely as tenderness and all the love in his great heart stared back at her and suddenly all this was so new she felt like a virgin with her first love when he surged a great wave of love and need into her and they both flew, together. Staring into his glittering gaze, full of shadows and light all at the same time, she really felt as if they *could* fly, that there was nothing but air under their feet, as if wings were bearing them up so they could bask in the heat and glory of the sun and flex again and again in this mighty triumph of the senses. Skin to skin and breath to breath, with wide open eyes on each other to share, to convulse and strive, then drift down together in heat and joy.

'I should have been more careful with you,' he muttered the moment they had sense enough to realise where they were.

'You great gallant idiot,' she told him fondly

as she luxuriated in the feel of his hands shaking as he smoothed them appreciatively over her lawn-and-lace-covered thighs. 'I liked you driven and out of control, couldn't you tell?'

'Not half as much as I did you.'

'Oh? Now I think we were about equal,' she said, feeling the sadness of being just Hetta again as he withdrew from them and so gently lifted her down from the side table in the hall she felt cherished and glowing as her feet hit the floor, and he didn't let her go until she could stand on them again without feeling as if her knees were suddenly made of jelly. He was so different she banished her only other lover from their lives as a half-forgotten fool who gave her a son. Bran never even got close to the intimacy she was going to share with Magnus for the time they were granted together on this earth. She felt sorry for him for a brief moment because he had been too selfish to ever share so much with another being. Then she waved him goodbye without regret.

'We need a fire,' Magnus said as the dim light of the lantern she now saw was on the floor near the door said what a hasty, love-driven pair they were.

'Maybe upstairs,' she said and why bother to be coy when they only had a few hours before she had to be back at Lady Carrowe's breakfast table looking as if she had no idea how it felt to want her lover so much they could barely get in through the door before falling on one another like wild animals in the spring. 'When is your birthday?' she asked, suddenly upset she didn't know so many things about this man she knew so deeply and intimately the answer ought to be already in her mind, as if they gave all the keys to their inner selves to one another with such a climax of love.

'July. I was celebrating it in my own unique fashion the day we met for the second time, Mrs Champion.'

'Were you, now? No more birthdays like that one for you, then,' she said sternly. 'And I don't want to be Mrs Champion any more,' she added with a moue of distaste.

'Mrs Haile, then, in two days' time.'

'I can't wait.'

'I had noticed.

'You're just as bad.'

'Worse,' he said and Hetta could see from the raffish gleam in his eyes he wanted her again

already, but was being gallant about it and trying to pretend he was quite happy to play the
gentleman if once had been enough for her.

'My feet really are cold now,' she said as she
thought about the options open to them with
an empty house and only a few more hours to
make best use of it. 'Race you upstairs?' she
offered and he barely gave himself time to pick
up the lantern, but she was already off and
running, laughing like a fool as she got to the
landing first and dashed for the first door that
was open and plunged inside shedding clothes
as she went in order to save time.

'I am going to light the fire this time,' he informed her gruffly, averting his eyes from her
scattering layers of clothing as she went like a
very impatient wanton, so he could hold on to
his willpower and his rampant masculine needs
long enough to find a taper, light it from their
lantern, then set a flame to the invitingly laid
fire. He even managed to wait beside it long
enough to feed it some coal as it built and put a
guard in front of it as she sulked about his self-
control, but loved the care of it all the same.

'You could at least have shut the door,' he
complained as he did it for her, then turned

round at last to see her hold up the bedcovers invitingly as she lay back on the bed with as much of her naked body on show as she dared leave out on such a cool and typically English night.

'How comfortable for me to have a bed-warmer. Only think how useful you will be while we tramp about the country on Isabella's business,' he said pompously even as he rid himself of his clothes so fast she had visions of sewing buttons and hooks back on for the next week.

'It's cold in here,' she told him with a frown as she tried not to gloat over every new glimpse of manly grace and urgency.

'It's cold everywhere. Do you want to go back to your beloved Mediterranean?'

'No, I want to be with my beloved Mr Haile in our beloved British Isles.'

'You don't mind, then?'

'I think the trade is in my credit, and if you will only keep me warm instead of the sun, I shall hardly even notice it above once or twice a week.'

'We could go back. I can find something else to do.'

'Nothing that suits you so well. You love this land and have taught me to like it, too. If you try hard enough, I dare say I shall love it by Christmas.'

'We could be with child by then,' he said rather impassively as he got all his layers stripped off at last and slid into bed beside her.

'Would that matter?' she said as she forgot seducing him for a moment to consider the idea and decided she loved it. Toby had been her saving grace from an unhappy marriage, but Magnus's child would be such a joy to add to the ones she already had.

'No, I would like you to myself for a while, or as much as we can be just us when we have a ready-made family, but I do want more children if we should be granted them. I am a greedy man and I certainly can't get enough of you.'

'You are a good man, Magnus Haile,' she informed him with shaken tenderness as she loomed over him in this very comfortable bed she suspected belonged to the master and mistress of the house. She hoped they wouldn't mind another pair of lovers taking advantage of it for the night. 'Even if you are lying there like a sultan in a harem, expecting to be seduced.'

'Well, there's a challenge for you, Henrietta Haile.'

'Hmm, it could be, couldn't it?' she said, and it turned out she was equal to every single one he threw at her and even a few he forgot to mention.

* * * * *

LET'S TALK

Romance

For exclusive extracts, competitions
and special offers, find us online:

f facebook.com/millsandboon

⊙ @millsandboonuk

𝕏 @millsandboon

Or get in touch on 0844 844 1351*

For all the latest titles coming soon,
visit millsandboon.co.uk/nextmonth

*Calls cost 7p per minute plus your phone company's price per
minute access charge

Want even more
ROMANCE?

Join our bookclub today!

'Mills & Boon books, the perfect way to escape for an hour or so.'

Miss W. Dyer

'Excellent service, promptly delivered and very good subscription choices.'

Miss A. Pearson

'You get fantastic special offers and the chance to get books before they hit the shops'

Mrs V. Hall

Visit millsandbook.co.uk/Bookclub and save on brand new books.

MILLS & BOON